REVENGE

Blood Runs Deep

by

Mitchell and Mitchell

ISBN 978-1-9993733-0-6

Second Edition

mitchellauthors@gmail.com

Cover images:

London Bridge 1600 © Simon Edwards 3dartvision.co.uk

Lady in Red I D37197840©captblack76/Dreamtime.com

Book cover-design © Elizabeth E Mitchell

Acknowledgements

We have many people to thank: our friends at Bexley Scribblers, who have given their time and offered advice along the way; Bexley Adult Education, where we met at a class led by the inspirational Donald Daby; and, of course, our families, without whose support nothing would be possible.

A special thank you to Simon Edwards for allowing us to use his beautiful design of the 17th century London Bridge.

Elizabeth & Linda

Mitchell & Mitchell

Chapter 1

Tiredness was slowing my pace but it could not mar my excitement. I couldn't wait to get home, what great news I had to tell: the king was to return. Charles Stuart would soon leave France and take his rightful place on the throne of England. What joy - no more living in terror of the hated soldiers who took such pleasure in enforcing the restrictive laws that bound our lives.

Home; it was odd to call Hamblemere Farm home, but such it was to be. All our things should be in place when I arrived after my dallying behind in Kingsdown.

I smiled to myself as I thought of father digging up the wine when I gave my news of the king, he was sure to have buried it in the garden just as he had done in our old home. My sisters and I would help mother prepare a meal such as the Christmas feasts we had heard about when she and father told us of the time before Cromwell and the Protectorate. And later we would dance and Henry would sing in that lovely baritone voice of his. I teased Hope sometimes that she married him because when he sang his voice was as smooth as flowing honey.

"Oh!" I winced as a stone bit into my foot. I dropped my bag and stood wobbling on one foot as I removed it from my shoe, brought back from my reverie of kings and celebrations to the path before me with its ruts and potholes and multitude of stones. The fields on either side were greening with the maturing spring, all except the old elm tree in the far field which legend had it had been struck by lightning the day the first King Charles had been executed and now stood stark on the horizon.

Glancing up I caught a glimpse of the ancient farmhouse through the trees, just a short way off, grandfather's home until his death but three weeks earlier. Beyond it stood the great oak tree, its mantle in budding leaf; as I walked on I tried to recall the odd name I had heard grandfather give it once, but forgot the thought as I became aware of voices. A visitor. Could it be Sir Edward, the man Henry regarded as a brother, who I had seen but once at some distance yet whom I had found myself heartily wishing to see again? My tiredness fell away from me as I hurried forward, wishing I wasn't all dusty after my walk up the lane. Why hadn't I let the carter bring me up to the farmyard instead of walking, insisting I needed to stretch my legs after my long bumpy ride? Oh no - if it was him he would have told them my news. Perhaps he had seen the king, perhaps he knew when… But I could hear more voices as I got closer, the occasional clatter of horses' hooves, could Edward have brought friends? fellow supporters of the king? What a party there would be. Perhaps he would dance with me; my heart skipped a beat at the thought.

At last the farmhouse came into view above the hedge. My excited smile froze on my lips. I stood open-mouthed as I saw two flaming torches arc against the sky, crashing into the thatch of the roof, the dry rushes igniting instantly. I could not move, unable to comprehend what I saw as patches of flame consumed the reeds. Smoke began to pour forth, rolling like thunderclouds. I was jolted into action. "No! no!" I screamed, dropping my bag, grabbing at my skirts and running into the yard. I heard raised voices, horses snorting with fear as smoke bellowed in every direction, smothering my breath, stinging my eyes. Men in the remnants of army uniform milled around, some carrying chairs, others curtains, pots and wall hangings. Looters! I raised my eyes and saw tongues of flame licking at the upstairs windows of the old house. Where was my family? God in heaven where were they?

Two men came out of the house, one with a dark scar above his right eye. "It was a good day that brought us here," the other said as they paused on the front step to wipe the blood from their swords.

I dropped to my knees in despair and covered my ears as I heard such terrible, terrible screams, as from a soul in torment. Someone shouted a command, pointing in my direction, "Stop her wailing!" Until that moment I had not known the screams were my own. I scrambled to my feet in terror, stumbling on the cobblestones, choking in the acrid air, looking all about to find a way of escape but through the smoke I could see no route between the angry looters and the restless horses. A man rushed forward raising his sabre and in dread I threw my outer skirt over my head to block out what was coming.

Chapter 2

I woke to the bitter smell of burning and the stink of smouldering wood. Nothing made sense to me as I lay there amidst the straw. I tried to move but gasped as a sharp stabbing pain shot through my head; my hand instantly found the wound and was bathed in blood. My body ached with every tiny movement. I forced myself to raise my head a little and open my eyes. I was in a barn. I couldn't remember how I had got there or what had happened to me.

Some dark instinct made me lift the rough horse blanket covering me. My clothes were slit through from neck to hem, the halves parted like a butchered pig. Vivid red weals covered my arms and breasts, my thighs were smeared with blood. Despite the pain I grabbed at the straw and tried to rub away the sign of my shame but my movements froze, my eyes straining in fear, as the dark shape of a man blocked out the light from the half-open door. I looked up in horror, my heart pounding in my chest. I held my breath and shrank back, forcing my lips to suppress a sob, praying he had not seen me in the gloom.

"In here, sergeant," the man called, "we have a survivor."

A fever took me, burned me, drained me. When slowly it retreated it left nothing but the shell of a person behind.

A week had passed and I had remained silent, unable to speak. My mind was as bruised as my body and every thought caused me pain. I slept little, fearful of the dreams that left me weeping, stemming my tears in the pillow so as not to wake the house. The vicarage in West Penton where I had been taken in was not large, and the Reverend Matthew Davidson and his wife Margaret slept next door. I had no recollection of my past life, of who I was, or what had happened to me, remembering nothing beyond a pair of strong arms scooping me up from the ground and holding me safe, but neither the kindness of my saviour nor the blanket in which I was wrapped could disguise the outrage that had befallen me. My memory had mercifully escaped me but the fire in my room had but to flare, a log to crackle and send forth a spray of sparks, for my hands to fly to my face and cover my eyes and mouth.

"Do not be afraid." Margaret encased my hand with her own, bending her long fingers over my upturned palm, smoothing away my trembling. She habitually wore dark clothes of the simplest kind, always with a stiff white collar, but was as gentle as her garb was stark. I opened my eyes when she was with me but I preferred to keep them closed; I preferred night to day, stillness to movement, rain to sunlight, for its beat against the window reinforced the limits of my world.

"You know, do you, that you are a member of the Courtney family?" I shook my head. Margaret sat at my bedside in the light of early morning. Each day I felt anew the chasm of sadness within me and was as afraid of remembering as I was of having forgotten. "Arthur, the old cowman who worked at the farm in your grandfather's time, says he saw your family's wagon the day they moved to the farm. You girls all have your mother's colouring. It's a pity that not one person in the

5

village could tell me more about you but no-one had seen you or your sisters for many a year. Some remember your father as a young man and I saw him at your grandfather's funeral of course. You must know you had a family who loved you," she said, as tears of frustration ran down my face for I could not picture them, however hard I tried, though I knew every effort at remembering was restricted by my dread of what memory might reveal.

They were all lost, everything was lost, I understood that.

A noise from the street made me gasp. Margaret saw the fear in my eyes and took hold of my hand. "It is nothing, child." She went to the window, pulling the curtain aside. "It's the maypole," she explained. "There are at least a dozen men carrying it, it must have been hidden in a barn all these years. Now Charles Stuart is to take the throne there'll be dancing on the village green once more." She glanced at me and I nodded. "I hope this does not mean cockfighting will start again," Margaret continued, "or the drunkenness I saw about me when I was a girl. But your wellbeing is my only thought today. All I ask is a step or two – just to the chair." She pulled back the bedding and held my elbow, ready to take my weight. Reluctantly I twisted my body round so that my feet touched the floor. My legs shook from both weakness and fear. "Lean on me, I will not allow you fall." I shuffled forward until my outstretched hand touched the arm of the chair.

I slid down into the seat. Pain embraced me: along my back, down my legs, and in, in and through me, to the centre of my being.

"Did I not say you would reach it?" Margaret laid a shawl over my shoulders, for I was shivering despite the sweat dampening my hair. "You must eat, I'll bring you some of the broth I made yesterday."

I slept from exhaustion in the chair until darkness took my room again and Margaret helped me back to bed.

"A little more each day," she said. "That is all it takes."

And so it proved. Despite my fears, despite my weakness and pain and cowardice, as the weeks progressed life reclaimed me.

"You must have something to wear for your first day downstairs." Margaret was bent over, removing some clothing from a trunk while I stood nearby in my shift. She slipped my arms into a bodice. "It's too big, I know, but if I add some darts," her fingers quickly put the pins in place, "and move the ties over, it will do until I have fattened you up, just you see." She began tying the many bows holding the stiff stomacher panel in place covering the front opening, bringing the top together and flattening the appearance of my chest. "There, I knew this russet colour would suit you." She pulled at the fabric. I stepped into the skirt and Margaret skilfully pinned darts into the material so they could be unpicked again when necessary. "You'll feel better soon," she said while admiring her handiwork. She took my hand in hers and held it fast and I could feel her trying to will life back into me.

"I have to make a visit this morning," Margaret said the following day as she brought in my breakfast. "But if I leave you my needle and thread I am sure you could sit in the chair and finish the skirt." She gave me a kiss and was gone. I regarded the closed door like an infant left alone for the first time. I did not know if I could hold a needle steady or push it through the fabric but I knew I could not disappoint her: my every effort – to eat, to sleep, to walk - was for Margaret; I did not care for myself, or my life, but wished only to take from her some of the responsibility of caring for me.

At dinner, dressed in my new clothes, I sat with my head bowed. Matthew was there. I did not wish to be seen, could not raise my eyes from my plate. He and Margaret spoke quietly of the day's events and allowed me my silence.

When we had finished and I went to creep back to my room I noted ink, a quill and a sheet of paper on the side table; Margaret observed my hesitation. "When you are ready, my dear, if you cannot speak, can you not write down at least your name and the name of any kinsman you may have?" I shook my head - I regarded the paper as if it were my greatest enemy; I was afraid of what I should write. Would the memories that refused to come to the surface of my mind spill out like blood on the page? I shook my head again and moved away. Margaret stood and I heard her scoop up the writing materials and place them in the drawer.

"Why can't she give us a hand - the silent one?" It was Aggie, the widow who lived in the village and came in a few days each week to assist Margaret with the household chores. There was a pause in the sounds coming from the scullery into the kitchen where I sat, my sewing on my lap.

"Do not speak of her in that manner," Margaret reprimanded her. "You know she is one of the Courtney girls from Hamblemere Farm. If you need help you should ask me, I will happily assist you - my guest is still very weak."

"Huh!" Aggie cried. "She doesn't seem too poorly to me."

I heard the heavy slap of linen against board, the sound of water from the squeezed sheets running back into the tub.

I had done that job: twist the laundry between my hands, the coil loosening the moment my grip slackened, unfurling like a flower, half-dry. The image flashed through my mind and was gone again before I could grasp it.

"And where was she when it happened?" Aggie asked.

Yes, where was I? that was the question.

"There are those who ask how it is she managed to survive," Aggie continued.

The sounds from the scullery were silenced for a moment. "Hush! Do not repeat such things, Aggie. Judge not that you may not be judged."

Matthew's church sat across the road from the vicarage on the edge of the village, its grey outline filling the windows at the front of the house. I was grateful neither he nor Margaret had suggested I attend the services, for if they had, how would I have been able to refuse them? Their kindness extended to knowing I was fearful of all the world saving the two people who allowed me to share their home. Everything I knew of the world outside was gathered from quick glances from those windows. I had not the courage to see for myself, or to be seen.

Nonetheless waking with the first notes of the dawn chorus one morning I felt myself drawn towards the church. I stepped across the road, pulling my shawl tightly around me. The tower of the church was short and squat, built as if to hold up heaven unaided if so required. The latch on the door thundered as I slipped inside. I had to pray, I had to pray for my family, though I knew not who they were, and for myself, though I knew not who I was - one of the Courtney girls would have to suffice for now - God, at least, would know me.

"We have caught the men who raided the farm." The words rang out from Matthew's study where he wrote his sermons and advised his parishioners. I recognised the voice with a shudder, causing the water to spill from the vase of flowers I was carrying: it was the officer in charge of the soldiers who had rescued me. "They had the stolen items. The previous servants who ran the farmhouse in old man Courtney's time recognised the candlesticks and tapestry."

"Excellent, Major Lawson, we shall all sleep safely in our beds from now on," said Matthew.

"Indeed! The leader, Sergeant Miller, maintains they had just marched back from the north; disgruntled parliamentarians, all of them; said he and his men were merely passing through the area on their way home. He claimed he bought the goods from a group of former soldiers as presents for his family and his troops knew nothing of what happened at Hamblemere Farm."

"Do you believe him?" asked Matthew.

"Certainly not. Some of the stolen items had been sold and Miller and his men have been identified as the sellers but the witnesses are afraid to speak out in case of reprisals."

"In that case do you believe you have enough evidence to go forward with a trial?"

"I do." Major Lawson's tone was confident as I heard him move about the room. "And with the Courtney girl's help they will be brought to justice tomorrow in the square."

"We will see that she is there - if you have no doubts."

"You would not ask that if you had heard them talking last night as I did - they didn't know I could hear them. They were complaining how General Lambert had let them down, it was plain they would see none of the pay they were owed."

There was a pause. "You are aware our visitor has not spoken since you brought her here from that scene of carnage?"

"Yes, but if she recognises the men she can surely indicate them. We need her, she is the only witness."

Abandoning the flowers, I gathered my skirts and ran to the kitchen, out the back door, across the vegetable garden and did not stop until I found myself on the reed-lined banks of the river where I collapsed gasping for breath, rubbing my bodice to alleviate the stitch in my side. I sat staring at the river and lost myself in watching the currents and eddies of the swiftly flowing water, a low-hanging branch cutting in to it, disturbing the patterns of light and shade. When the scene had calmed me and the sun was high, I shook myself and slowly made my way back to the vicarage.

Matthew was in the garden when I got back. "We have been searching for you, my dear," he said. "Margaret said she thought you may have overheard?" He left the question in the air. I nodded guiltily. "You know then we need you to identify the men at the farm that day. The men who…" I shook my head wildly, gasping for breath.

He held my hands gently as he whispered, "It will be all right, we will be by your side."

All faces turned towards me as the crowd filling the small market square parted to let me through. I kept my eyes on the ground, wanting to see nothing of this day. The accused men stood with their backs to me as Major Lawson came forward. "Now Mistress, I regret it is necessary for you to confront these men," he said as he took me firmly by the arm. "Have no fear, they cannot harm you, their hands are tied." The men stood a couple of feet apart, linked to each other by a single rope.

Major Lawson led me forward to face the accused; how would I know them? my mind was a dark cavern. "You must look up, mistress," the major gently rebuked me. I raised my eyes.

The man before me curled his lip, his eyes filled with hatred. The sight of him made me quake and my legs buckle. I felt Lawson place his arm around me, holding me securely.

I found myself once more standing on the cobbles of Hamblemere Farm, smoke all about me, watching as this man stepped out of the farmhouse door, blood dripping from his sword.

I shrank away from him in horror. An involuntary cry escaped my lips as I lifted my arm and pointed a shaking finger at him.

"Sergeant Miller has been identified by the witness," Major Lawson declared. Tears blinded me. Margaret stepped forward, took me in her arms and tenderly moved me a little away from the line of men.

"The woman's deranged. I never saw her before," screeched Miller. "She is a half-wit, she can't even speak. You can't take a mad woman's word against mine."

His voice made me feel sick with fear as memories flooded back, images tumbling into my brain, immersing me in the past.

I lay in the straw on the floor of a barn, my head pounding, my eyes unable to focus. As they cleared I saw a man standing over me, a gleaming knife clenched in his fist. He leaned forward laughing at me; terrified, I tried to move away. Placing a booted foot on my lower legs he pushed down hard, causing a searing pain to shoot through my body. I screamed but the sound became muffled as vomit rose in my throat. Dropping to his knees he pressed the knife against my face so I could feel its sharpness before he slit it down through the front of my garments. "Let's see what we have here." He straddled my knees and thighs, his weight pinning me to the ground. I could see the gleam in his fathomless black eyes. I tried to squirm away from him as his hands reached out towards my breasts. I tasted blood as he hit me hard across the face. I spat at him and he struck me again before I slipped into oblivion.

The memories were so clear I gasped and swayed under the weight of them. I clung on to Margaret's arm.

My assailant stood with his back to me, fixing his clothing. "I will see you later my girl."

A rectangle of light lit the floor as the barn door was pushed open by the man who bore a scar above his eye. "My horse is prepared, Captain Jacob."

"Good. Say we shall not be more than a day or two behind you; some clearing up to do."

I raised my head a little and the movement, though so small, gave me away. "Not leaving her alive, are you, sir?" he asked, seeing the officer making ready to leave.

"I thought to have my pleasure once more," my violator said. "But you are correct, we should leave no-one alive. Be gone now, on your way."

The barn door scraped over the ground as it closed and I heard the clatter of hooves on the cobbles of the yard. In an effort to rise I pushed down, my shaking hand falling on a rough wooden handle buried in the hay. The man bent forward to pick up the helmet he had left on the floor by my side. Without a thought I lifted my arm swiftly with as much force as I could muster and a pitchfork rose from its resting place, straw falling from between its tines. His eyes opened wide as one sharp prong penetrated his chest and he lost his balance. Staggering forward he dropped to his knees impaling himself and slumped away from me.

"Forgive us, mistress." A young boy's voice cried out in the market square and jolted me back to the present. "Forgive me, I did not know what they were going to do to you and your family, we wronged you so dreadfully." He broke down, fell to his knees, still imploring me to forgive him. He could not have been more than fourteen years old. The men who stood either side of him began to kick at him viciously for speaking out. Major Lawson stepped in to stop them.

"I've heard enough," he announced, "these men are condemned for their downright wickedness."

"We're soldiers," one protested.

"We fought for Cromwell."

"We fought for the people."

"Fought against the king."

"And now they bring back his son."

"But we won the war."

"He's not *our* king,"

"We have no king."

A chant sprung up between them. "No king, no king." The people standing nearby shuffled their feet, uneasy. Some of them had doubtless been Cromwell's men once, had cheered his victories, now they were set to cheer as a king resumed the throne.

I sought amongst the men for the one I had seen coming from the house, the one with the scar across his face, but did not find him among the angry faces that stared back at me as the guards quickly moved to restrain them. Margaret hurried me away, heading for home as their voices rang out behind me.

"They're stealing the country away from us."

"We only took what was owed us."

A silence descended on the little village square when those words were uttered and the men were led away to meet their fate.

Chapter 3

As darkness began to fall, with only the fire lighting the room, Matthew entered the parlour where I lay on the settle after my ordeal, my shivering yet to stop. "Those men will never harm you or anyone else ever again," he said, patting my hand. "I heard their confessions; the ones who had the good grace to admit their crimes made their peace with God. Justice was swift – all were executed by hanging half an hour ago."

"God have mercy," Margaret whispered as tears overwhelmed me.

"I was sorry for the lad but he was part of the gang and therefore just as guilty in the eyes of the law," Matthew continued. "He signed a confession saying what happened before the raid. He said Sergeant Miller had told his men they should take what they could from those who had sat safely at home while he and his men had risked their lives in battle. He'd argued that General Monck's soldiers had been promised their back pay by the king but Miller's men would get none of what was owing to them, and it was time to take care of themselves. Oh, Margaret," Matthew finished, and I could hear the pain in his voice, "I pray there may now be peace."

They had hanged the boy: the words went around and around my brain. His face shot into my vision and his voice filled my ears. "Forgive me," he had pleaded, "forgive me." I remembered now with aching clarity. I remembered, but too late.

After my assailant had fallen over, the pitchfork in his chest, and his choking breaths had died away, the boy had pulled open the barn door, calling out "Captain Jacob?" as he entered. Peering into the sudden darkness of the barn he paused before rushing over to the body on the floor. "Captain Jacob?" he said again, a whisper now, his eyes but not his hands checking the captain was dead. A catch in my breath made his eyes dart in my direction, to where I had painfully crawled as far from the body as I could manage. I pulled my clothes over me as best I could, cringing in fear. He saw me in all my pain and understood. "Hush" he said, "I'll hide you."

He covered me with straw and tossed a horse blanket over me, so it lay crumpled, before whispering, "Stay very still, I'll tell them you escaped through a hole in the back wall." I heard him kicking at the boards until they broke. He ran to the door shouting, "Sergeant Miller, quick in here! The girl has killed the captain and escaped!" I slipped gently into unconsciousness once more.

I let out a great sob from the centre of my being. I had remembered too late how he had saved my life, and they had hanged the boy.

A few weeks after the trial Major Lawson again called on Matthew; they were a long time conversing in the study.

"Lawson has been asked to make enquiries into the rightful owner of Hamblemere Farm," Matthew said when we started dinner. "Now that…" He did not finish the sentence: *now that all my family were dead.* "He is trying to find the nearest living male relative on your father's side."

"You know as a woman you cannot inherit the farm, my dear?" Margaret said as she helped me to more rabbit stew.

I nodded.

"Maybe he will take you in as kin," Matthew continued. Margaret gave me a half-smile, she knew this was the best I could expect. "But if not, you must not worry; you may stay here with Margaret and myself for as long as you wish."

For some reason, a denial of the future, I had not thought of what I would do in the days to come. It appeared it had been assumed I would go back to live at the farm if the new owner would be kind enough to offer me a home. What was left of the farm; the house had gone so I had been told but the barn was still standing and with some work could be made into a comfortable enough dwelling, and many of the animals had survived the raid. But how could I bear to see that place again? "Do you have any recollection, my dear," Margaret asked as she began to remove the plates from the table, "who is your nearest male relative? An uncle, a cousin perhaps?" I shook my head. I could not recall my mother or father, nor the sisters they told me I had, never mind an uncle or cousin. The family bible, with a copy of the family tree, had undoubtedly gone up in smoke with the house. *The family bible.* I could see its great leather covers, the inner page, written in different hands, listing our family members, though the names were but a blur - another fragment of memory.

It was not until Margaret asked me, a few days later, if I needed any new rags for my monthly curse I realised I hadn't given it a thought. I shook my head. "Haven't you had any?"

18

Again, I shook my head. "Well, maybe the shock of all that happened has upset your body and they will return soon. Yes, certainly, that is what it is."

It was more than three months since the raid and still my monthly curse had not returned. I sat in my usual haunt by the river, the mossy stump of a tree felled in a storm. The water was fast, ruffled by a chill breeze. I drew my shawl tightly about my shoulders. I held myself still, aware only of the racing of my heart; I raised my hand and allowed it to slide slowly across my belly. I felt it, the slight but unmistakable hint of smooth roundness beneath the thin material of my dress. A child!

I let go of my shawl and ran both hands across my stomach as I had done with my mother when she was pregnant with Jessie. *Oh Lord, Jessie!* Her face appeared before me, my little sister.

"Here, girls," mother had said, "quickly, before your father comes back. Here is your little brother or sister." Hope and I ran our hands across our mother's stomach. It was smooth and round like the bowls in the kitchen cupboard. "One day you too will be mothers, my dear girls, you first Hope, then you Ruth," she added, stroking my hair. "It is the most wonderful thing."

My breath seemed to stop in my chest. But Hope would never be a mother. I would, but in circumstances beyond my mother's worst imaginings. Tears of joy and sadness coursed down my face as now they were all there, clear in my memory: my elder sister Hope, only a year older than myself, and little Jessie, born with an abundance of the same auburn hair as all the women in the family. I could see in my mind our old home in Kingsdown, mother and us girls occupied in the field out back providing the family's milk, eggs and vegetables while father was in the yard working as a wheelwright, busy at his wood lathe, preparing a new spoke for a broken wheel with Henry helping him, learning the trade. Henry, who had been disowned by his father, a squire living many miles away, who had wanted his son to marry an heiress, not a humble country girl. But they had been so in love... Dead, all dead. Dead at the farm. I could see the searing orange of the flames, smell the smoke and hear the cries of terrified animals. How father and Henry would have fought for the women they loved. Poor little Jessie, only nine years old - she had seen so little of life.

How could I live without them? And how could I live with the memory of them? If I had not begged to stay a few extra days with my cousin Penny I would have been at home with my family that day and after the moments of pain and terror, I would have died with them, and been at peace, never to be parted from them again. My survival was an accident, a mistake I could now, should now, make right. I knotted my shawl behind my neck and reached out, gathering stones to fill it, and stood awkwardly holding on to the weighty bundle as I walked towards the river, careful not to disturb my burden. The river was flowing fast after the recent summer rains; it should not take long and would quickly envelope me. I stepped into the shallows; the water stung me with its chill and took my breath away as it touched my belly. I immersed myself slowly. As my hands rose with the level of the water the knot in my shawl unravelled and the stones fell about my feet. The water was clear and I could watch the current tug at my skirts as they began to float to the surface, air trapped within them. My foot slipped on the slimy stones as the water finally reached to my neck and quietly I fell back and allowed it to cover me. I felt the pain as it started to fill my lungs. "Not long," I prayed, though when the current carried me round the bend in the river's course and I momentarily bobbed to the surface I gasped for air as my body fought to live as I strove to die. There seemed to be shouting, a figure, then nothingness.

I could feel the warmth and embrace of a soft woollen blanket holding me close. There were voices murmuring on the other side of the room. I forced myself to open my eyes a little, but they sank shut once more. I slept. When I opened my eyes again I was on the cot in the parlour before a blazing fire. Major Lawson sat nearby wrapped in a blanket with a hot drink in his hands, his grey hair still tousled from being dried.

"You're safe, mistress," he said quickly as he saw my eyelids flutter. "You must have slipped and fallen into the river."

I understood he knew what I'd done but for some reason wished to shield me from the consequences.

"You are awake, my dear," Margaret said as she came across the room to me. "If it had not been for Major Lawson…"

"I thank God I saw you." Lawson stood, throwing off his blanket, revealing borrowed clothing beneath instead of his bright red uniform.

Matthew came into the room saying, "I thought I heard voices. I thank God for your bravery, major, and for bringing our guest back to our hearth."

"Do not speak of it, I pray you," Lawson replied.

"I'll bring in some soup," Margaret said. "You must eat, it will warm you."

"And I must bring more coals," Matthew said, "for you both must still be chilled through."

The major moved forward the moment we were alone. "All will be well," he said. "Your secret is safe with me." A tear fell from my eye. "Some years ago, when the last of our three wars broke out, my daughter was in a similar position." He smiled gently, adding, "And she went on to have a good life. You must not give up hope; all life is a special gift and has to be lived as best you can." He took my hand in his. "Please give life a chance, have courage."

I drifted in and out of sleep. Margaret had put me to bed, smoothing the sheet and blankets under which I lay, stroking my head. "You must take care," she said softly, "you will not go so close to the river bank again, will you, my dear? It is difficult, I know, but you must think of others." I started when I heard those words, and she must have seen the enquiry in my eyes. "Matthew and I would be so sad if we were to lose you," she continued. "You are not alone. You may never have spoken a word to me but I feel you are my dearest friend."

"Have courage," Major Lawson had said. Was that what I lacked: the courage to go on alone? Margaret for all her kindness, for all her gentle words, could not keep the harshness of the world from me. Everything was clear to me now, everything but the path ahead. What if it had been Hope who had been away from the farm that afternoon, if it had been my blood on the sword and her screaming in the yard? Would I have wanted her to believe the only remedy for her pain was the river? "No!" The word rang out like a bell, its sound skating over the whitewashed walls of my room, vibrating against the water jug. Had my voice returned at last? "No," I whispered to myself, "no," in a voice I did not recognise.

What would the boy, the poor young boy, who had risked his life to save my own, what would he say to me if he could speak? Not throw away the gift I have given you, never that. Had Margaret guessed my secret? "You are not alone," she had said. My hand slid automatically to my stomach with its gentle arch. Indeed, I was not alone. I must tell Margaret - I trusted her with my life, and with my child's. And life it must be. If it had been Hope who had lived, I would have wanted, no, I would have demanded, that she live the life so bravely saved. Live it for us all.

But the child, surely it would not be possible to love the child. Yet what else did I have?

That night I prayed for mother and father, for Hope and Henry, for sweet little Jessie. And I prayed for the boy who had saved my life and through my lack of recollection I had condemned to die.

The first rays of the morning sun lit my little room and I opened my eyes. As I moved to sit up my hand brushed against my stomach but this time I did not recoil from the knowledge of the child within me. I carefully placed my hands on my hips and drew them across my belly. I was caressing my child. The curve of my abdomen filled the hollow in the palm of my hand and by some force of nature I found it filled the hollow at the centre of my being. How could I have thought to destroy it along with myself? It was my child, the one possession remaining to me. It was meant to be a curse, but I would make it into a blessing, a gift, someone to love, and someone to love me. My daughter. My son.

My son - if my child was to be a boy the farm should be his. Why should he be denied? As my father's grandson he should be his heir, as Hope's son would have been.

My mind was made up, I resolved I would be strong for both our sakes. Hope would forgive me for what I was about to do.

"Margaret," I whispered to check my voice had not deserted me while I slept. The word hung in the air. I could feel my voice in my mouth and in my throat and in my chest; it was there, waiting to be heard. It had waited till now, until my memories in all their horror had returned, until I had decided to live despite them. My voice had a wisdom I did not possess - it had waited until my mind was clear and now it was time to speak. As I thought of my future, my child's future, I knew my silence had protected me.

I ran down the stairs and caught sight of Margaret walking across the hall with her hands full of linen to be washed. "Margaret," I called out.

"What is it, my dear? Did you sleep…?" She stopped, surprise lighting her face. She dropped the linen and ran to me, her arms open wide. "At last, at last, thank God."

"Margaret," I repeated but my words were buried in her embrace. As she released me I found I could not confine the smile that overtook me. "Thank you, thank you, thank you," I said. "What would have become of me but for your kindness, yours and Matthew's?"

"Matthew!" Margaret grabbed hold of my hand and led me, almost pulled me, towards his study. She opened the door without knocking. "Matthew, it's a miracle."

"Sir," I said with a curtsy.

Matthew jumped up from his desk, leaving his quill to roll across his papers, dripping ink. "An answer to your prayers, Margaret," he said.

Tears formed in my eyes when I heard those words. "I do not deserve all the kindness you have shown me, sir."

"Of course you deserve kindness," Margaret reproved me. "Everyone does. It was what happened to you before you came to us that you did not deserve."

"All my memories are clear to me now," I said.

Matthew's face was grave. "It must be hard to bear such memories."

"Yes, it is, but I would not be without the good ones, even though it means braving the worst of them."

"Oh come, my dear," Margaret said. "You must eat." She paused. "I am so used to calling you my dear, and my dear you are, but pray what is your name?"

"Hope," I replied. "Hope, wife of Henry Ashton." My stomach fluttered as I spoke the lie and I said a silent prayer for there could be no going back.

"Hope," Margaret said, leaning forward and kissing me on the cheek. "What an appropriate name you have."

"You two must wish to talk about many things," Matthew said.

"Indeed we do," his wife replied, "and I suppose you wish to have some peace in your study."

"Hope," Matthew said, "it is good to hear your voice at last."

"Sir," I nodded as we turned to go.

"And you must call me by my name, for we are all family within this house, are we not?"

"Hope Ashton," Margaret repeated as she closed the door behind us. "I heard one of the Courtney girls was married, but did not think it was you as you wear no ring."

I looked at my naked hand as a gasp escaped me. A ring! How could I not have thought of that?

"Wait, wait." Margaret flew from the room while I stood in confusion in the centre of the kitchen, distraught that my lie had been discovered by my one friend. My wish was to run, to hide, but I heard Margaret's footsteps beating down the stairs.

"Here," she said, holding a gold ring between her thumb and forefinger. "It was my mother's."

Sobs exploded within me. She slipped the ring on to my finger. "It must have been lost in the attack or stolen perhaps when you lay dead to the world."

She wrapped me in her arms. "I know," she said, "you have lost so much, at least this one thing I can replace." I shook my head in misery at having so deceived her but Hope I must become and confine Ruth to some secret part of myself. "Not replace, of course," she continued, as if scolding herself, "it could never do that, it can but be a symbol of what was once yours." I was as dumb as I had been before my awakening. After a few minutes she led me to a chair by the fire. "I heard there was a young man at the farm," she said gently.

"Henry," I whispered. I was lost in memories for a moment. "He sang as he worked with father, whenever the two of them were alone, at least until father told him to be quiet." Words drifted away from me.

Margaret smiled. "It sounds as if he was a very happy man."

I nodded. I had told Matthew that all my memories were clear to me now, and so they were, but if they were clear they were also distant. When I pictured my family, it seemed they were on a hilltop far away, lit by the sun, but the valley between us prevented me, would ever prevent me, from being more than a spectator in the lives they had lived. Or perhaps they were a hundred years in the past so unreachable did they feel, and every moment was dragging me further away from them. My pain was tempered by this distance, leaving me both relieved and distressed.

Margaret and I sat at the table with the kettle beginning to warm over the fire while my head buzzed with thoughts pulling me in every direction. Finally I said, "My name is even more appropriate than you know." I took a moment to steady myself. "I believe I am with child." Margaret's hands flew to her face as she received the news. I knew I must continue with the speech I had rehearsed in my head though my voice was shaking as I did so. "I was almost certain we were to have a child before the attack on the farm. The child I'm sure is my husband's - Henry's."

"Of course, of course." Margaret's voice was soothing, as if comforting a child.

"So," Margaret continued when we had spent much time staring at the fire flickering before us, "we know you have no near relatives on your father's side but what of your mother's family?"

27

"It was my mother's family leaving England that saved me," I said. "I did not journey to the farm with the others but stayed a few days more in Kingsdown to help my aunt with her preparations."

"And Henry agreed?"

My breath caught in my throat, I had not thought of myself as Hope, a married woman. "He knew how fond I was of my cousin Penny, she is exactly my age." I had shared all my eighteen summers with her, and had begged my father to have those last days with her, for surely I would never see her again. "Her family were leaving the village too, going to the Americas," I said. I was quiet awhile and Margaret did not press me to say more but held my hand fast within hers. Speaking was difficult, words felt awkward in my mouth after so many weeks of silence, but I must give my explanation. "I did not get to the farm until they - the men - were about to leave. I remained behind in Kingsdown not knowing I was sacrificing my last days with my own family. I would not have stayed if I had known," I said, my eyes lowered to my lap.

"I thank God you did," Margaret replied. She reached up and took my face in her hands and with her thumbs wiped away the tears as they began to slide down my face. "And so must you."

Chapter 4

"Hope, you will have a difficult fight on your hands." Matthew stood resting his hand on the back of the kitchen chair as he made his way towards his study the following day. I had ventured to ask whether, if my child was a boy, he might inherit Hamblemere Farm.

"I have been speaking to Major Lawson, he has been approached by a male relative of yours, by the name of Oliver Whitby; I hear he is to claim the farm as his inheritance. The point is - I mean to say - Oliver Whitby is unlikely, well, he may not accept your child is your husband's. There is unfortunately," he broke off and ran his fingers across the back of his neck, "I am sorry to say this, but there is room for doubt. You have several months to wait until the child is born and if it is not a boy there will be no chance of regaining the farm in any case." He raised his hands in the air as if powerless to do anything about the situation.

"How can it be this man is called Whitby and not Courtney if the farm is to be his?"

"I gather there was a change of family name many years ago following a second marriage." Matthew paused. "There are good and charitable people in this world so perhaps we should trust in Oliver Whitby's kindness for now."

My mind was full of this supposed kinsman, this Oliver Whitby, wondering whether he would be willing to take me under his roof in such a state, a double burden? If my story was not believed would I ever find a husband, deflowered and with a child in tow? Whitby might be anxious to rid himself of my presence and marry me off to whoever needed a free cook or farm hand, little better than a skivvy: then what sort of life could I give my child?

"Do you know him?" Matthew interrupted my thoughts. "Did your father speak of him?"

"No, I do not know the name. I have no idea who he is or how he can be related to my father. The family bible would have held a clue perhaps if it had survived the fire. I have seen it but once or twice."

Matthew could see my dismay. "Try to put the matter out of your mind."

But how was it possible for me to do that? I did not I know if this man had any legitimate claim to the farm.

"Come sit with me," Margaret said, distracting me, "I find my workbox is full to overflowing." I took up my needle and a pair of stockings and upon her enquiry began to tell her a little of my father's wheelwright yard atop the hill in Kingsdown.

"Henry's family," Margaret said not glancing up from her work, "you have made no mention of them."

It took me a moment to gather myself. Henry, my husband, or so I had said. I must answer for my decision; it had seemed such a simple deception.

"Henry had a family," I began in little more than a whisper. "His father is Squire Ashton. His mother died when Henry was very young and later his father married Lady Somerville, a widow with a son of her own, ten years older than Henry, Sir Edward." *Sir Edward - I had given him no thought since the day when I had excitedly imagined he might be paying us a call, but it had been death and destruction waiting for me as I walked into the yard of the farm. I had not understood what riches in family I already had and had yearned for more.* I noticed Margaret's needle was stilled as she waited for me to continue. "Yes, Henry has a living father, or so I presume, not that I have ever met him. They were not a wealthy family but Henry's father spent heavily on his education hoping he would marry well. But one day Henry's horse went lame on the road and he came into father's yard, and ..." And he had fallen in love with Hope. "Ashton disapproved of the marriage," I continued, "and in his anger cut Henry off without a shilling." I dropped my thimble and I took my time recovering it from the floor. "I saw Sir Edward once, he was talking to Henry in Kingsdown, that was not long before my grandfather died. They did not see me and he did not come to the house."

"It is always sad when a family falls out."

"Henry regarded Edward as an older brother," I said. Memory took me back to the lane in Kingsdown, Henry in his leather apron, speaking to Sir Edward, a dashing figure in his short cloak and with his sword at his side. "I believe he supported the marriage but he spent his time away on important missions. It was never spoken of openly but I believe Sir Edward was often at the king's court in exile."

"Why not approach Henry's father, Squire Ashton? After all, if he knew of your plight he might be willing to help. A grandchild surely would soften his heart and Sir Edward might plead your case."

"No, I could not." The thought sent a shudder through me and I pricked my finger with the needle, a dot of blood appearing on my fingertip. "Squire Ashton obviously despises my family and would do so all the more if he knew the shame of what has happened to me. I could never go to him for assistance." I knew, with a chill, that my own deception made that doubly true.

"Hush, my dear, do not speak so," Margaret said, dropping her sewing as she stretched out her arms to hug me. "I am surprised this Sir Edward hasn't sought you out," she continued, releasing me, "does he know of your move to Hamblemere Farm?"

"Oh yes, Henry wrote to him, but as he climbed on his horse to leave I heard Sir Edward say, 'Between ourselves,' he said, 'I am on my way north. It is a dangerous mission but God willing I shall return in better times'. Henry did not speak of the encounter at home, so nor did I, I had been eavesdropping."

There was a long silence between Margaret and myself into which I found myself saying "I fear Sir Edward may not have survived his commission from the king."

We continued with our sewing: buttons were replaced, rips mended, hems re-sewn.

"There is something…" Margaret said.

"Yes?"

"I trust you will approve."

"Approve? I cannot imagine what…"

"I do not believe you are aware - your family, my dear, they have been laid to rest within the church. There, I have told you, you do not object, do you?"

"Oh!" I could say no more.

"It was while you were ill, when it seemed you did not know who you were – we feared you might never remember, and something needed to be done. There were much distress and sympathy in the village - that such a terrible thing should happen here. Come, I must show you."

She removed my apron for me and took my hand, leading me across the road to the church.

"There," she said, pointing to the newly-laid stone halfway along the side aisle. "Of course we did not know who was - " Her voice faded away. "We can have it changed." In neat, precise letters the stone declared:

> "In memory of the Courtney family
> of Hamblemere Farm
> cruelly murdered 21st April 1660
> With God"

"No, do not change it," I said.

"Will you come to market with me today?" Margaret asked me one bright morning a week later. "Now you are so much better."

"But I cannot..."

"Hope, you must not hide away, you cannot live merely within this house. You have your life before you, the sooner you take your place in the village the less..." Margaret stumbled over her words as she saw I understood her meaning. "You must know you are the subject of much interest," she continued. "It cannot be helped. The events that overtook you were the worst ever to happen here, even during the wars. It is only human to be curious. Once you are a common sight in the village the curiosity will move on to another subject. It is a hurdle that cannot be avoided, I'm sorry to say."

She spoke nothing but the obvious truth, yet I found it hard to take.

"I have asked my good friend Mrs Adams to accompany us," she said. "She is the miller's wife - you must have often seen the great wheel of the mill in the distance." I nodded; silence had become a habit with me. "Do not be so concerned, she is the kindest of people."

No, that is you, I thought.

Polly Adams put a smile on my face the moment she blew into the house like a gust of fresh, outdoor air, dropping her shawl over the back of a chair, shaking her head so her bright golden hair danced about her face. "Beautiful day," she said with a wave of her hand. "And you are Hope, Hope Ashton, I knew your grandfather, of course, a grand old man, so tall, the years barely seemed to make a difference to him, even after his brothers died leaving him to manage the farm on his own. Loved his farm and the old house, he did. Everyone knew him - everyone liked him. George, that is my husband, always enjoyed chatting with him - though George enjoys nothing more than talking, no matter to whom - and you will think the same of me, if I do not hush myself and say merely it is a pleasure to meet you."

I could not but smile. She spoke not of my situation, and I was grateful for it.

Margaret and Polly kept me between them as we went about the market; if introduced I curtsied to my new acquaintance, reminding myself I was innocent in all that had happened to me. I was introduced as the granddaughter of Seth Courtney and had the comfort of hearing my name given as Mistress Ashton, widow of Henry Ashton, but would that be sufficient to quell the gossip when my condition became more apparent? The situation in which I was found was common knowledge and that left me uneasy and grateful when I reached the vicarage door once more.

"It was not so bad, was it?" Margaret said, when we were alone again.

"I could not have done it without your companionship," I replied. "And… and I thought I saw Aggie walk away when she caught sight of me."

"Do not mind Aggie," Margaret explained. "She is as full of resentments as a rotten apple is full of maggots. I asked her to assist me here out of Christian charity, there's many another I would have preferred, but she lost her employment when your grandfather died, her son also. Did you not know she kept house for him?"

Aggie had her group of friends in the village, and Margaret hers - whenever I walked outside it became obvious which were which.

"Do not give a care for such people," Margaret advised me following another trip to the market. We had finished putting our purchases away in the store cupboard and Margaret dusted off the table and brought downstairs a package, unwrapping it carefully. "This piece of material comes from a dress length I had before the wars," she said, hoping to distract me, "but I had to put it away." She held the light blue material in her hands, lost in memory. "It was to be a rather frivolous dress." She dropped the material on to the table and picked up a thimble. Her voice resumed its everyday tone. "I think it will do well for the baby." We sat in silence sewing, each with our private thoughts. Now I could remember I missed the constant chatter of my sisters and mother but it was Margaret's peaceful company that kept me from despair as I waited for both my baby and Oliver Whitby to arrive.

But the longer I waited the more I found a certain resolve settling within me: I must see this Oliver Whitby for myself, I must go to the farm, though the thought of seeing it filled me with the utmost dread, for I could not feel settled until I had seen Whitby and his family documents for myself. But the farm? Would I not rather run back to the safety of the vicarage than walk along the path and see the ruins of the house? I must do it, I must, when the time came, though I could not see how I would have the strength - but it was for my child, and where my child was concerned strength would always overcome fear.

Chapter 5

"We are to be joined by a visitor for supper," Matthew announced brushing the rain from his coat as he entered the house.

"And who is that to be?" Margaret answered.

"Sir Neville Lattimer."

"Do you know him?"

"Barely," Matthew replied. "He was a good friend of my late uncle and added generously to the funds for the church repairs a few years back."

"And when is he to come?"

"This very night."

"Tonight! But Matthew?"

"I know, but he seemed to invite himself, there was little I could do after I commiserated with him about the food at the inn where he has been staying for the last week. Once he reminded me how my uncle always praised your cooking, how could I refrain from asking him to supper?" Matthew shrugged his shoulders. "You must have seen his coach - black with a gold crest with his initials on the side."

I knew the coach he meant, it was far superior to any I had ever seen before; it was drawn by a fine matched pair of horses.

"You are making me feel no better," Margaret said. "And what does he want with us?"

"I do not know, but we could do with further funds for the church."

"But Matthew?" Margaret repeated. "This Sir Neville Lattimer, he will not want the left-overs from yesterday's stew."

"I know you will do your best, Margaret."

"I am not sure my best will be good enough for this Sir Neville. What is he doing here and where does he come from?"

"A far part of Kent, I gather he has a grand manor house and a large estate."

"And half a dozen cooks, no doubt. Tell me no more, husband, I have heard enough."

"I happened to see George in the street and have asked him and his wife to join us this evening. George will keep the conversation flowing whatever the difficulty."

"That's the first good thing you have said since you came in the door," Margaret replied. "Now go away, Hope and I have much to do."

As darkness gathered over the house I watched from my bedroom window as the black coach drew up outside the vicarage and the passenger alighted. Sir Neville was about sixty years of age and quite a handsome man. He was dressed in silk and velvet, in greens of various shades, his moustache waxed. He wore the latest fashion - a short jacket and flared breeches gathered in at the knee with ribbon frills down the seams. His shoes had two-inch heels and bows on the front in a style I heard say favoured by the new king. I had never spoken to such a fine gentleman, rarely even seen one. Did he know how quietly Matthew and Margaret lived? We would all be dressed in black. I had said I would stay in my room, or serve the meal, but Margaret insisted I sit with them.

"Remember, he knows nothing of your history, you are our guest, that is all."

I curtsied when introduced to Sir Neville, as my mother had taught me. She had been a stickler for manners, having been a lady's maid before she married my father. Margaret and I placed the pigeon and bacon pie, minted peas and potatoes on the table and left the cheeses and apples for dessert on the sideboard before taking our seats. Mr Adams was as good as his fame for never being short of an opinion and there were no uncomfortable breaks in conversation Mr Adams did not fill with a hundred words or two, but when pretty little Polly Adams put out her hand to touch her husband's, he would smile and say, "But there, I must not hog the conversation." I smiled and relaxed a little.

"Mistress Hope," Sir Neville addressed me, "where did you live before your father inherited Hamblemere Farm?"

"I..." I started with nothing more than a whisper. Margaret was wrong, this gentleman knew my story; I could not feel more uncomfortable.

"Come, Mistress Ashton, do not be afraid, you are among friends."

The faces at the table were smiling, encouraging, and I tried to steady myself. I began again. "I was raised in Kingsdown."

"I know it not," Sir Neville replied.

"It is a small village, high on a ridge, the land falling away on all sides."

"It sounds charming," Polly said.

"It was my home."

"Everything changes, does it not?" Sir Neville added. "The king returns - so much death and destruction, families torn to pieces, and the king returns and takes the place of his father."

"But he will be a different monarch to his father, parliament will make sure of it," Matthew replied. "The pain of the nation has not been totally in vain."

The others gathered in the little room nodded, and after a moment's silence Margaret brought in the blancmange and Mr Adams spoke of the price of flour, and we left the tender subject of loss behind.

Sir Neville became a frequent visitor to the vicarage and Margaret felt her days being filled with the attention she must pay such a distinguished guest.

"Has he told you why he stays here so long?" Margaret asked Matthew one evening.

"I do not feel it my place to ask. To speak honestly there is much parish business to attend to so I am happy he is as pleased to spend his time with you and Hope as he is with me."

And so it seemed. I spent hours in the kitchen making elderflower cordial and preparing little dumplings flavoured with apple and cinnamon under Margaret's tuition to make Sir Neville welcome. Each time he visited he would bring some small gift - flowers, a trinket, or embroidered handkerchief both for Margaret and myself.

One afternoon Sir Neville suggested he and I should walk along the riverbank, a place I had avoided since the day when I had thought no good could come of my life. I took a deep breath knowing I should have faced that fear before now.

"As you wish," I said.

"Mistress Hope, I believe we are bound together in the loss of our loved ones," he said as we walked slowly along the path.

I did not wish to speak of my family, the pain too strong, too private, to be shared, but was surprised to learn that he, too, was mourning family members.

"I had sons, strong and handsome young men, cruelly taken from their father. I had two sons - the elder, Robert, fought for the royalists in our war and my younger son for Cromwell. I did not take sides between them, they were both my sons, and both were killed. Neither was married, I have no grandsons, no heir."

"I am sorry, Sir Neville, to hear you speak so sadly."

"I may have had another son, younger, too young to join the terrible fighting but the child died with my wife in childbirth fifteen years ago." Sir Neville sighed. "At least she was spared the news of the loss of her sons, she would have been as broken-hearted as I am."

"I know the loneliness of losing a family," I said.

"Yes, you do. That is doubtless why I feel I may speak to you with such ease. Naturally, a house as large as mine has many servants but they cannot take the place of family." He clapped his hands lightly together and lifted his eyes towards the heavens. "Come," he said, "let us speak of other things this fine day, we must enjoy the sunshine while we may, but I can see from your eyes there are many matters concerning you yet."

"Indeed. The issue of the farm is uppermost in my mind at the moment."

"My dear," he said, regarding me with kindly eyes, "I would not get my hopes up if I were you. You have had no experience of the wider world and you will learn women have no say whatsoever in the world of men. Your word counts for little. It would be a long and bitter battle if you were to contest Whitby's rights and it would cost money to pursue through the courts even if there was a chance you could prevail. And Master Whitby may well have the resources to fight off any challenge."

This was not the response I had hoped for. Everywhere I turned there seemed to be a wall of men.

"But please, do not fret yourself, I would not have a frown upon your pretty face."

Chapter 6

"There you are!" Matthew hurried into the parlour and warmed his hands by the fire. "There's a fierce cold wind blowing this afternoon."

"Where else would we be but happily occupied in the warm," Margaret said, her cheeks rosy from her proximity to the fire.

"What is it you are doing?" Matthew asked.

"Don't you recognise a …?" I fell quiet.

"This is a baby's layette and we are each embroidering a bonnet," Margaret continued on my behalf. I had never voiced my question about whether Margaret and Matthew wished for a child - my position made it impossible. "And why are you in such a hurry, may I ask?" Margaret carried on calmly, lifting her long neck.

"Well, I am informed Oliver Whitby has arrived at Hamblemere Farm and he has brought with him his family and a cart load of belongings."

"Oh no," I said. "I have been dreading this moment."

I told no-one of my resolve to see Whitby: this was an act I must do for myself, even if it brought no satisfactory outcome I must put my mind at rest. I set out in the early afternoon, my cloak battling against the sharp wind. I kept my head down, for I was battling with myself also. It was not thoughts of Oliver Whitby which filled me, but the images of that day, the house ablaze, the raiders swaggering with their bloody swords. I must dispel such thoughts. I held my cloak with clenched fists and walked on.

I stepped aside as I heard a coach rattle up behind me. "Mistress Ashton."

"Sir Neville!"

To my surprise he stepped down from the coach and came to stand beside me. "Where are you going with such determination may I ask?"

"I..." I did not wish to say but could not avoid the direct question. "I thought I should see Oliver Whitby."

"Please, please allow me to offer you the use of my coach."

"I cannot."

"Do not refuse me." He held the door open for me waving the coachman back to his seat. He took my hand as I stepped inside and sat down.

"Ah, I see my advice concerning the farm was not to your liking. I do not blame you. It is hard to believe your family home must go to someone else - I have the same difficulty myself. Having no heir my own house - Wilderness Hall - will go to a cousin I barely know and do not like. Permit me to assist you in this matter, allow me to do you that service. I do not wish to see you upset yourself - I shall speak to Whitby on your behalf. I am sure you will agree a visit from me is more likely to bring forth information than one from yourself. He will not be able to ignore me. I shall willingly undertake this mission for you."

"But..."

"Turn about!" Sir Neville shouted, and while I gathered my arguments the horses circled at the crossroads and I felt myself being carried back to the village and dragged away from my purpose. I was in turmoil: the fear of seeing the farm was being lifted from me and the burden of possible dispute, but I was being deprived of settling my own account, of discovering the truth for myself. "It will be my honour to do this for you, Mistress Hope. Your first duty must be to keep yourself and your child from harm."

I was back at the vicarage door before Margaret had missed me.

I heard a familiar sound an hour later and I went to my bedroom window and saw Sir Neville's ornate black coach draw to a halt outside. Sir Neville climbed down and shook hands with Matthew. The pair walked past the house and into the garden, conversing as they disappeared from view but not before I had noticed Matthew rubbing the back of his neck, as he did when worried.

I sat myself down in the parlour to wait but instead of the expected footsteps I heard the coach pull away across the gravel. Sir Neville had not come in to speak to me, instead Matthew entered alone. He did not seem happy as he asked me to sit down next to him at the table while Margaret prepared the bread and soup. "Hope, Sir Neville has seen the documents relating to Whitby's right to your farm - Hamblemere Farm, that is. He said there is no doubt of his entitlement. He said Oliver Whitby was an uncouth, ill-mannered lout who stood flanked by his two burly sons as he tried to put your case to him."

"How did he respond?"

"The man laughed."

"He laughed at Sir Neville?"

"Apparently, Whitby said he had heard all about you from Aggie Douglas when he met her in the village. She told him how you managed - no, I cannot say."

"Please tell me, tell me the truth – all of it."

"She told him," he began, and I could feel his reluctant to speak, "that you managed to save yourself by – you must guess the rest, I will not repeat it."

"Oh, God," I said, feeling sick, choking on my tears. "I knew the woman disliked me but to say that. No, no, how could she?"

"Sir Neville told me he lunged at the man but his sons intervened. He demanded Whitby watch his tongue, telling him spreading such lies and listening to gossip could lead him into serious trouble, but Whitby would have none of it, he said no bastard was going to take the farm from him and walked off without another word. I'm sorry Hope." I could see my own disappointment reflected on Matthew's face. "I'm so sorry." He stood up and went to help Margaret carry in the soup bowls as I contemplated the hopelessness of my situation.

I was in the garden when next I saw Sir Neville. It was a cold bright day in October and he found me tilting my face to the sun in a nook where there was shelter from the wind.

"Hope, may I join you for a few minutes?" he asked.

"But of course." I noted the serious expression on his face as he sat down next to me.

"You may be wondering why I left Matthew to tell you about Oliver Whitby. It was because I felt I had failed you. I can see no way forward with the man, unfortunately he has the law on his side, and the man is a brute, you can expect no generosity from him."

"Please, do not trouble yourself further. You warned me I was unlikely to prevail. I am most grateful for the effort you have made on my behalf."

We sat quietly awhile. A blackbird singing from the bare bough above us softened the silence between us as crisp leaves scuttled across the path. Sir Neville cleared his throat. "I have brought some of my late wife's clothes with me and have left them at the house. She was a larger woman than you, and they're a little old fashioned in style," he said, "but I'm sure they can be altered. After all, you will need clothes that fit for these last three months of your term. You may use them as you please, for baby clothes or for yourself and Margaret to wear."

"Thank you, you are so kind," I said "though I fear they may be a little grand for me."

"Not at all," Sir Neville replied. "I shall be visiting West Penton again in two months, and shall be calling on Matthew and - and I shall see you then, I trust."

"I have nowhere else to go at present, though I must not depend upon his charity for too long, I must make plans for my future," I finished in a whisper, "when I am able to see what that may be."

"Make no plans for now," Sir Neville said, taking hold of my hand, "other than to stay here with your friends. I have business to deal with but when I see you next I have something to ask you, but now I must depart." He kissed my hand and with a bow left me in my sheltered nook. So the farm would not become my home. If Sir Neville could not obtain so much as a civil answer from Whitby, what chance had I of ever learning exactly what claim he had to the place? I had no money and it seemed I had no chance. I must learn to accept it. Acceptance: a simple word, but a difficult way to live I had found. I should no longer trouble Sir Neville or Matthew with my forlorn hopes. I should instead concentrate on being grateful for all the love and generosity I had received, and from strangers at that, like the dresses Sir Neville had so thoughtfully left at the house for me. I rose and made my way indoors, leaving the blackbird sole ownership of the garden. I was in need of the dresses; in truth the one I was wearing was tight even though I had already let it out twice.

What was it, I wondered as I stepped inside, Sir Neville was going to ask me?

Chapter 7

I had told Margaret of Sir Neville's curious words to me and she had spoken to Matthew of the matter and they had decided it was possible Sir Neville would offer me a position at Wilderness Hall. "Be prepared for the question, consider what your reply would be, but I may have misjudged the case, so do not depend upon it. And if he should ask you do not feel obliged to accept," Matthew had declared, "we should be sorry to see you leave, this is your home now."

"Do try it on," said Margaret. She was sitting on the floor in the large front bedroom, having just finished the last dart in the dark green, fine woollen gown. She had done an excellent job, embellishing it with a green satin overskirt.

"Isn't it the most wonderful dress," I said, "but should I be wearing it? I am still in mourning for my family."

"And you are still young," Margaret put in. "It is a sober enough colour and the lace is a quiet decoration. Sir Neville, having been so generous, will expect us to make use of the material and fashion is changing as much as the times, whether for better or worse we know not yet. Stand still now, I've not finished," she continued, standing up and shaking her long limbs to loosen her stiffness. "Here." She draped a chiffon scarf over my shoulders and tucked it in the neckline to complete the style.

I reached up and kissed Margaret's pale cheek. "Come," I picked up the blue bodice and matching petticoat lying on the chair, "we must start work on your gown now and one evening we can surprise Matthew by sitting together in the parlour as grand as any two ladies in the land." We laughed, and for a moment I was young and carefree again.

We had spent several enjoyable days working on Lady Lattimer's gowns; these obviously had been put away before the late king's death judging by the style and the reek of lavender that filled the room as we unpacked them. My senses revelled in the sensuous feel of satin and velvet against my skin; the vibrant colours blazed against the quiet shades of my bedroom. We had had drabness forced upon us all for so many years such vivid colours seemed almost a sin.

"Before we continue with my dress," Margaret said, "we should alter the black gown to fit you. If Sir Neville does ask you to become a member of his household as Matthew thinks, you will need such a gown though I doubt you could take up the position before the baby is born."

It would soon be the last day of November and my baby was due near the end of January. As I got up slowly from the fireside my back ached, as it did most days when I exerted myself. Polly Adams, sitting with me one afternoon, informed me that as I carried the infant high, it was sure to be a boy. Each day I wondered when Sir Neville would return, and what that return would mean for me. There had been snow and it had settled, perhaps that had kept him away.

Christmas was no more than three weeks hence. It was wonderful to think we would be able to enjoy the festival once more, to give and receive presents, to listen to music and sing and dance. There were no restrictions now, apart from those on me due to my size. I would have to be content to watch the dancing.

All the preparations for Christmas were well underway. I sat tying bunches of mistletoe as part of the church decoration when I heard the crunch of gravel outside. I cast my eyes toward the window and saw Sir Neville and Matthew alight from the coach. "See who I found in the village!" shouted Matthew as the pair entered the house and hung up their cloaks. Matthew ushered Sir Neville into the parlour. I struggled to get to my feet but Sir Neville hurried to my side and insisted I sit down again. Margaret came in from the kitchen with glasses of mulled wine. We all sat close by the fire and listened eagerly to Sir Neville as he told us about his travels and what was going on further afield. "The date has been announced for the king's coronation," he said. "It is to take place on the 23rd April and I shall be there to swear allegiance to our new monarch."

"How wonderful to be present when the king is crowned," I said, awed by the prospect.

"Indeed, though it will cause much expense - new clothes in the latest fashion for all the festivities. I shall have to reside at my house in London, though I prefer to be at Wilderness Hall."

"You will stay for supper, Sir Neville?" Matthew asked while I thought what it must be like to own two homes.

"Thank you, Matthew, that would be most agreeable. I had intended to visit tomorrow but our meeting in the village has brought matters forward. I would like a word with Mistress Hope if I may?"

Matthew smiled. "Of course, we shall leave you in peace," and he picked up the empty glasses and followed Margaret into the kitchen.

"Hope, you may recall I said I would have something to ask you when I visited you once more."

"Why yes," I replied, it was a matter to which I had given much time and thought. I could not remain with Matthew and Margaret indefinitely despite their protestations to the contrary. I must make my own way. Sir Neville's estate was many miles away, no-one would know me there. If I was introduced as a young widow, I could leave my present circumstances behind me and my child would have a start in life unburdened by the horror of my past.

Sir Neville moved to sit next to me. "As you know I am a wealthy man and have a large estate and various other properties. I have many servants but I have no family now." An expression of profound sadness crossed his face and I lowered my eyes as I felt tears dampen my lashes. "The house feels empty and is a lonely place. It is a good house but lacks a mistress. Hope, will you marry me?"

My hand flew to my mouth as I regarded him in wide-eyed alarm.

"Hope, I see I have surprised you, did you not guess? Did Matthew not warn you of my intentions?"

"He didn't realise you meant this and no such thought crossed my mind," I stuttered as he took hold of my shaking hands.

"Hope, I am many years your senior and would not call on you to act as a wife but to be more of a companion. Let me be a father to your child. If we marry before the child is born it shall have my name and the rights that would bring. None of the stigma of possible bastardry would touch it. As you are aware there is little or no chance you would be able to repossess the farm. Instead you would be able to live in splendour and want for nothing. There is time before Christmas to call the banns and to have Matthew marry us. And in the new year we would journey to Wilderness Hall in time for the birth." He paused. "With you as my wife. What do you say, will you marry me?"

"Sir Neville..." I gasped for breath as my head whirled. "It is a great responsibility you ask of me. I have never lived in society, my family, though respectable and hardworking, were country people, would it be proper for me to marry you? How would I fit in with your friends?"

"Well, Henry Ashton thought you good enough to be his wife and his father was a squire married to a lady of breeding, I believe. Her son, Sir Edward, fought with my older son Robert back in '48 at Berwick and Preston - a fine soldier."

My breath caught in my chest – a double blow had struck me with his words: the mention of Sir Edward had made my heart lurch, confounding my confusion, for in my surprise at Sir Neville's proposal I had thought of myself as Ruth Courtney rather than the widow of Henry Ashton, a mistake I must not repeat. "Yes," I began gravely, "but Henry's family disapproved of the marriage and his father disowned him."

"Hope, there is no-one to gainsay me." He regarded me with fierce eyes, telling me I should not compare his position with Henry's. Then he smiled and his eyes warmed. "My friends will be envious of my pretty young wife and the expected child, the heir I shall have thanks to you."

"It is great honour you do me, Sir Neville." I spoke formally, nervous because of my previous error. "Please, may I ask for time to think?" At this moment I needed time merely to breathe; my thoughts were a wild jumble. "May I give you my reply tomorrow?"

"Of course, we will say no more of it tonight." He let go of my hand and stood before me. "You must take your time, we shall not speak of it over dinner." He smiled. "I am looking forward to one of Margaret's meals, they could do with a cook as good at the inn." He bowed and left me alone.

Marriage! Nothing could have been further from my thoughts. I would need both love and tenderness to make myself vulnerable to a man again. Sir Neville was most pleasant but there was no hint of love between us, nor could there ever be, I was sure of that. Could I spend my life separated from love? My mind was filled with the image of Hope and Henry on their wedding day, their love apparent in every glance and gesture. If I were to marry Sir Neville such emotions would never be mine. But then, what chance had I of a true love? What man would want me now? Sir Neville? Why? Why me? My baby gave me a sharp kick below my ribs, reminding me that if, in a sense, I felt my life was over, my child's was yet to begin.

When supper was finished and Sir Neville had left for the inn, I decided to ask Margaret and Matthew for their advice. We sat together in the light of the dying fire. My hands twisted the handkerchief I held into a tight knot.

"What's wrong, Hope?" asked Margaret gently placing her hands on mine to stop their nervous twiddling.

"Sir Neville has asked me to… marry him."

Both appeared stunned by my news. "But that is wonderful," said Matthew, the first to gather his wits. "I had thought…"

"Yes, that he might want me to work in the household in some capacity. That would be more appropriate, don't you think? And more than I had any right to expect in my position."

"Hope, you are a lovely young woman and life has been unkind to you but you were in no way to blame and Sir Neville has obviously seen that," said Margaret, squeezing my hand as she smiled broadly at me. "You should have the chance to enjoy the good things in life."

"Margaret, he says my child will bear his name if we marry now. But he is so much older than I. He has proved himself a good friend but I find it difficult to think of him as anything more."

"Are you worried about being a wife, sharing his bed and having his children, is that what vexes you?"

"Partly, though he said he wants me only as a companion. But perhaps one day it is just possible I could find someone to love, more of my own age, but I would be already trapped in marriage. Would it be fair to me, or indeed to Sir Neville?"

Matthew moved to my side. "Hope, you have to think of your child, of the start in life you will be able to give it. You will see your child grow up, well fed, clothed and healthy. There are many marriages made for convenience, especially in society, and I have seen such couples grow to love one another in time. As for maybe finding love, remember it is most likely Sir Neville will die before you, leaving you to pursue your heart. My dear child, you have nothing. In all honesty, the idea of owning the farm was but a dream. If anything happened to Margaret and I, God forbid, where would you be? At least with Sir Neville, you would have security. I have known him but a short while but have found him to be a good man."

I nodded. My heart and my mind were being forced along paths I had never imagined they would have to follow. Matthew's arguments were those I should make to myself. The future offered to me was far above anything I could have expected in my present situation, or indeed any other, a future not even dreamed of, but the lack of love weighed on my heart, and the thought of physical contact, of the marriage bed, made my stomach churn. But Matthew was right; my child's future must be my prime concern. I knew Matthew was a true friend and would not recommend a course of action if he did not genuinely believe it to be to my advantage. "Your thoughts are my own," I admitted after a silence that encompassed my spinning round and facing an entirely different future. "I must do the best for my child."

"And your comfort will be assured," Margaret said, "and will not happiness follow?"

"It is a great honour, I know," I burst out. "If my mother had ever thought I should become the mistress of such a house…" but I could say no more, tears spilled down my face and dropped on to my gown. It was somehow so much more than I had ever dreamed, and at the same time, so much less. "In truth, I cannot quite believe it," I said.

Margaret stood and came to my chair and hugged me. "It is not surprising your mind is confused on hearing such an unexpected declaration. You must give yourself time to get used to the idea."

"But I promised Sir Neville I would give him my answer tomorrow."

"I am sure he would wait for a little if you are still unsure."

"No," I determined. "I should count this as a blessing, should I not? I shall accept Sir Neville on the morrow. Will you marry us, Matthew? Sir Neville spoke of the banns having to be read."

"I would have it no other way."

"A Christmas wedding," said Margaret, "a double celebration."

When I had Margaret to myself early the next morning I told her of my concern about being accepted as mistress of Sir Neville's home.

"You must believe in yourself," she scolded me, "as Sir Neville obviously does."

I nodded. "Yes, yes, you are right. You are always right, Margaret, I do not think I could have survived without you."

"You are young and strong, Hope. I do not believe there is anything you cannot do."

"I shall trust your judgement on this as on all things," I said with a smile. I began to think of my future as Sir Neville's wife, in his home, with some sense of reality. "Will you be able to come to visit me, it would give me such pleasure. How far away is his estate?"

"I believe Matthew said it was near the Kent coast, more than a day's travel from here, but that would not stop me were I to receive an invitation. You know that, don't you?"

I did not reply, but held her close and as ever gathered strength from her love.

A private wedding was arranged for the early afternoon of Christmas day. The banns were read for the required three Sundays and I attended the earliest service on each occasion, not wishing to hear the murmurs that would accompany the reading at the later, more crowded, services. And I went to the church alone at other times, to sit beside the Courtney stone, to think of them and pray they understood all I had decided to do - understood and approved.

Margaret eased me into the beautiful green dress on Christmas afternoon and lent me a white Spanish lace veil that had been her aunt's. "You look lovely," she said.

"As do you," I replied, for she had relinquished her normal strict dark attire and her angular frame was draped with the rich ruby material of one of Lady Lattimer's gowns. "But I am so big," I added as I caught sight of myself in the glass; my skin was pale so my eyes seemed large and bright, but they did not smile back at me; I gave my attention to my gown instead - it would not disgrace my groom though my size might be thought to do otherwise. So, I thought, this woman, this woman fashionably dressed in expensive materials was the woman I was about to become. I would have to learn to live with her.

"Oh, there is a letter on the mantle downstairs, I almost forgot," I told Margaret. "It is for Mr and Mrs Adams, to thank them for their generosity in providing the wedding feast at the mill. I have a family, I realise that now," I said, the glory of my dress forgotten. "Mr Adams will give me away, you will be beside me and Matthew will perform the service. I feel as I would if it had been my own father, my own family - I feel loved. And here, I must give you back your ring," I finished, my voice wavering, "its replacement will soon be upon my finger."

Twilight was gathering in the trees as I walked across the road to the church, its tower outlined against the sky, clouds hurrying past the rising crescent moon. Mr Adams, silenced by the occasion, supported me with his arm and with his gentle smile. The heavy wooden church door stood open, and with a nod of encouragement from Mr Adams I began my walk towards the altar. I could not prevent my eyes from straying towards the stone in the floor bearing my family's name, but, my fingers tightening around Mr Adams' hand, I forced myself forward. In the soft candlelight the church, filled with holly, ivy and mistletoe, seemed changed into a private, quiet, bower filled only with my friends - few, but loved all the more for that.

My groom stood waiting for me, elegant in a short silver jacket and grey satin breeches decorated with folded ribbons. This was a happy occasion I chided myself as I advanced towards him. The dye was cast and I should take some pleasure in this special day in my life; one to be remembered as a new start, a putting away of all my travails.

I said a silent prayer that I was doing the right thing as I gave my responses. Matthew smiled as he pronounced us man and wife.

I sat at the wedding feast smiling, everyone so happy for me. I smiled for my husband, smiled for my hosts, smiled for Matthew and Margaret. My own smiles, the smiles that came from within, would have to wait until I was sure what my new life would entail. At the back of my mind while I ate my way through duck and asparagus, dried fruit and custard, was my disquiet at what would happen to me now, now I was Sir Neville's property. My husband, how strange that sounded, could, despite his kind reassurance, could, despite my condition, demand his marital rights.

Sir Neville and I went back to the vicarage in his coach. We did not speak, the day spoke for us - we were married. It was late as I made my way to my bedroom. Margaret waited there for me and helped me undress. She slipped me out of my gown and underskirts and into a nightdress of white linen. She kissed me. She had brought me thus far but the future I would have to face alone. She left the room and closed the door quietly behind her. I could hear the creaking floor boards as Sir Neville moved about in the next room, no doubt disrobing for bed - but whose bed? Alone in my bed in the moonlight I fidgeted with the wedding ring on my finger and felt the baby move within me. "You are safe, little one," I whispered. "There is no discomfort I would not endure to keep you so." How my feelings had changed for my unborn child, I loved it now beyond anything I could imagine, though it was nothing more than a bulge that weighed me down and a kick that made me gasp.

I lay in my bed; the sounds from next door had ceased. I waited anxiously but I need not have worried, as finally, I heard Sir Neville snoring. I relaxed and exhausted fell asleep.

Chapter 8

"I have informed Matthew we will be leaving in an hour," Sir Neville said as I reached the foot of the stairs.

"An hour!" I gasped. "What of my packing, my farewells?"

"I do not imagine you will need much time for either," Sir Neville replied. "As I said we should leave in an hour if we are to make the inn as arranged by nightfall."

He dismissed my plea and went outside to speak to the coachman.

"Margaret, Margaret," I cried, catching sight of her in the kitchen doorway.

"I know. Eat your breakfast."

"I can't eat."

"You know you must, for the baby. Meanwhile I shall begin packing your things, if you will permit me to do so."

"Permit? Oh Margaret."

She saw the tears forming in my eyes. "You must keep the black dress," I said, "it may be of use to you."

"If you wish, my dear. Fear not," she said, "I shan't forget to pack the baby things, after all the hours we spent making them. Eat your breakfast and I'll pack, Sir Neville has had his driver drop off a box for you." She explained the matter as if to a child. I felt like a child, a lost child.

I did as I was bid, and within the hour my trunk, only half-full, was placed on the back of the coach. I stood at the door, reluctant to move.

"The weather is none too bad," Sir Neville said, gazing up at the grey clouds covering the sky from horizon to horizon. "It is important we get to Wilderness Hall as soon as possible, for the sake of the child," he added. For a moment I could only think what was to my baby's advantage seemed always to be to my detriment. "Here, put on your cloak, it is a cold morning."

I felt myself being hurried to the door. "No, not yet. Margaret! Margaret!" I called. Margaret appeared, running down the stairs. We hugged each other close. I was leaving the only safety I knew. "Here," I whispered, "I thought I should be here on Twelfth Night to give you my present." She opened the package I handed her and took out the draw-string bag I had made to match her ruby dress. I could see from the smile on her face that it pleased her.

"Dear Hope," she said quietly, words just between the two of us, "it is beautiful and," she handed me a small trinket box, "I have a present for you." I lifted the lid and found within a gold cross on a chain. "Like the ring you returned to me it was my mother's, I have no children to hand it on to, I want you to have it."

My mouth made the words 'thank you' but my voice had disappeared.

"I'll be here, if you ever need me, please remember that," she whispered. Then she held me away from her. "You will write to us and let us know how you fare and all about the baby?"

I swallowed and tried to gather myself. "Oh, yes. You shall know all about my child, and my child shall know all about you. I can never repay you and Matthew for what you have done for me."

Matthew was standing on the doorstep, blowing his hands to keep them warm. "Come," he said, "let me help you into the coach."

I embraced Margaret one last time. "You have been a daughter to me," she whispered.

I stepped outside and took the few steps that led me to Sir Neville's coach. He waited patiently within. With the assistance of Matthew I climbed up and sat down heavily. Matthew laid a blanket over my lap. "Be happy. God bless you both," he said, as he closed the door, shouting, "Drive on," to the coachman.

Sir Neville spoke a few words as the horses pulled away from the vicarage but I heard them not. I craned my neck to catch the last sight of Matthew on the gravel drive, Margaret beside him now, waving, both waving. I tried to reply in like kind but the limitations of the coach meant I could no more than move my hand an inch or two. I craned my neck to catch a last sight of the church tower until its greyness merged with the heavy sky and I felt as lost as the tower was to my sight. I sat back, holding myself tight in case I should dissolve in tears. I closed my eyes for a moment.

"You understand how important it is we are settled in Wilderness Hall as man and wife before the infant is born," Sir Neville was saying. I nodded, afraid my voice would give away the emotions within me. "Fear not," he said, "we shall make the journey in easy stages, and all the necessary arrangements have been made along the route."

"It is most thoughtful of you, Sir Neville," I said.

"I will do anything for the benefit of the child," he replied.

I sat back. I was glad to be in the comfort of such a splendid coach; previously I had always travelled in father's cart or a farmer's wagon, now I was resting on leather seats with silk lining the walls, yet my heart was discomforted and no silk lining could compensate. Sir Neville spoke occasionally of the villages we drove through but I found I could not listen. By afternoon I was uncomfortable and restless.

"Are you unwell?" Sir Neville asked.

"Not unwell," I replied, "but my back is aching and I am afraid the jostling of the coach could bring the child on too soon."

Sir Neville, my husband as I found it impossible to think of him, was much concerned and immediately shouted an order for the coachman to go more slowly and he gathered all the cushions about me until I felt almost smothered. "We must take all possible care," he said.

We stopped occasionally to give the horses a rest, stretch our legs and to eat the food Margaret had prepared for us. The cold had crept into my bones by the time we reached the inn. I was relieved the first of the two-day journey had been safely completed.

There was already a light covering of snow over the Kent countryside and the lanterns of the inn blazed cheerfully against the darkening sky. I struggled out of the coach, stiff and aching. The warmth of the main room hit me as I walked in and the clatter and noise of the other guests assailed my ears. A table was ready for us, placed close to the fire, and a good meal soon followed. As soon as we had finished the landlord showed us to a chamber at the back of the building on the ground floor. There was one question in my head and I dare not ask it. I smiled to see a glowing fire and my smile deepened when Sir Neville said his own room was on the floor above and I must be sure to keep my door bolted; I was more than happy to comply. Sir Neville returned to drink with other revellers in the main saloon and I was soon asleep despite the noise.

Immediately after breakfast we travelled on, just as a gentle snow started to fall. After a brief stop at a hostelry for some dinner we were on our way once more. But the closer we got to Wilderness Hall the more anxious I became.

The days were short and we had hoped to arrive at the house by mid-afternoon but the bad weather had slowed us, the horses' hooves slipping as they filled with compacted snow, and I was weary from the rocking of the coach as the wheels hit the ruts caused by other coaches and wagons.

"Not long now," said Sir Neville. "The gatehouse is up ahead."

I gazed out of the window; the snow had ceased to fall and a weak pink sun had finally shown its face as it began to set. Ahead stood the most magnificent house I had ever seen, two storeys high, topped with tall twisted chimneys, a dusky red E-shaped building, a manor house of Queen Elizabeth's time seeming to sit but lightly upon the earth, banded as it was with great mullioned windows. At that moment the walls of glass were reflecting the deep pink of the glowing sunset and my breath caught in my throat to see something so glorious. From the long drive I saw someone run to the house, no doubt to warn of our approach.

Chapter 9

"Hope, I know how tired you are but tradition requires I present the new mistress to her staff on her arrival," Sir Neville explained. "It won't take long. There is one thing I must demand of you," he said, taking my hand, holding it too tight. "You must never speak to anyone of your past life - never. Do you hear me? Never a word."

I nodded my assent, waiting for him to free my hand.

"You must say it."

"I must never speak of my past life - to anyone."

His grip upon my hand loosened. "We do not wish the child to learn of your unhappy past, I am sure you agree."

"Of course. It is for the best."

I assented, but did not understand. There were many things I had no wish to speak of – but of my family? Of the farm? Of the village where we lived, or Matthew and Margaret? What would I be allowed to say when they visited, as they promised they would? How could I ever become acquainted with Sir Neville's circle of friends if my life up until that moment had to be blank? How should I answer the commonest of questions? The baby kicked and I reminded myself I had more immediate concerns than idle conversations in the months to come.

The coach drew to a halt outside the entrance in the central wing where the double doors stood open. I took a deep breath to steady the fears taking possession of me. The coachman pulled the weary horses to a stop and two liveried footmen stepped forward to open the door of the coach. Sir Neville alighted and held out his hand for me. *Lady Lattimer! I must be Lady Lattimer - not the girl from Hamblemere Farm. Sir Neville said I must never be her again - but surely that meant I was no-one at all.* Sir Neville's hand waited for me to take it. I descended from the coach with as much grace as I could find. The way to the great doors had been swept clear of snow. Sir Neville was a man who had his path made clear for him, as it was now clear for me, as his wife. Sir Neville glanced in my direction - his expression was neither of tenderness nor affection, but it seemed, of pride. I held myself as tall and straight as I could in my condition and we climbed the three steps and moved within.

I had never imagined I would walk through the front entrance of such a house. I could not refrain from tilting back my head to take in the height of the hall. The servants stood in a line, the broad staircase of gleaming dark wood rising above them. Sir Neville guided me across the black and white chequerboard floor to a spot beneath the portrait of a man in Tudor doublet and hose standing with his dogs at his feet. I turned to face the assembly. My back was aching and the child kicked as I gave a faint smile.

"As you know," announced Sir Neville, "I have been away for most of the last year and in that time," he raised my hand, guiding me forward, "I have married. I present to you, the new mistress of Wilderness Hall - Lady Lattimer." A cheer rose from the assembly; the women curtsied and the men lowered their heads in a bow. I was unsure how I should respond, but found myself nodding in acknowledgement. "I charge you all," Sir Neville continued, "to take great care of my lady and my future heir." I heard a sound, an intake of breath, perhaps, at the unexpected declaration: I was so wrapped up against the cold it had not been immediately apparent I was pregnant. The cheering grew stronger and I could feel a blush take hold of my cheeks.

"I must appoint a maid for her ladyship," Sir Neville declared as the hall fell quiet. I saw an expression of pointed interest from half a dozen of the women before me. "Gwen, you will take that position." I could see the disappointment, verging on anger, written on their faces as a young redheaded girl, standing towards the back, raised her eyes in surprise. "Look sharp," Sir Neville commanded, "and make sure there is a warming pan provided for her bed and a bowl of hot water." The girl gave a bob and beamed at me. "Her ladyship will retire shortly as she is tired after the journey. Cook," he barked, "a light meal on a tray for Lady Lattimer and I will eat once I have seen my wife safely to her room. Steward, what are you waiting for, man? See to it the men bring in the luggage from the coach and take the trunks to our rooms. And show the new coach driver to his quarters.

"Your ladyship," said Sir Neville, offering me his arm on which I leaned gratefully, "I shall escort you to your room."

We climbed the stairs slowly behind a footman carrying an ornate candelabra, my hand sliding over the smooth polished wood of the handrail. We made our way to a room at the far end of a long gallery, candles flickering as we passed.

"This is your room, my dear," Sir Neville said, opening a door. He entered the darkened bedroom and waited while the footman proceeded to light candles, the room slowly taking shape before me. The girl who was to be my maid slipped in and placed a pan of hot coals on the hearth using a few of them to light the fire. Moving quickly and silently she placed a small table and a chair close by. "I shall say good night." Sir Neville kissed my hand as I stood there in some bewilderment. "Your supper will be here shortly. I shall see you in the morning."

I felt my whole body weaken as the door closed behind him. The girl must have observed the movement and hurried to my side; she was not as tall as I and had to stand on tiptoe to help me off with my cloak. She gave me her arm as I made my way unsteadily to the chair. I took a quick glance at the huge bed, darkly canopied, so it seemed almost a small room unto itself. There was a tapping at the door and the maid collected a tray from the serving man and carried it to the table. It held a mug of hot milk laced with honey, a few pieces of chicken and a small apple tart. "Thank you" I said, "this is very welcome, I did not know I was so hungry."

"If you will excuse me, your ladyship," the girl said, keeping her head bowed, "I have to go downstairs." She left the room coming back a few minutes later with a jug of hot water and a parcel under one arm. She placed the jug by the bowl on its stand and the parcel on the bed's rose-pink coverlet.

"Have you finished, my lady?" she asked seeing the empty plate before me.

"Yes, thank you," I said. She removed the plate, scooping it up and placing it on the other side of the room. My baby gave a kick that made me catch my breath.

"My lady?"

"All is well, perhaps you could show me to the water closet."

"Of course, my lady."

"I am sorry," I said, "but I have forgotten your name."

"Gwen, my lady."

A slight groan escaped me as I stood and I was unsure whether it was from exertion or the thought I had seemingly lost my name: I was 'Lady Lattimer' or 'my lady', my every wish attended to almost before it had taken shape in my mind. I felt fenced in by civility.

A little later Gwen gently helped me off with my clothes so I could wash. "These are for you, my lady," she said, unwrapping the parcel and holding up a fine nightdress of soft wool, slippers and a shawl of the most delicate fabric. "Sir Neville said you should wear these," she explained. I felt a momentary chill as I heard those words but she added, "The master said you were to be kept warm." She dressed me, her small hands dancing about me, and settled me into the chair in the glow of the blazing fire. I could hardly keep my eyes open as I saw her run the warming pan slowly over the sheets until satisfied. She helped me up the step and on to the bed carefully lifting my feet into the warm cocoon, closing the side curtains, but leaving open the end facing the blazing fire. I settled down and started to drift off while she carried the tray quietly from the room, snuffing out the candles on her way. I fell instantly into a deep and much needed sleep.

It was very early and my bladder was bursting. It took some effort to pull back the curtain around the bed and climb down into the chill air of the room. I searched for the chamber pot but could find no sign of it so put on my slippers and picked up my shawl. Moonlight flooded in through the great windows as I stepped outside but moving down the long gallery I could not recall which door led to the water closet. Not wishing to rouse the household if I made a wrong guess I decided to go back to my room. I sighed; there was always the jug or the bowl as the last resort. As I walked back in the bright moonlight I noticed something stir on the other side of my doorway - it was Gwen lying next to my trunk. She raised her head from her straw pallet at my approach.

"My lady, are you all right?" She struggled to her feet, grabbing at her blanket.

"I need the water closet, where is it?" I said urgently. "I can't remember which door."

"It's just along here, my lady," Gwen replied, "but there's a chamber pot under the bed at the front end, behind a small door. I'll show you."

I saw the girl's tired face. "Why are you sleeping here, on the floor?"

"I have to sleep nearby in case you should need anything, my lady," she said, picking up her candle and lighting it. I was getting cold and we hurried back to my room and retrieved the chamber pot. Gwen busied herself while I made use of it, adding some thin rags and kindling to revive the dying embers, bringing the fire back into life, gradually adding coal and sticks to it.

"Gwen, please bring your pallet in here, the corridor is freezing, but first help me up the step and back into bed."

She took my arm. "Are you sure the master won't mind me being in your room? I would not wish to make him angry."

"Angry? But I have never seen Sir Neville angry," I said. Gwen's expression changed to one of surprise. "Of course, your ladyship," she said. "I will do as you say."

"It will be fine," I reassured her. "I shall tell him I felt I might need your assistance again. Now go on, fetch your pallet and place it near the fire." The room was warming up once more as I pulled the covers close around me.

"Yes, my lady." I heard her drag her pallet into my room before I drifted into sleep once more.

The following morning well rested, I rose early. The room I had barely been able to discern the night before was nigh on half the size of our entire house in Kingsdown. All this space - for me alone? The thought of it did not make me happy. But I would not be on my own – my child's presence would fill this room in time. Gwen had opened the heavy pink curtains to let in a chill white light, illuminating the pale primrose yellow painted walls. Having removed her pallet, she dragged my trunk before the fire and I went through it with her, unpacking the baby clothes and my few dresses. Sitting beside her, watching her move, the speedy flow of expressions crossing her face, Gwen reminded me of Jessie; she was small and quick with a ready smile she tried to repress when she spoke to me, obviously feeling it would be inappropriate when addressing the lady of the house. Did some fine lace and a few ribbons mean she could not see I was but a young woman like herself? As she sat below me, bent over my trunk, I felt the urge to place my hand upon her shoulder. Margaret had always protected me, made me feel almost a child, but with Gwen I felt as if she had been put in my charge, I must protect her, guard her. I smiled to myself, perhaps I was merely preparing for motherhood.

When we had finished Gwen went downstairs to tell the cook what I would like to break my fast. I spent a moment at the window: the sky was pale with winter sunshine and below me I could see the rose garden covered in snow, stark and bare now, but how pretty it would be when summer came. I could sit there with my child. I must be content.

"Ouch." The baby gave a hefty kick just below my ribs. "Steady on little one, we will both be fed soon, I promise." I walked the length the long gallery and met Gwen on her way to find me.

"My lady, Sir Neville is in the dining hall waiting for you to join him. I told him you intended to go down to breakfast." I refused her arm, feeling quite fit and well after my night's sleep. "Please lean on me when we get to the stairs otherwise Sir Neville may be cross with me for not caring for you properly," pleaded Gwen.

"Surely not?" I saw the worried expression on her face and reluctantly took her arm.

Gwen led me to a large dining hall with a long dark table at its centre. Serving men stood between richly carved sideboards. Sir Neville indicated a tall chair opposite his own which a footman pulled out for me. I was uncomfortable with such attention, unused to such formality. Breakfast was good, the bread freshly baked and the eggs just the way I liked them. As I finished a serving girl leant over me to remove my plate but her hand slipped and the plate fell to the floor, crashing beside me. Sir Neville jumped up forcefully pushing the girl away. "Be more careful in future, idiot, you might have injured the baby," he shouted.

"Sir Neville, please." I said no more, warned from continuing by the sharp glance he sent in my direction.

"Was your chamber to your liking?" he asked when he had resumed his chair and the girl had disappeared from the room.

"Oh yes, it is very comfortable, thank you," I replied shakily. "And there will be plenty of space for the baby's crib."

"The child will have his own room," Sir Neville said as he took more bread.

"Not in my room?"

"Certainly not. The steward has been busy while you slept, the room is being prepared. You will find many items there for the infant, including a christening gown that has been in my family for many years."

The nursery was a small room with a window giving a view of the gardens. I felt a sense of relief when I saw there was a bedroom leading off it - so I could sleep close to my child after all. Sir Neville saw me wander over to it.

"That is the wet nurse's bedroom and will eventually be the nursemaid's room."

"Wet nurse! But I want to nurse the child myself; I'm young and fit enough to do it."

"No, not possible, it cannot be done, not by the mistress of the house." He opened the first drawer of a tall chest and revealed a complete layette.

"But I have a layette, the one Margaret and I made."

"You can't believe I would allow a child of mine to use anything sewn by you and that vicar's wife."

"But it's lovely, you haven't even seen it." I frowned, tears welling up.

"Why not give it to some member of the local poor. Yes, that would be a good idea and would go down well with the

74

villagers, it won't be wasted. See, here is the Lattimer christening gown, I wore it, as did my sons."

Sir Neville removed the gown with careful hands and I could see why he would disdain anything Margaret and I had made, however fine the stitching, however much emotion was wrapped up in it. I stretched out my hand to feel the intricate lace and the tiny bobbles of the seed pearls. "It is very fine," I said. "I shall do as you suggest." I understood I must take this lesson; this world was not the world I knew. Nothing of mine would be good enough, and nor, I feared, would I. Carefully I replaced the layette and closed the drawer.

"You have a new life now," Sir Neville said. "No one here knows what happened to you. I even changed the coachman at the last minute before we left West Penton, the new one is from London and knows nothing of the events in the village. It will be acknowledged I have married beneath my station, but you are of good family, there is no need for it to be known how great that distance is if you follow me in all things. You understand?" I nodded. "And you will never, ever, question my actions again as you did at breakfast, or you will face my wrath. I forgive you this time because it's all new to you." I kept my eyes down, staring at the floor, confused, alarmed, and bit my lip. "And I won't have sulking," he added as he spun on his heels and left the room.

Chapter 10

I reasoned the sharp words from Sir Neville were but a momentary flare, for he continued to be as courteous as before, as if nothing had happened when next we dined together. I considered I had much to learn about being the mistress of the house and set to teaching myself all I could, not from questioning but from observation. I knew I must act as if I had always lived in a home of some quality and must not gaze in wonder at the comfort and beauty that was now all about me. Sir Neville had chosen well in nominating Gwen as my especial maid for she brought a smile to my face. The colour of her hair was not one I had ever seen before: it was a fiery red and the hair itself was wiry and oft-times it had difficulty staying beneath her cap.

"You have been running," I said as she entered my room one morning.

"No-one was about. Oh," she caught herself, "I mean, I'm sorry, my lady." She tried to keep her eyes lowered, but her glance kept bobbing up, subservience was a lesson she had not learned, I realized, and was glad of it. "But I wasn't carrying anything." She thought better of it and stopped there. Little did she know if it had not been for the advanced state of my pregnancy I would have been tempted to join her in a race the length of the long gallery.

When I felt rested, and the baby was quiet in my womb, I explored the house. I ran my fingers over the gleaming wood panelling, each small square displaying the skill of the carpenter with the wood seemingly folded like linen. I bent my neck to gaze at the elaborate mixture of squares and circles of the moulded plaster ceilings and tried to puzzle out who the figures might be on the heavy tapestries lining the walls. The fires were kept well-stoked with no thought for the cost. Candles lit the way once the sky darkened and I could hear my mother's voice scolding at the extravagance I saw all about me. The food was plentiful, well prepared and tasty, though the cook's puddings were not as fine as my mother's. I smiled to myself when I heard her comments in my head, smiled to know she was still with me, and would ever be.

One afternoon when the frost had faded beneath a gentle sun I gathered my cloak and stepped outside. The gardens were laid out with a fine precision of hedges and plants. Close to the kitchen there was a herb garden and in the distance I could see the shimmer of a lake. Mostly the inclement weather meant I must stay within doors but I could explore the countryside with my eyes from the long gallery. One day as I gazed at the far horizon a flash of sunlight, pushing its way between grey clouds, caught a mark in the glass before me. I studied it and thought I could make out an I or J entwined with an L with something resembling ivy leaves. Some forbear of Sir Neville's idling the day away, I thought, and I longed to make my own mark on the window glass to show I too had walked and waited here. I should write HL for Hope Lattimer but in truth I wished to write RC, for in my heart I was still Ruth Courtney, the girl who loved to help her father in his wheelwright's shed when not told she was in the way, who had been taught to milk a cow and make cheese, whose family's position in life had improved on inheriting

Hamblemere Farm, but was still of little consequence in Sir Neville's world.

"I have guests arriving today for the twelfth-night revels," Sir Neville informed me over breakfast. "Local gentry staying for the hunt."

"I should be happy to make their acquaintance," I replied.

"That will not be necessary," Sir Neville informed me. "In your condition you will not be expected to join us, indeed, as you know, it is customary at this stage of your pregnancy to keep within your own chamber at all times. Your meals will be brought to you on a tray from now on."

"Of course," I said quickly, not wishing to show my ignorance of the fact, but thinking of the farmer's wives working indoors and out until their pains began.

"You may greet my guests on their arrival this evening though, I wish them to see my wife."

You wish them to see my condition, I thought, but nodded.

I asked Gwen to help me dress in the new gown Sir Neville had presented me with specially for the evening - a cream satin bodice, heavily embroidered with intertwining leaves, with lace at the cuffs and about the neck which was cut low over my breasts, a cream petticoat and an overskirt of pale green to match the embroidery. There was a knock at the door and Gwen paused from brushing my hair.

"Come in," I called.

The door opened and one of my husband's gentlemen entered carrying a velvet box. "Sir Neville requests her ladyship wear this tonight." He opened the box and I beheld a glittering necklace, bright clear stones surrounding dark blue ones.

"Please thank Sir Neville," I whispered.

As soon as the footman had disappeared Gwen came forward to see the jewels. "Diamonds and sapphires," she said, entranced. "Oh, my lady, forgive me. I have never seen such things before."

"Nor I," I replied too quickly, wishing I had not spoken but Gwen hardly seemed to have heard.

"I've heard talk of them, the Lattimer jewels, but of course there has been no-one to wear them since..." Now it was Gwen who wished she had not spoken.

"You must fasten it for me, Gwen, when you have finished my hair."

My gown was perforce large but it flowed prettily around my feet when I walked, and with my hair loose and shining, and the brilliant stones about my neck I felt I would not be out of place in this splendid house for once.

"Ah, my wife!" Sir Neville announced as I carefully made my way down the great staircase into the brightly lit hall. I stopped on the third step, my eyes lowered. Sir Neville took my hand. "My lords, gentlemen, I introduce Lady Lattimer." Something of a roar of approval made me raise my eyes. "My wife has had a busy day, so you must excuse her if she retires to her room."

Sir Neville led me to the first landing, kissed my hand, and I continued up, holding my voluminous skirt, unable to wipe away the tears forming in my eyes.

"You sly old dog," I heard a rasping voice below me declare, "so that's why we haven't seen much of you this last year. You kept it pretty quiet, claiming you were away on estate business."

"I wouldn't mind such work myself," another voice said and laughter rang out.

"I didn't believe it when they said you'd married your mistress…" were the last words that assailed me as I reached the gallery and though I listened, I heard no word of protest from Sir Neville.

Despite my misgivings, I could see Sir Neville had been successful in his aim of making his friends believe the child was his own and knew I should be grateful.

Early the next morning when the air was almost white with frost I watched from the gallery windows as Sir Neville and his guests, some of the older ones with considerable assistance, mounted their gleaming horses. I caught fragments of conversation of favourite horses and long-dead dogs. They trotted away in search of ermine and deer to the sound of the hunting horn, the hounds milling about, anxious to be given the freedom of the hills and woods, as was I.

On the way back from the water closet I passed a maid carrying bed linen and spied she had left the door to Sir Neville's room slightly ajar. I decided upon an impulse to sate my curiosity and stepped within. It was a far larger and grander chamber than my own. My eyes roved from the rich reds of the carpet to the blues and greens of the tapestry; to the huge bed with its embroidered hangings, to the fire burning in the grate; to the writing desk beneath the window. On the far wall I spied three pictures each draped in black silk. Carefully I lifted the corner of the covering of the one nearest to hand to reveal the portrait of a handsome fair-haired young man with kindly grey eyes, reminding me of Sir Neville. The name on the brass plate was Robert Lattimer and I recalled that was the name of his elder son who had died fighting for the royalists. I tried to understand Sir Neville's decision of covering the portrait - if I were lucky enough to have the image of my loved one, would I not wish to have it gazing down on me when I was in the quiet of my own chamber? "Everyone mourns in their own way," I remembered my mother saying, and doubtless she was correct in that as in all things.

I let go of the silk and it fell back into position. I moved to the second picture and raised its silken shroud. It was the portrait of a woman, Sir Neville's late wife, Edwina, according to the name-plate; she was handsome without being beautiful; haughty, unsmiling. Her hair was dark brown and her eyes were even darker, almost black. She was dressed in blue satin trimmed with intricate lace in the fashion of the first King Charles, and on her bosom lay the resplendent Lattimer jewels. I noted how she wore them; it was with an utter conviction of ownership I knew I could never aspire to. I heard a noise, probably Gwen I thought or maybe the linen maid. I made sure the paintings were as I found them and hurried back to my room.

Chapter 11

The guests departed, rather to my relief, and the house was quiet once more. Sir Neville came not near me; all my meals were brought to my room. "Do not take the stairs in case you should fall," he had told me one afternoon when I longed to step outside. If he did not want my companionship it would have been better if he had taken me on as a servant, I thought.

"Do sit down, Gwen," I said one morning, weary of sitting alone.

"But, my lady."

"I shall strain my neck if I have always to look up to you."

"Well, you don't have to look up very high," Gwen retorted, then stopped, covering her mouth with her hand. "I beg your pardon, my lady, I forgot myself."

"Gwen, you have merely spoken to me as a human being, one woman to another. Now sit down beside me. You mentioned yesterday your mother worked here, how long ago was that?"

Gwen sat down carefully, as if this could all be some trick. "My mother was employed here as a seamstress before she married," she began, quite formally, as if under close questioning, but then she warmed to her subject. "Well, that's not quite right, she started as a scullery maid but when they saw how good her sewing was she was employed as a seamstress - so much better, she said, for one thing she could sit down all day, but she told me it was a case of aching hands in place of aching feet. Of course, she was but an assistant to

Mary who was the chief seamstress, but I am sure she would have taken that position in time, if she had not met my father when he was delivering meat. He was a labourer at Old Lodge Farm and mother says the most handsome man she ever saw, so she married him at barely twenty and went from mending the finest linen to darning my father's socks, that is what she always says."

"And where is this, where do they live?" I sat back in my chair, happy to be having a real conversation; a genuine conversation with someone for the first time since I had kissed Margaret goodbye.

"My father lives not at all, he died with a rattling chest that took his breath away."

"I am so sorry. I did not mean to upset you."

Gwen shot to her feet, as if afraid she had said too much. "Is there anything else, my lady?"

Call me by my name, I longed to say, and sit with me and tell me more of your family, but "No, that will be all, thank you, Gwen," I said, and she made a curtsy and left the room.

I waited until she was bathing me one morning, running the cloth over my back where I could not reach, to ask her more.

"How long have you been here at Wilderness Hall?"

"More than five years now, my lady."

"You must have been very young when you first came."

"Ten I was, after father died." I felt the hand pause on my back. "They took me in as a favour to my mother, no pay to speak of, but one less mouth for her to feed, though she says she missed my help when my brothers and sisters were younger."

"Do you have many?"

"Brothers and sisters? Five of them." The hand speeded up on my back. "Lively as a bag of kittens, mother says."

"I'm sure." I smiled as the image of Gwen's home came into my mind. "I had sisters," I replied. "Two sisters, I always wanted a brother, a big brother, I was so happy when..." I swallowed the words that were to follow, remembering Sir Neville's one order to me - that I never speak of my past. "Could you help me out, Gwen, I'm getting cold."

Seeing true conversation with Gwen was nigh on impossible as I could not speak of myself and was wary of any questions from her, yet desirous of her company, I asked her one day if she could write a note for me.

"But I cannot," she replied, as I had expected.

"Then let me teach you."

"My lady?"

"I shall write out the letters of the alphabet for you to copy. Here, sit down with me, firstly you must learn how to hold the quill."

"Could you show me how to write my name?"

"Only if you come to sit by me."

I smiled at the success of my plan; I had a companion by my side and my mind was happily distracted by her eager willingness to be taught. When I rallied myself from a short nap the following afternoon she thrust a piece of paper into my hands.

"Is this not right?" she asked.

"It is, Gwen Dixon. You must be proud of yourself. I shall show Sir Neville when next I see him," I said, not knowing when that would be.

"Please don't! Learning is something not always happily shared," she said.

I nodded. "Then I shall not speak of it. Now what words do you want to write next?"

It was a sunny morning late in the second week of January and I was bored, missing Gwen who had gone to visit her mother. I opened the window a little to breathe the cold fresh air when I saw Sir Neville in the rose garden below with a glass in his hand. He gestured as he spoke to someone and my curiosity made me push the window open a little more. "You are more than welcome, of course, but I am sure there's a good reason behind your visit."

A tall man stepped into my line of sight - I was staring down directly at his long light brown hair and broad shoulders.

"You are correct, sir," the visitor said as he turned to survey the garden and I saw once more the face that had remained with me since that day he had met with Henry in Kingsdown.

"The king takes full advantage of your loyalty, Sir Edward. I gather your time is much taken travelling on his commissions."

"My duty is to the king, as ever." Surprise made me draw back from the window. "But it is true," Sir Edward continued, "I have not been home for more than a day in this last year but once the coronation is over I shall be a free man. But now I need to ask you if you have heard of any dissent in the countryside hereabouts - the king wishes to feel the temperature of the land as he takes the throne."

The gravel beneath their feet crunched as they moved away.

My heart beat wildly - Edward still lived. I had decided he had either died or abandoned his brother, but the truth was he had had no time for anything other than his duty. How was it this unsettled me so? Did he know what had happened to his brother, I wondered, but in my heart I doubted it. I sat down heavily on the bed. Once I had wanted nothing more than to see him again, dance with him, feel his arms around me. I shook myself - those days were far behind me, I had been a mere girl then, now I was a woman, a married woman, soon to be a mother. I forced myself to accept it would be best if I was never to see Sir Edward again.

Chapter 12

"Only a couple of weeks to go," said Gwen. "I can't wait, it's so exciting, a baby to care for."

My own excitement was tempered with some degree of fear, and not of the birth only. I had dreamt of my baby's eyes. Eyes as dark as night. As dark as *his*.

I took a deep breath and gave Gwen a weak smile. "I think the baby can't wait for much longer, not the way it has been kicking me, I feel it's digging its way out," I said grumpily, rubbing my midriff, "and the sharp twinges in my back certainly don't help."

"Shall I massage your back for you?"

"Please, I would like that." As I stood up I felt water running down my legs. "Oh no, now my bladder is playing up as well."

Gwen laughed, "It's your waters, they have broken and the baby's coming."

"You know?"

"Of course, I've seen all my brothers and sisters born. I'll get a towel and I'll ask the steward to send someone for the midwife from the village; it's only a mile away."

"You will stay with me, Gwen - during the labour," I took her hand, "I'm afraid. Will it take long?"

"If you want me to, your ladyship, of course I shall be here. It won't be for hours yet, though. When I get back you can tell me how long it is between the pains."

The pains soared repeatedly throughout the morning, lasting a short while before mercifully retreating, but as time passed the pains grew stronger and the relief between them was brief.

"Hold my hand, Gwen," I pleaded, as the pains took me over yet again.

Gwen grasped my hand between both of hers as I struggled to keep from crying out. "The midwife is here," she said. The pain abated and I breathed more regularly for a moment. "I don't know her, she's not from the village."

"As long as she knows her business," I managed to say before the pain hit me once again. A moment later a woman of older years entered, bringing with her a birthing chair, similar to the one I had seen my mother place on the wagon when we moved to the farm. It had a shallow seat, a mere perch, and arms like low wings with hand-holds cut into them. A shiver of apprehension went through my body now the time was nigh.

"My name is Robinson," the midwife said. "It won't be long, my lady," she reassured me seeing how frequently and how strongly the pains were taking possession of me. "But I still have time to go and arrange for some warm water to wash the infant, more than enough."

"My mother had a chair like that," I told Gwen between panting breaths, "but I don't know anything about it – she isn't here to tell me." I began to weep.

"Don't worry, mistress, here, you hold on to the arms while leaning forward trying to push the child out. Just do what the midwife tells you."

I gave a cry as the pains hit me again, even more strongly than before. "Has Sir Neville been told the labour has started?" I asked.

"I sent someone to find him," said Gwen, wiping my brow with a cloth soaked in rose water as the sweat poured off me. "The wet nurse has just arrived, she is not from the village, either. I saw her sharing a mug of grog with the midwife to fortify her for the night to come, or so she claimed."

"Lie on the bed, mistress, let me examine you," said the midwife. Between bouts of pain Gwen helped me up the step and on to the bed. The midwife ran her hands over my abdomen. "A pity," she said when she had finished, lowering my shift and clicking her tongue as she did so.

"What's wrong?" I asked, my voice shaking.

"The babe is in the breech position so I'll have to try to turn it, it won't come out if left arse first."

"Oh God!" I screamed as another pain racked me.

"Don't worry, my lady, the midwife has done this before," Gwen said, squeezing my hand but I had seen the worried glance that passed between them. If only my mother was here, or Margaret, I thought. The pains were now coming every minute and I was exhausted.

"Here, swallow this," the midwife said, raising a glass to my parched lips. "Tis brandy and will help you through." She lowered my head and moved away.

I clasped Gwen's hand as hard as I knew how. "Don't leave me, will you?" I pleaded. "Don't."

"I'm here, and here I'll stay," Gwen promised. She reached down and picked up a sturdy leather strap. "You may need this, my lady," she said.

The midwife stood beside the bed once more, lifted my shift and placed one hand inside me moving the baby further up and with the other outside pushed the babe slowly this way and that. The pain was unbearable and I bit down on the leather strap until I felt I would bite it in two.

I sat on the chair holding tightly to its arms, my knuckles white. "The babe is coming," the midwife said. "Push, push hard." My body was now one great seizure trying to expel the child. Then I felt it slither out; I waited only to hear its first faint cry and passed out.

When I came to my senses I found I had been lifted back to my bed and washed and placed in a clean nightgown. Gwen smiled at me and patted my hand, "It's all over and you have a fine boy, they will bring him to you shortly."

I was more tired than I had ever known possible. "A drink," I whispered.

"Perhaps the draft the midwife left for you will help you recover," Gwen said, and lifted my head and put the glass to my bruised lips. I slid gratefully into sleep.

Captain Jacob! He stood over me, his face twisted as it was in death, lowering itself to mine, forcing me back against the pillow, coming closer and closer, until I screamed and my arms flailed weakly above my head, trying to beat him off. But it was not Captain Jacob who stood before me but the midwife and wet nurse who held my arms and legs, fixing them with leather straps.

"What's wrong?" cried Gwen.

"The birth has affected her mind," the wet nurse said. "I have seen it happen before. The child must be kept away from her at all costs. The last mother I saw in such a state killed her child. We must keep her door locked whenever she is alone, otherwise who knows what she might do. You remember, girl, she must be kept locked in," said the midwife as she gave Gwen a forceful shake. Leaving the room the midwife placed the key in the lock on the outside.

"Here, my lady, 'tis a sleeping draft, take this and all will be well in the morning." Wishing to escape this new horror I forced it down.

Chapter 13

When I woke it was many hours later and the restraints had gone. "How do you feel, my lady?" Gwen asked.

"Weak," I replied. "Where is my son? I want to see my baby." I had to see my baby, he felt so totally mine but still I had to check, check that he did not have his father's eyes.

"Shush now," said Gwen, "if you make a fuss they will restrain you again."

"The nightmare has passed," I said, though its echo still reverberated in my mind. "Where it came from I know not, it was horrible, Gwen," I whispered. "But I'm fine now, really I am. So where is he? My baby, please fetch him to me."

"Stay quietly and I will see what I can do." I watched as she left the room and waited, my heart pounding. My arms ached for lack of my infant. The pain I had so recently gone through was pushed into memory, my mind had room only for thoughts of my child.

Gwen came back a few minutes later cradling the sleeping baby and quickly placed him in my arms and then stood guard at the door. I held him close; so tiny, so sweet, making small, snuffling noise, as if surprised to find himself alive and breathing. He was beautiful, his downy hair the colour of ripened wheat. His eyes flickered open for a moment and I could feel a smile of absolute joy spread across my face.

"The wet nurse and the midwife are having breakfast, I believe," said Gwen, "but they are sure to get back shortly. If they find out I brought him to you I will be dismissed on the spot." I did not wish to hear her words - I was greedy for every moment with my baby. "I must put him back, I can hear voices," Gwen said urgently, scooping the infant from my embrace. I let out a cry of dismay to find my arms empty once more and tears slid down my cheeks.

"Goodbye, my little one," I murmured as Gwen hurried away, reappearing a minute later as footsteps echoed down the long gallery.

Gwen sat on the side of my bed and held my hands. "You have to convince them you are well, until then do not tell them you have seen him. Just ask when you can see him or they will be suspicious."

When the midwife came back to my room she leant over me to feel my forehead. "How is my lady today?"

"I am quite well. Where is my son? I want to see him."

She stood up straight and regarded me, her face hard. "We need to wait a while longer; to be sure you will not have more violent fits. We cannot take the chance. You need to sleep and fully recover. I have a sedative and restorative potion for you to take later. Try to eat something - you will need your strength. I will go and give cook orders for your food."

"Should I help the mistress wash?" Gwen asked Robinson. I noticed Gwen was careful to act in a submissive manner to the midwife, even giving a little curtsy when addressing her.

"Yes, and get on with it quickly, you foolish girl," the midwife replied, sweeping out of the room as if it was she who was mistress of the house.

"We have to mind the midwife for now," Gwen explained when we were alone once more. "She should be gone in a few days, but for now she could make life difficult for us." As she carefully bathed me with a flannel and warm water I squeezed her hand for that last word; I was not alone after all.

Evening came again and the curtains were drawn. Gwen gave me the little food I could manage. "This drink came up from the kitchen for you, my lady, the midwife said it will give you a good night's sleep." She smiled. "Tomorrow you shall have your son all day long, just you see." I took the cup and drank the bitter draught in one go. Any medicine that brought my child closer to my arms was welcome to me. "I'll wait the night here by the fire," Gwen said, "and watch over you." My heavy lids sank down and I relaxed to be in such tender care. I slept, a heavy, oppressive sleep, but my demons were awake. They plagued and tortured me. I thought myself outside a church, Matthew's church. I could hear voices within but when I tried the door it was closed against me. I felt pulled from the ground into the air and I floated up to the church window, but stones flew up and filled the space as I grew near. I heard laughter behind me and a voice crying, "I'm waiting, waiting."

"I was waiting for you to wake," Gwen said but broke off when she saw the sweat that bathed my body, the terror in my eyes. "It is all right, my lady," she said, smoothing the wet strands of hair from my face, "you are awake now."

I covered my face with my hands. "It has happened again," I whispered. "Am I going mad?"

She hugged me. "It was a bad dream, my lady, nothing more, brought on by the pain of childbirth. Lie back and I shall fetch your breakfast." She opened the curtains to let in a cold grey light. I tried to force my attention onto the everyday

94

things about me: the jug and bowl and towels, the poker in its place beside the fire, the little table at which I ate my meals, neatly placed to the side with my chair; all was in order - this was my room and I must put all other images out of my mind.

"I have just seen the wet nurse and midwife go downstairs for breakfast," Gwen said when she brought in the breakfast tray. "I overheard some of what they were saying, it seems they are going out about 11 of the clock."

"When they are out couldn't you bring my son to me for a while?" I implored.

"I will try but I don't expect they will be away for long."

I closed my eyes when I had eaten my porridge and drifted into a peaceful sleep until Gwen woke me saying, "It is time, my lady. I heard the midwife and wet nurse going downstairs. Here, let me help you." She assisted me to my feet and I walked slowly, painfully, to the door. "My lady, you must keep watch while I go into the nursery and warn me if anyone comes."

Gwen was back in a moment, frowning, "He's not there. The cot is empty."

"Why have they taken him away? Where is he? I must know."

"Perhaps they have gone for a little walk, it is a nice morning, if on the cold side," Gwen reasoned.

"But he should be with me. Gwen, go downstairs and see what you can find out, please."

"Yes, I will, my lady. But you must get back in bed, you are still very weak." She took my hand and helped me climb on to the bed. "You know I must lock the door after me, don't you? If anyone was to come to your room and find it unlocked, they would know I..."

"They would know you are my friend. Yes," I said, "I understand, but please hurry."

Gwen rushed into the room a few minutes later, panting from having run up the stairs. "They have gone to church to have your baby baptised," she told me.

"No! Not without me! How could they? The baby, he isn't unwell, is he? Say it's not so, for why else would they hold the christening so soon?"

"I will go back and wait for them," said Gwen. "No one said he was ill. Please do not fret." She disappeared once more.

I could not remain in bed. I pulled the blankets back and got shakily to my feet. I paced back and forth between the small table and the bedpost, tears brimming over as I thought of my son in his christening robe. Surely Sir Neville would not have deliberately left me out from my own son's baptism? Did they believe he would not survive, was that the reason for the haste, but why no word to me, his mother? But he had not seemed ill when I held him, he was not weak, had no fever, no doctor had been called. Sir Neville, why did he not consult with me in the matter of my son's name? I had not seen my husband since before the birth, I realised, unless of course he had called in while I slept, the sleeping potions were powerful. I'll ask Gwen, I resolved, surely that would be the answer. I had done nothing to make Sir Neville cross, I reassured myself.

"The christening party are back," Gwen said coming into my room, smiling. "I've brought you a slice of the cake made especially by the cook to celebrate. There's quite a merry party downstairs, a few neighbours, along with Sir Neville's sister and her husband, who are the godparents, were toasting the baby's health as I left," she said. "He looks grand in his christening robe."

"And me not there?" I was angry, sad, perplexed. "And why has my husband not been to see me? He hasn't visited while I slept, has he?"

"I don't believe so. Perhaps, he will bring little Jacob to see you dressed in his robe when the others have gone."

My mouth fell open and I felt my face drain of colour, "Jacob!" I sat down shaking. "No, he must have known I would hate that name above all others. How could he?"

"Are you feeling unwell? You are very pale, my lady. Jacob is a traditional name in the Lattimer family."

"Gwen, if you only knew why I hate that name. Maybe that's why he kept me away from the christening, so I could not protest, how dare he?"

Early in the evening the midwife came into my chamber, bringing another sleeping draught for the night to come.

"You need not wait," she said to Gwen, without a glance at me. "The master has given you the evening off so you may join in the celebrations." Gwen did not move. "You're expected downstairs, girl," she said with an impatient wave of her hand. I could see Gwen was reluctant to go.

"You should not forgo a chance to enjoy yourself," I said.

Once Gwen had left, the midwife handed me the drink and I sipped a little. I screwed up my face at the taste and asked her to bring me the slice of cake as it would help kill the unpleasant flavour, which she did with a cross word before departing the room. I ate a little, yawned and put down the cup. I felt sleepy and reached for the potion again but knocked it over, spilling the rest. I stood the cup up once more and wiped the table as best I could with my handkerchief. I half opened my eyes when I heard the door open and Robinson peered in. She closed the door quietly and I heard her footsteps receding. I did not hear her twist the key in the lock but felt too drowsy to get up.

I woke later, alone, and decided I must try to see my son; surely he would be in his bed by now. Was my memory correct, had Robinson failed to lock the door when she left? Placing my shawl over my shoulders and taking my candle, I went to the door, pushed down on the handle and to my pleasure it opened. I stepped out and checked that the gallery was clear. I crept towards the nursery but when I hurried to the cot and reached out my arms I beheld it was empty. The sound of music and laughter wafted up to me from the rooms below.

Shaking with disbelief at the way I had been treated I passed Sir Neville's room and without a thought I tried the handle. The door opened. I tiptoed across the room, still feeling a little drowsy. I held my candle above the desk and there before me was the christening certificate for Jacob Robert Lattimer. As I made to leave I noticed the black silk had been slightly drawn back from the third of the paintings. I reached up with one hand and pulled the material away. I screamed as the black eyes of Captain Jacob, the man who attacked me and murdered my family, gazed down at me. "No, no, not him, not him!" I screamed falling, insensible, to the floor.

Chapter 14

A moment later, or an hour, I know not, Sir Neville strode into the room with the midwife and wet nurse running in his wake. The women grabbed me and began dragging me across the floor. "How could you let this happen?" he cried. "You two told me the drugs would keep her under control until I was ready to deal with her."

"Sir, things were going to plan, I don't know what went wrong; I saw her drink the potion."

I heard, but I did not comprehend. In my room I was dumped on my bed, a coverlet was thrown over me and the door was slammed shut and locked.

"Perhaps you will be able to see your son today if all goes well, your ladyship," Gwen said the next morning, brushing my hair as I sat up in bed. "Did you not sleep last night? you seem very tired."

"I slept well enough," I replied, not wishing to tell her of the nightmare that had possessed me while I slept, though I could still see the face of Captain Jacob in the portrait and hear the conversation between Sir Neville and the women in my head. How long would these hallucinations haunt me? I must not speak of them if I was to be allowed my freedom again.

The door flew open and Sir Neville entered. Gwen curtsied and left us alone.

"How are you this morning?" he asked, bringing a chair to my bedside.

"I feel better," I said and smiled. "Maybe I will be able to get up later and visit my son."

"Hope, you have been very unwell and have had violent fits. It is too soon for you to see him while there is any chance of you being a danger to him. You would not want to cause him injury, now would you?"

"I would not hurt him. I need to see him, please, Sir Neville." Tears slipped silently down my face.

"You obviously do not remember lashing out for no reason at the wet nurse and leaving her badly bruised."

"No, I would do no such thing," I said, but even as I uttered those words there was a doubt in my mind; there was so much I did not comprehend.

"But you did, Hope, believe me. I found you flailing about wildly quite close to the nursery."

"I feel so much better, today, honestly I do."

"I'm pleased you do but it will take time for you to recover completely. I wish you to go to one of my properties with a small household, there you will be free to move around, and a doctor will visit."

"But my baby, will he come too?"

"No, Hope, when you have had the treatment I will bring him to see you; it is for the best. You would not forgive yourself if he were to come to harm."

I couldn't believe what I was hearing; could I be a danger to my son when I was filled with such love for him? But what if I was to hurt him? I reluctantly nodded my head in agreement.

"Gwen will accompany you, remain with you."

"Thank you," I began, but stopped. I did not want her to suffer for being my friend. "She seems a good enough servant," I finished.

"I shall visit regularly and give you news of the child," Sir Neville continued, "and see how you are doing. Now rest, my dear. The coach will collect you tomorrow morning. Rest." He patted my hand. "Do not concern yourself; there is no trouble I would not take for my heir." He said those last words with such sincerity I could not doubt him. "We shall leave early in the morning," he said. He pushed himself up and out of the chair and left me alone, locking the door.

Gwen was informed she was to accompany me. "I'm so pleased I'm going with you, my lady," she told me, "I've never been away before. We're going to another of Sir Neville's estates some distance away, so I've heard. I wanted to say goodbye to my mother but there's no time for I hear we are to leave tomorrow - would, my lady, would you write to her for me, tell her where we are and when she can expect me to get home again?"

"But of course, and we shall have time to continue with our lessons, you shall be writing your own letters soon enough."

"I doubt we shall be away that long," Gwen said with a smile. "Do you think it will be as grand a house as this, or even better?" I knew not, and cared not, my son and my distance from him were my one concern. "I was allowed to go to the nursery," she continued as she began to pack my trunk, folding my gowns neatly, placing lavender between them. "He's like you, my lady, and they say he is feeding well." I sighed: I could feel the useless heaviness of my breasts: they ached with milk.

Before dawn I was awoken and dressed and carried down the stairs on a chair feeling very sleepy; due to the early hour, few servants were about as we made our way out of the great entrance hall. I was lifted into the coach by the driver as if I was but a child and placed on the seat next to Sir Neville, Gwen being seated opposite.

My heart was breaking because I was leaving my son behind, not knowing how long it would be before we were reunited. After a few hours the coach stopped and the others got out and stretched their legs and ate from a hamper while I dozed fitfully. Gwen brought me some bread and cheese together with a flask of porter and I drank deeply and handed it back to her to drink also. As soon as the coach moved off I found I could not keep my eyes open and saw Gwen too had fallen asleep.

It was dark when I woke up. I lay on a pallet as did Gwen next to me. Sitting opposite me was Sir Neville smiling a bitter smile. "Awake at last," he said. I took in my surroundings: rough plastered walls, a table and chairs and a dresser that had seen better days, all with a home-made appearance. We were in an old farmhouse - a large single room. In an alcove I spied a curtained-off bed. Was this another illusion, yet another nightmare? When I touched Gwen she felt solid enough, though. Shaking and scared and very confused I saw the expression of triumph on Sir Neville's face.

"My dear wife. Now you will see I am as good as my word. I have installed you in a property of mine where you can spend the rest of your days repenting your actions. You seem puzzled, my dear."

"Sir Neville, what have I done that you treat me so?"

"Murdered my son, Jacob!" he shouted, standing up. I thought he was going to kick me and cringed. "Jacob is your baby's father and now he belongs to me."

"Captain Jacob, the man who violated me? The man who murdered my family?" I struggled to my feet, regarding him with disgust as I recalled the painting in Sir Neville's room and the black eyes of my attacker. It was not a nightmare - it was real. It was all real: the painting, Sir Neville and two old crones talking, the drugs they spoke of - real. Anger was brimming over within me. "How could anyone blame me for defending myself?" I yelled.

Sir Neville came over to me and struck me hard across the face. I staggered backwards. "You are nothing but a farm girl and there for the use of, you dullard. Though how my Jacob could lower himself to couple with such a creature I know not."

"So why do you want my child? He is Henry's son."

"No, he is Jacob's all right and even if he wasn't, you took my last remaining son from me, so it's only justice that I take yours: an eye for an eye."

"It is you who are mad, I will go to law."

He started to laugh, a mean cackle. "Oh Hope, you are a fool. You are my wife, I can do whatever I like with you."

"But ..."

"There are no buts. Whatever I like, do you hear me?" He paused. "And if that is not enough I have in my possession confessions signed by you and Gwen stating you were caught in the act of stealing."

"No!"

"Stealing from me," he resumed, "and as your punishment you have both agreed to work here, on this pig farm, without pay rather than take your chances in court. Meanwhile everyone knows my poor stricken wife and her faithful maid are being taken care of far away."

"But I am your wife." I held up my hand but my wedding ring was gone.

He regarded me with a gaze so cold it chilled my blood. "How could that be – you are Hope Courtney – thief."

"Do you think you can keep me here?"

"Oh, if you were to leave I would put up reward posters for your return dead or alive; after all the two of you are proven criminals. Well, it's time I was leaving. You will not find your trunk, it goes back with me, you have only the clothes you stand up in and the farm garb your master sees fit to give you."

A muffled sound, almost a word, came from Gwen's throat. "But must she suffer too?" I asked.

"It is your choice she is here, not mine." He pushed his foot at the slumbering girl and rolled her over on to her back. "You persuaded her to help you, she was seen replacing the baby in his crib. I cannot know how much you may have confided in her but you have sealed her fate along with your own."

Sir Neville walked to the door. "One thing more, let me introduce you to your new owner. Skinner!" A tall man entered the room. I gasped. It was the man with the scar I had seen leaving my home through the smoke, laughing, as he wiped his sword free of my family's blood. A cry escaped me, I stumbled back and hit my head on the wall - stunned I slid down. Sir Neville pierced me with a look of utter hatred as he left.

Skinner kicked the door shut behind him.

Chapter 15

"You are mine now, girl," Skinner said as I heard the coachman outside crack his whip and the horses begin to draw Sir Neville's coach away across the frozen land. Gwen let out a groan as she began to wake. "And her too, my property, you hear me?" He enjoyed his moment of triumph, standing over me, so close I could smell him.

Gwen lifted her head. "Where are we?" she asked. She stood a little shakily, brushing the dust from her dress and adjusting her cap as if she had merely woken from a nap, unaware she had been drugged and unconscious for hours. "I'm sorry, your ladyship," she said, ignoring Skinner's words. "I must have fallen asleep. Is there anything I can get you?" She looked about her, trying to understand why we should be here. "Has the coach broken an axle or a horse gone lame?" she asked. "Have you had any supper?"

"Supper!" Skinner scoffed. "If there is any supper for that hussy she must do the getting of it and feed the pigs and every other chore that needs to be done!"

"Mistress?" Gwen began again, paying Skinner no attention.

"Don't call her mistress, she is no better than a whore, a murdering whore at that."

Gwen regarded Skinner for the first time. "You!" she cried.

Skinner smiled, a mean smile showing his blackened teeth.

"Remember me now, do you, girl? Remember me from my visits to Wilderness Hall, eh?" Gwen nodded. "I can see you are no longer the scrawny child you used to be, you've filled out a bit these last few months." He reached out an arm to grab at her. "Yes, a comely wench you are, I'm sure I could allow you to share my bed."

"Never!" Gwen shouted back at him, standing as tall as her fifteen years would allow. "I will tell Sir Neville, he will…"

"Sir Neville! Do not speak of Sir Neville; he is the one who put you here, in my power. I am lord here. You two have agreed to be my servants for twenty years in return for not being charged with the attempted theft of the Lattimer jewels. That's a hanging offence so you see you've got away lightly. Your signed statements were witnessed by Sir Neville himself."

"But I didn't try to steal anything," Gwen protested. "I never would. And how could Lady Lattimer…"

Skinner sniggered. "Lady Lattimer! Everyone knows that poor lady is locked up in an asylum."

"I don't understand. Lady Lattimer is here and… and I didn't put my mark to anything. What's happening?" Gwen's eyes pleaded with me to explain.

"Tell her all about it," Skinner said, pointing a finger at me. "Tell her this farm is my reward for giving Sir Neville the news of his grandson." I saw how he enjoyed confusion spread across Gwen's face. "I must see to my horse, some animals are deserving of their food. When I get back you are coming around the farm with me so you can see where you will be working. It's bounded by marsh and bog so I wouldn't be in a hurry to leave if I were you. And you may not have

107

noticed but I have taken your shoes, there are rags and string over there to cover your feet. Something for you to do while I'm away." He took a key on a chain from his pocket as he moved towards the door. "Go on, tell her why she is here for your sins," he added as he left. The key twisted in the lock and Gwen and I were alone in the farmhouse.

"My lady?" Gwen asked as if I had some easy answer to all that had overtaken us. "It is not true, is it? That we are trapped here? It cannot be."

Energy had evaporated from my body. I fell on to one of the kitchen chairs in despair and closed my eyes. "I fear it is true; all my nightmares are true."

"My lady?" Gwen repeated.

"Please sit down," I said, my voice shaking as much as my legs. "I must try to explain." Gwen perched on the chair opposite me. I took a deep breath. "My name is Hope Ashton," I said.

"But you are Lady Lattimer."

"In name only, Gwen."

"But, my lady."

"I am Hope Ashton, widow."

"Widow?"

"My husband was murdered." Gwen let out a cry of surprise. I sighed as I set about putting the horrors of my recent past into words for her. I watched her anxious face as she absorbed all that had happened to my family. Tears fell from both our faces as I concluded the terrors of the raid.

"Thank God you managed to escape," said Gwen clutching my hand.

"I did not escape, Gwen, it was not as easy as that."

"Mistress?"

"Before they left Sir Neville's son, Jacob, raped me."

"Oh my Lord!" Gwen's hands flew to her mouth. I sat without moving while Gwen placed the pieces of the puzzle together. "So Sir Neville thinks the child, your child, is Jacob's? That is why Skinner spoke of Sir Neville's grandson."

"Yes, but I believe the child to be my husband's."

"But you married Sir Neville a year ago, did you not?"

I shook my head. "Sir Neville led you all to believe that, but it was not so."

Gwen rubbed her eyes as if to wipe away the confusion. "But if Captain Jacob forced himself on you why would you marry his father?"

"Gwen, the truth is Sir Neville tricked me into marrying him this last Christmas, but five weeks ago." I thought of all that had happened in those weeks. "I had no idea Sir Neville's son was my attacker until I saw that painting." I felt sick as I recalled the moment. "What a fool I was! How easily deceived! Sir Neville misled everyone. I had been given a home by the vicar of West Penton and his wife - such good people - but they believed Sir Neville's lies and told me to forget what doubts I had about the marriage." *It had been so easy for him, I thought: we had been flattered into being fools.* I stood to face Gwen. "Sir Neville told me he would give the child his name. I had lost everything." I was in such need for her to believe me. "I had lost everyone I loved but my baby would need a home and thinking of my child I felt bound to accept him. I thought him such a generous man." I sat down heavily. "How wrong I was," I finished in a whisper. I felt a hand on my shoulder but did not look up. "I have lost my child now and he has lost his mother. I was deceived by Sir Neville and have given him my son." I felt the desolation of my words, too deep for tears.

"Such a story," Gwen said, her hand moving slowly across my shoulders. "Who would believe it?"

"Who indeed?" I echoed.

Sir Neville had changed more than I had ever thought a human being could. How had he pretended so well to be a gentleman of kindness and generosity? How stupid had I been to believe that such a man could wish to marry me and care for my child? Had some vanity been my undoing? Did I believe my youth and my fair face had won his heart, or had at least, awoken a genuine tenderness? How many prettier girls must there be in his village, how many more sad tales of widows must he have been able to hear if he had wished? Yet he had deceived Matthew, who had believed his kindly declarations - Margaret too. What would Margaret think if she could see me in my present state?

"My lady," Gwen began, but I shook my head to hear that title.

"You must call me Hope, that is my name."

"You will see your child again - somehow we will find a way. Surely Sir Neville will not leave us here in this place for long with such a vile man. Someone will listen to us, to you at least, if not to me, you are Lady Lattimer after all."

"Did you not hear what Skinner said? Sir Neville says he has our confession. He could have us hanged."

"Sir Neville has the baby; could he not just let us go?"

"Not when he has taken so much trouble to imprison us."

"But when shall I see my family?" Gwen asked, her voice breaking. I could not speak - to my shame I had no reply. "A fortnight does not pass without me going home. What will my mother think?"

"That you are with me, in some place where I have been sent for my health, I'm sure that will be the story told. Sir Neville will not want more gossip than necessary - he will put out some believable explanation."

"And my pay? How will mother manage without my pay? Little though it is, it helps keep the roof over her head."

"Sir Neville will pay her, I am sure of that. The last thing he wants is for questions to be asked."

"But why? Why all this?"

"Oh Gwen," I whispered. "It is because he values his good name. He would not want me telling my story, saying how his son raped me, how he himself had tricked me into marriage and stolen my child. He has been very clever. The drugs they gave me after the birth made me seem quite mad, now he can say he has put me away so I cannot harm the child. And you, dear Gwen," I said, "you are here for being kind, for helping me." The words died on my lips: surely I was driving her away with my every utterance. "Someone saw you leaving the baby's room, they are afraid of what you might know." I forced myself to continue. "For my sake you are condemned to this dreadful place at the mercy of that murderer. They cannot keep me and let you go. As our lives were intertwined so is our fate. The worse thing in all my woes is what I have done to bring pain on those who have helped me." I stopped as I thought of the boy, the poor hanged boy. "Or not done," I added, my words choking me.

"At least we are together, my lady," said Gwen.

"For your sake I can only wish it were not so."

111

The key scraped in the lock and we fell quiet as Skinner entered the room, filling the doorway, nonetheless letting in a rush of freezing air. "Right," he said, "you must see where you will be working. Not put the rags on your feet, yet, eh? Well, that's your choice. Quick now," he picked up a stick that was leaning against the wall and waved it at us. "Out!"

Hurriedly we rose and followed him outside, regretting not having done what he said as the ground was frozen hard and the cold instantly penetrated our stocking feet. There were a few snowflakes in the air, the day was coming to a close and we could see little but a vast open sky heavy with snow. A few small bare trees were dotted close to the farm and in the distance I could make out the skeleton of a meagre orchard. I spun round, making a complete circle; apart from the farmhouse and the outbuildings I could see no sign of further habitation. The land rolled away, seeming to reflect the dullness of the sky. It was as if we had arrived at the end of the world. I had no idea where we were.

I tightened my shawl over my shoulders and hurried to catch up with Gwen.

"Make sure you understand this," Skinner declared, "you two are my property now, my servants. For taking him news of the child and you, girl," Skinner said poking me with his long finger, "my reward from Sir Neville was this farm and any profit I make and the two of you to work it. You," he said and I took a step back to avoid the touch of his finger for the second time, "you are of value to me, Sir Neville pays me a pension to hold you here, so you see it's in my interest for you to stay alive. But Gwen," he gave his twisted smile, "she means nothing to me, a burden, as an extra mouth to feed. You will need to earn your keep and she hers, if she wants to be fed."

I made to make a move towards Gwen, but she stood her ground. "You do not own me," she said.

"But I do," Skinner growled.

He moved on and we followed.

"This is the bake-house," he said, lifting the latch and throwing open the door to a large dark building. "There's the oven and grate for cooking, the well and the animal feed's in the far corner - feeding the animals will be your first task every morning. Next door is the provisions store for vegetables, salted fish - things you will need to make my dinner. You must be up before dawn to start your duties, for now I have the two of you I shall be a gentleman of leisure." He kicked the door shut and led us over to the stable which backed onto the cowshed with its stack of straw. Beyond stood a block of sties each one alive with brown, wiry-haired pigs, their bright eyes watching us as their long snouts twitched. They snorted with interest as they watched us hurry to step on to the few strands of straw for momentary relief from the icy earth. "You must feed the pigs and chickens and milk the cow before you get my breakfast," he said. "Leave the boar to me. Your work clothes are in the house, you can't wear this," his fingers picked at my sleeve, "now you're a servant." Skinner waved his hand aloft, showing his ownership of this place. "The chicken coop is at the back of the pig sties," he added. "The pigs need to be herded into the fenced-off field each day, if the snow is not too thick and the chickens can go there too." Finally, he pointed out the privy and the piss pots standing a little way off. A few other huts stood nearby; no doubt we would find out later what they were

113

for. The cold seemed to be reaching Skinner now and he headed back to the farmhouse and after making use of the privy we followed gratefully in his wake.

Inside once more we hurried to the fire to stop our shivering. Behind us Skinner picked up a plate of ham and bread. "Here," he said, throwing some dry crusts on to the table, "eat that, then get to bed, I can't be wasting candles on you." We grabbed the bread and took it to the fire, eating greedily.

Skinner retired to his alcove, pulling a rough curtain across. We dragged the straw-stuffed pallet from the floor to the far corner where there was a gap between a large dresser and the wall making another alcove for the two of us. "You go in first," I whispered to Gwen, "nearest the wall, then I will know if he…" There was no need for me to finish the sentence. "At least we are close to the chimney breast, it might help keep our feet warm." While Gwen settled, I opened the door of the nearest cupboard and was surprised to see it held two neatly folded blankets, odd household items and a few plates. Were these Skinner's? I wondered; it all seemed too orderly to be his doing. I threw the blankets over our pallet and crawled in beside Gwen.

"We shall be all right," I whispered.

"I know," Gwen replied with a certainty she surely could not feel.

A little later, when Skinner's snores and snorts vibrated through the room, Gwen turned to me, though I could see nothing of her in the darkness except the curve of her plump cheek as it caught the last glow of the fire.

"I think I understand now," she whispered, "I heard talk how, many years ago, when the war was still raging, Jacob and some of his men went off to join Cromwell's army. Jacob was young, but the leader of a nasty little gang including Skinner. Everyone at the Hall was pleased to see the back of them." She pulled herself up on her elbow, pausing to check Skinner's snores were steady. "They say Jacob was jealous of his brother and opposed him in everything, even to taking the Parliamentary side in the war. Jacob visited his father from time to time. I saw him that last time when Sir Neville had Jacob's portrait painted. Cook told me to avoid him as much as I could - he was likely to grab a serving girl if she pleased him - or throw a tankard at her head if she didn't. The Hall was not a good place when he was there. 'He infects all he touches, like poison in a pie,' cook said. Then Skinner came back last April-time, alone. He stayed a week and we were all expecting Captain Jacob and the others to follow, but when there was no sighting of him or his men Skinner went off to search for news of him. When Skinner came back we were told Jacob had been killed in a skirmish."

I stifled a bitter laugh as I heard the story that had been told at Wilderness Hall. "Sir Neville and Skinner set off to find the body," Gwen continued, "to bring it home to rest in the family mausoleum but they never found him."

"That is because he is buried in unhallowed ground, as fitting for a murderer. The rest of his group were caught and hanged. Skinner escaped a hanging more's the pity because he was ordered back to Wilderness Hall during the raid."

"But why wasn't Captain Jacob given a Christian burial if he was killed on duty?"

"He wasn't Gwen, I killed him. Killed him with a pitchfork before he could kill me."

Chapter 16

When I opened my eyes I could see nothing. I felt utterly lost. Where was I? It was like those days before my memory came back to me, the sensation that nothing was real, that I was but a spirit adrift in the world and could disappear with the next breeze.

There was a movement behind me, and there was Gwen, breathing gently, and I felt strangely safe.

A snort burst from the other side of the room and I shuddered to think of the malignancy at the heart of this place, the person who made it a prison. Skinner was rising from his bed, roused no doubt by the cockerel greeting the dawn. He kicked at my feet. "Out, you two," he bellowed, "lie abed half the day, will you? Not while I'm your master." Throwing aside his blanket he moved to the door as we hurriedly dressed in the clothing that had been thrown over a chair for us to wear, our own gowns nowhere to be seen. Shivering we laced the bodices over our shifts and climbed into the rough woollen skirts. We searched about as best we could in the half-dark but finding no jackets or kerchiefs we gathered the threadbare shawls around our shoulders knowing these would not be sufficient to keep us warm in such bitter weather. I pushed my hair into a cap and bent to cover my feet in layers of rags, binding them tightly with string. "Out!" Skinner shouted again, opening the door wide to let in the freezing air as he drove us from the house, his stick raised above his head.

"How could anyone expect us to face the frozen ground without shoes?" I grumbled.

"Where to?" Gwen asked, half-asleep. I pointed to the pigsties. A little snow had fallen overnight and we shuffled off in our rags holding ourselves tight and huddled against the searing cold. Daylight was only the faintest glimmer on the horizon; everything was still, frozen, as we drove the pigs into the field. We found the brushes and I opened the gate to the first of the six pigsties. "Careful," I cried as my foot slipped in the mess. Despite the overpowering smell we were grateful for the small amount of shelter from the biting wind given to us by the cowshed, the sties being set back from the wall, protecting the small hut where each sow slept. We stood a moment to gather ourselves. "I think we should do as Skinner says for now," I began, "till we discover how we can leave this place."

"So how long do you think we'll have to live like this?"

It was a question I could not answer and another surge of guilt grabbed at me. "We must wait until the snow has gone, we could die in this weather without shelter."

We regarded the frozen earth, the sky threatening more snow. Gwen stepped forward and began sweeping out the dirty straw with long strokes of her broom. "Come on, Hope," she said, "we will get warm if we work."

I smiled to hear my name; she knew we were sisters now.

The vigorous action of gathering the soiled straw refreshed the pain of childbirth, but it warmed me by a few degrees and my teeth stopped chattering. I found a wheelbarrow and loaded the waste, spadeful by spadeful, grateful for the work to keep me from freezing, to keep my mind occupied. There was a pale grey light now and I stopped to look about; the scene was almost featureless, the horizon lost in the mist.

"Where are we, I wonder?" I questioned.

"Lost," Gwen replied in a whisper.

"Do you have no idea where this place could be? Did Sir Neville ever mention his estates in your hearing?"

"Never. He owns much property I've heard it said, but I know not where." We headed into the field carrying buckets of feed for the pigs. Gwen broke the ice on the water trough with a heavy stick and emptied the pig swill buckets into a second trough. "How can it be so cold and us with so little by way of clothing?" she asked more of the air than myself, the immediate need for warmth more pressing than the far-off desire for rescue.

Now the pigs were fed and their sties cleaned we moved towards the henhouse carrying the empty buckets, pulling at our shawls with frozen fingers. "We must get the feed stuff first," I said, and we moved on in silence to the bake-house I remembered Skinner pointing out to us the day before.

"I suppose we will have to do the baking," Gwen said.

"Something to look forward to."

I left Gwen sheltering in the bake-house adding corn and oats to the buckets ready for the next feeding time while I fed the greedy hens and searched amidst the straw to find any precious eggs.

"I'll do it tomorrow while you shelter," Gwen said when I got back to the bake-house.

"Now for the milking." I made my way towards the cowshed, Gwen hurrying to catch up with me. "I hope the cows have a better temperament than their master, they can be awkward if they want to be."

I pulled open the heavy door, scraping it across the ground; the mooing within ceased and a pair of enormous soft eyes met mine.

"I think we shall be all right," I said, stretching out my hand to stroke the calf's head. The calf's mother came wandering up and I could see her udders were over-ready for milking. I found the stool and Gwen brought over the pail. The steady rhythm slowed my breathing and brought a moment of serenity to my mind. I could feel my own milk flowing and felt an unexpected sisterhood with the placid animal before me and when I finished I rested my head against her dark flank.

"Here, I've found a ladle," Gwen interrupted my idle thoughts. "Fresh warm milk from Betsy, I haven't tasted it since I left home."

"Betsy?"

"Yes, Betsy and Bonnie."

I would agree to anything if it made Gwen smile, even for a moment. "As you wish, now come on, drink your fill, we must get back to make Skinner his breakfast, clear the grate and re-lay the fire, then perhaps we may be fed, too."

"All the animals before us," Gwen added, including Skinner with the other beasts of the field.

"As you say."

The beast in question was pulling on his breeches when we opened the heavy door and stepped inside, the snow dropping from the rags on our feet.

"Where is my breakfast, you idle wench?" he roared at me. Before I could reply I felt the weight of his belt fall across my shoulders, my knees buckling. I staggered forward but balanced myself against a chair.

"I..." I began but decided not to waste my words. For the moment he was determined to show who was the master and there was nothing we could do against him; any rebellion on my part would only give him more reason to lash out.

Skinner took another key from his chain and unlocked a narrow cupboard. "Now get my breakfast before I strike you again," he shouted. Gwen and I went forward, catching our breath at the sight of a large cheese, a whole loaf of bread and a small piece of ham. Our stomachs rumbling with hunger we found a plate and put some of each before him on the table with a tankard of weak beer that disappeared down his throat before the first wedge of bread and cheese had been eaten. He banged the tankard on the table by way of requesting it be refilled. Gwen and I moved quietly about the room, our hunger growing stronger as we watched each mouthful disappear.

"There," Skinner said, pushing his plate away as he finished his third small beer, "you can clear the plate before you go out - there are turnips in the field to be pulled."

"The ground's hard frozen, there's an inch of snow," Gwen cried.

"Then the work will keep you warm, I dare say you want to eat today and as turnip stew is what you'll be eating, I should get to work if I were you."

"Turnip stew!" Gwen exclaimed.

I put out my hand to hold her back. Skinner had put on his boots and now he grabbed his jacket, locked the cupboard and exited the door. "He's enjoying playing the master," I said. "We must let him have his way for now."

We beheld the thick crusts Skinner had left us on his plate. We regarded the bread where his blackened teeth had torn it

120

and momentarily shuddered before stretching out our hands and grabbing it, pushing it into our hungry mouths, devouring it quickly.

"We must get the turnips," I said with resignation as we cleared the last fragments from the plate.

"No turnips here," I said, once outside, "must be over yonder." It was too cold to waste our energy on words; our breath billowed in soft clouds before us. "We'll need the tools from the shed."

We hacked at the earth, my belly aching with every blow, to break the turnips free from their buried roots until a chill sweat froze on our faces and we had precious few turnips to place in the sack to show for our labour and the worst of those would be for the pigs. "Let's go to the bake-house to get some of the cold out of our bones," I proposed, and Gwen nodded her assent. The winter sun had broken through the clouds casting a dim gleaming light over the land and the snow had begun to melt a little; a few birds emitted melancholy cries as they moved across the sky. We picked out some potatoes, turnips, and salt fish from the food store, ready to cook later, not daring to take any fish for ourselves.

Gwen stood at the door of the bake-house. "I can't see Skinner, he must be in one of the sheds. Couldn't we run for it, we must meet someone on the road."

"What road? Where is there a road? And who would believe us? No, Gwen, we must bide our time, the winter is against us, a worse enemy than Skinner while the weather remains like this."

"But must we wait till spring, is that what you mean?"

We had not been here a day as yet, but there was despair in Gwen's voice. We made our way back to the turnip field and I raised my pick-axe to resume chipping at the ice-hard soil. My breasts were weeping tears of milk for my son. I must believe each fall of the axe meant I was working towards my return to him, so I lifted the axe time and time again with no image other than that of my son before me, and I heard Gwen working beside me until there was harmony in our rhythm.

We finished in the field, thanking God the daylight hours were so few and made our way back to the bake-house to finish preparing the meal. The wind was getting up as we headed to the house, our skirts beating against our legs, our shawls flapping at our shoulders like broken wings. We were within a dozen paces when the door opened and Skinner barred our entry.

"I should have had my dinner an hour ago! Here, give me the food," he said, grabbing it from our hands, "and go, get the pigs in and give them their evening feed, if you come inside, you lazy wenches, you'll not want to go out again. And see to the boar, there are rotted parsnips next to his sty." We kept our heads low and trudged towards the pigsties once more.

"They seem more content than we do," Gwen said, leaning over the fence surrounding their runs, watching a fat sow nuzzling the earth, finishing up the last of the rotten turnips we had thrown in earlier.

Not wishing to prolong our time outside by as much as a minute we hurried on. As I dropped the rotting vegetables into his pen, the boar's loud grunts were joined by a cry from Gwen.

"What is it?"

"That's why he said we were to leave the boar to him! It's my gown - and yours."

In the waning light I peered into the pigsty and there were the clothes we were wearing on our arrival; the last remnants of our time at Wilderness Hall. "But how do we leave here now?" I asked, more of myself than Gwen.

"In this I suppose," Gwen said, her hand going to her muddied bodice and torn skirt. "I hate that huge ugly animal." The boar let out a satisfied grunt and we saw he was munching on half a stale loaf. "And he's better fed than we are."

"You have destroyed our clothes," I shouted at Skinner the instant we entered the house, "given them to the pigs." I knew my protest was in vain but I could not contain my anger.

"Well," said Skinner, leaning back in his chair by the fire with an unaccustomed smile on his sallow face, "I knew you'd have no further use for them."

The next morning we were up and silently out of doors once we had coaxed the fire back to life. We were both hungry - Skinner had left us only a few pieces of turnip the night before. We had learnt our lesson - next time we would eat what we could in the bake house before we brought the food into the house.

We fed the chickens and chased the pigs into their field. Leaving them to their breakfast we went to feed the boar. I stared at our gowns beneath the straw and mess, the frill that had once draped so prettily about my neck was wrapped around his foot - he seemed ready to eat it.

"Oh no, you don't!" I cried and climbed over the wall with a turnip in my hand hoping to entice him away, throwing it some distance in front of him. The animal glared angrily at being disturbed. I knew what such a look could mean, a neighbour of ours in Kingsdown had once had his leg broken by a boar and had limped ever after.

"Here! Here!" Gwen shouted and began to rattle the feed bucket, throwing turnips on the ground. The boar moved in her direction and I grabbed my skirt and bodice.

"There, there!" Gwen said, pointing eagerly, "I think that's mine, over there." I moved slowly, keeping out of the pig's sight. I clambered back over the wall with the stinking rags that had once been our dresses. "I always liked this one, Margaret and I made it over and it took us hours," I said. I held it up and caught Gwen's eye and she shook her head at me and we both began to laugh.

"Surely, they are beyond help," Gwen said.

"Not at all." I held the bodice up before me as if I were happily about to try it on. "It will be fine - I believe pig-sty ornamentation is very popular in London this year." Laughter - I had not heard it in so long; it was the sweetest music and as nourishing as a good meal.

I gathered up the torn skirts, the ripped bodices, holding them at arm's length. "We must hide them somewhere till we can wash them," I said. "When they have dried some of the dirt will brush off."

"But they're full of holes," Gwen said.

"A coming fashion," I replied.

"You must learn to be quicker if you don't want a beating," Skinner shouted at us as we made our way back to the house from the cowshed and quiet minutes spent with Betsy and her calf. "I'm waiting for my breakfast and you've got to prepare the dough, the baking must be done today."

Gwen and I exchanged a glance of joy at the thought that today, at least, we would have some warmth, a little relief from the ever-present cold that had become instilled in our bones.

"Go then, prepare the oven." Skinner dismissed me with a wave of his hand. "You," he said to Gwen, "see to the fire and get my breakfast."

The bake house was large and dark and I lit a candle to work by, putting it to the twigs in the oven, blowing on them until they caught. When I had finished scrubbing the table with salt to ensure it was clean I found the yeast and flour and began mixing the dough. Gwen arrived, releasing the shutters to let in early morning light and the cool fresh air. Skinner appeared at the door a while later with a rabbit, skinned but not gutted. "Rabbit pie," he said, and left.

"I wonder if we shall get any of it," Gwen said.

"I'll make sure we do," I replied and with my knife I separated a fore portion and started cleaning out the innards, throwing them into the swill bucket.

"Hear that?" Gwen asked. There was a gentle swishing sound in the distance. "He's brushing his horse. I think Cassie is the only thing in this world that man cares about."

A while later we heard Skinner's heavy footsteps crashing across the yard. The bake-house door was pushed shut and we heard a key twist in the lock. The footsteps receded and were replaced by the clatter of horse's hooves.

"He's gone." Gwen ran to the door but there was not so much as a handle on the inside. She pushed against it valiantly but hopelessly. "What if he doesn't come back?" she asked.

"At least we shall be warm and well-fed," I replied, giving the proved dough its final kneading, shaping it into round loaves plus a couple of baps for us, putting them on the wooden paddles ready to be cooked. Gwen raked out the embers of the fire from the oven into a metal tray and quickly brushed it clean before we slipped in the dough. Together we placed the slate board at the entrance of the oven using two bricks to hold it there and sealed it, using the hot ashes to warm a tankard of milk. "I'll make the pastry for the pie," Gwen said, "before I became a maid I spent two years in the kitchen."

When we had time to rest we placed some old sacks on the floor and sat down loosening our shawls. Gwen spoke in a low voice. "We must find a way to escape."

"There is no need to whisper now," I said.

Gwen slept awhile, curled up on the floor, so young and innocent, a pink flush to her cheek as she absorbed the warmth of the bake house.

My son! I envied Gwen her innocent sleep. My son consumed my every quiet moment. My nameless son, for I could not call him by that most hated of names, did not have a mother's arms to hold him. There was but one comfort, I knew Sir Neville would protect my child as if he were his own. But that thought chilled me to my very marrow, for I alone knew without a doubt my son was indeed of Sir Neville's flesh and blood.

I jumped up when I smelt the bread burning and quickly removed it from the oven, replacing it with the second batch and the pie - now the oven had cooled slightly the next batch should be better. I sat down, my thoughts taking me once more to the ever-present dread of our changed lives.

The days took on a dull monotony of cold and hunger, of aching limbs, blistered hands and throbbing feet, a regularity broken only by baking day when Skinner would take off, locking us in the bake-house. I continued telling Gwen my story, day by day, as much as I could bear, and she hers to me: the conversations I had longed for at Wilderness Hall took place in frosted fields and pig pens: it was freedom of a sort.

Once I found Gwen scrawling her name in the snow with a stick. "I mustn't forget," she said before carefully rubbing it away with her foot.

"How to write?"

"Who I am. It is as if we no longer exist."

I shuddered when I heard her words, but I did not need them to see Gwen's spirit fighting against our confinement. At night when the wind let out a lonely howl as it circled the house and the only light came from the embers of the fire, Skinner always refusing us a candle, I prayed hard for her and for my son - two beings for whom I had responsibility and I must somehow save, though I knew not how.

"Hope! Hope!" Gwen called, racing to the henhouse one morning of flitting sunlight; the frost had gone and the land was hard after a week without rain. "He's gone to the top field, he can't see us from there."

"What?" I was busy raking over the rough piece of soil where the hens pecked their days away.

"This is our chance. We can make a run for it."

I paused.

"What have we to lose?" Gwen insisted and I could see the despair in her pleading eyes. Precious little, was the only reply I could find to her question. She saw me hesitate and started to run.

Chapter 17

"Wait," I cried but Gwen was racing away from me, lifting her skirts almost to her knees, running like a fox with the hunt in pursuit. I chased after her. "Gwen," I called, afraid to shout in case Skinner heard.

Gwen halted for a moment, allowing me to catch up with her, an anxious expression clouding her eyes. "Oh quickly, quickly!" she urged me. "While he's in the far field. He has a flagon of beer, if we're lucky he'll be gone awhile." Her hands were fluttering with impatience to be gone.

"But which way?" I asked, surveying the all too familiar landscape before us.

"Away from him!" Gwen could no longer bear my doubts and was gone. I could but follow.

Which way does he go when he leaves the farm? I asked myself but I could see no track across the earth as I pursued Gwen past the spring cabbages, showing their heads in bright green rows. We ran beyond the handful of apple trees we called the orchard, still waiting for the spring to awaken them. Gwen was faster than me, all her determination visible in the pounding footsteps that took no account of the stones littering the ground - running, running for her life. My eyes searched for hoof prints we might follow but found none. My breath was tearing at my lungs. It had been such a long time since I had last run: I had been chasing Jessie because she had said she would tell mother I was soft on the peddler boy - running and laughing then, happier than I knew.

The rags around my feet were starting to unwind. "Wait, wait," I cried. "Wait."

Gwen paused to see me bent double to relieve the stitch in my side. Her face was scarlet with effort and exhaustion. The only sound was our own struggling breaths. "Nothing," Gwen said, peering into the distance. "Surely we should be able to see a house, a church tower - something. But there's nothing."

"There are sheep, they must belong to someone." I searched the horizon but the cloud was hanging low: this was not the day to have run, but I could not utter that thought to Gwen. "We are bound to find some habitation," I said.

"Yes. Soon." Gwen wasted no breath on further comment; she picked up her skirt and ran as I followed in her footsteps.

The further we ran the softer the ground became, opening up, as if torn by some rough hand, riven with deep cracks, filled with dark water; reeds stood all about us, tall and stiff, the tallest structures in our landscape.

"Oh!" yelled Gwen as she slipped off a grassy mound into a trench of mud. I reached over and gave her my hand and she scrambled up to stand beside me. "I don't understand, it hasn't rained for days." Mud, water - it was all around us. Even the sheep were keeping their distance. "We can't go back, can we?" Gwen's face showed the anxiety I felt. Skinner's words that first day came to my mind, "This place is bounded by bog and marsh." It had been no idle threat.

"No," I replied, "we can't go back. I'm not even sure I could find the way back now." I tried to smile. "At least he can't come after us on horse-back because of the mud and we're not leaving any tracks. We will be all right, there must be a farmhouse somewhere near if only we can find it." A wide-winged bird floated low over the reeds, its wings gently arched; oh, to glide over the landscape as he did, to see all before us.

We could no longer run but had to watch our every footstep. The boggy ground was riddled with hollows, the water running between them in places, and we had to jump from mound to mound helping each other as best we could when we lost our footing. It was hard going, the sweat from our exertions adding to the chill of the day; we were aching and hungry and lost.

"It's getting worse," Gwen said, the islands of solid ground becoming smaller between deepening water.

"Listen!" Gwen stopped still. "Can you hear it? It must be a stream." We hoisted up our skirts yet again and ran, leaping over the rivulets, onward, the sound of water growing louder with every step. The earth beneath our feet changed as we began to trudge uphill between sandy mounds and tufts of long grass, until, climbing over a ridge, we found ourselves staring out over the flat dark expanse of the sea.

We moved down to where the water lapped gently at our feet. I had never seen the sea before; it ran towards us in long furrows, like a field brought alive with movement, until it spluttered at our feet, hissing in the shingle. It felt like a prison door slamming in our faces.

"Where is this? Where are we?" Gwen whispered. I fell down on the shore, all energy drained from my body, my legs shaking from exhaustion. Gwen flopped down beside me and we sat in silence in our hopelessness.

"We must find shelter before dark," I said as the light began to wane beneath the sombre clouds. We pulled ourselves up and began walking as above us a multitude of birds swirled and swooped as the darker hues of dusk soaked into the sky.

We traipsed onward, the mist creeping over us until soon little could be seen ahead. The ground became firmer as we walked on but we knew not which way to turn. We stumbled forward, exhausted and shivering as the mist slowly enveloped the landscape. Escape was no longer the force driving us but the simple dread of being caught outdoors when night came.

"Hope!" Gwen ran ahead and I feared she had caught sight of Skinner in the mist, but then "There!" she cried. My eyes were not as sharp as hers but I could just make out a dark outline. "It's a hut, we're saved." We had not spoken our fear until that moment - the fear we would die here, our bodies denied even the proper ceremony of Christian burial.

"Maybe fortune is not so cruel to us after all," I said. Gwen put her hand on the latch and to our joy the door opened. "Perhaps when the fog lifts we will be able to see a farmhouse." Could we be saved after all? We collapsed on to the floor, between the ancient rakes and shovels, too weary to stand a minute longer.

Tears of relief sprang up in Gwen's eyes. "I'm sorry Hope, it was a bad idea to run like that - without thinking, without planning." Her body, thin and worn, shook with sobs. "It's my fault," she mumbled, "but I so long to go home."

"Oh, Gwen!"

"I want to see my mother and the little ones. What if my mother thinks I'm dead? It would break her heart."

"No, no-one would tell her that, it would bring too many questions."

"I pray you're right," Gwen conceded.

With every nerve we could feel the darkness and isolation surrounding our tiny pool of safety.

"I must be sixteen now," Gwen whispered. "My birthday is at the beginning of February."

Guilt made it difficult for me to reply. "I'm sorry," I said.

"My mother always made me some little present..." I heard the words end in a stifled sob.

"Here, come here." I reached out my arms to her. "Come cuddle up with me, we're safe for now, and next year, just wait till next year."

We lay down on the unyielding cold earth of the floor and were asleep before we had time to think what another year might bring.

A sharp sound broke our exhausted slumber; daylight was seeping in between the wooden planks of the walls. "Dogs," I whispered, putting my fingers to my lips and moving quietly towards the door. I opened it warily: could this be the moment of our rescue? But the angry barking sent a shudder through my body.

I peeped out, and there stood Skinner, grappling with the leads of two ferocious dogs excited to claim their prey. I pulled the door shut. "Out!" he yelled, kicking the door open "or shall I let them in?" He moved back a pace and we crept out keeping our backs to the side of the hut, as far from the saliva-dripping teeth as space would allow. "Shall I set them on you?" he snarled, "though you'd barely make a decent meal for such hungry beasts." He started to laugh. "You stupid besoms, you are back on my land. It didn't take me long to track you down with these." He loosened his grip on the leads and the salivating animals took an eager step forward. "I will deal with you two later, now get back to the house." He pulled the dogs away and we followed him, aware now of the landscape that had been obscured from our sight the evening before, but barely taking it in, trudging along with our heads down, quiet, but our minds buzzing with fearful thoughts.

When we approached the farmhouse Skinner stopped and came towards us; I could see how he enjoyed our terror. "Get into the bake house and I don't want a sound out of you." We circled round the dogs and stepped inside. I held Gwen's hand and gave it a squeeze as I heard the door being locked behind us.

We did not move until we heard Skinner ride out and the barking decrease along with the hoof beats. There was fresh water in the bake house, but nothing to alleviate our cold and hunger. Fearfully, we sat together. "Where did he find those hunting hounds?" I wondered. "He must have borrowed them from someone, so there must be neighbours not so far away." Neighbours we now had no wish to meet.

It was several hours before we heard Skinner return, his faithful Cassie's steps thankfully not accompanied by the sound of the dogs. Gwen clung to me when we heard him approach the bake-house. He stopped outside the door. We heard the key clawing at the lock and cowed as far away as possible fearing what he would do. My heart beat wildly but then there was silence, followed by the sound of footsteps as he walked away, leaving us to our fears and the night.

Next morning we were stiff and weak from lack of food when he flung the door open. He jerked his head to show we were to follow him. We stepped out, the caked mud dropping from our clothes, glad to move, but afraid of what awaited us.

He motioned us towards the house and we walked with our heads bowed. If ever we had been in his power it was now - tired, starved, defeated. "Get my breakfast, you stupid wretches. Here, here's yours." He threw two mouldy crusts on to the floor and we grabbed them, gobbling them up like hungry dogs ourselves. We could smell the drink on him from the night before. Gwen added some wood to the small fire where the kettle hung. I put eggs into the pan for him and held it over the open flames. We dared not take anything for ourselves despite the groaning of our stomachs. "You, Hope, strip my bed and wash the linen." As I pulled his bedding apart he reached for his second tankard of beer.

Gathering up the sheets I hurried out, determined to get back as soon as I could, not wanting to leave Gwen alone with him. Moments later I heard what I had been dreading - a scream. I ran back to the house and burst through the door; Skinner had tied Gwen to the heavy oak chair and torn the back of her shift to expose her back. He stood over her, whip in hand.

"No, no!" I screamed, "please don't do it, leave her be." Gwen's eyes were wild with fear. I tried to get between them. "Blame me, I am older. Punish me," I begged. He swung out his hand and hit me in the face and I crumpled to the floor.

"Oh, you will be punished, you will sit there and watch as I chastise this bitch and if you interfere or you make a single sound I will beat her again tomorrow." He raised his riding whip and lashed out. Gwen screamed and begged him to stop. I saw her blood flick through the air and drops hit me in the face. My hands covered my mouth so tightly I could hardly breathe - I was terrified I would call out and be the source of more pain to my poor Gwen. Tears streamed down my cheeks as he lashed out once more. A coward, I closed my eyes to the scene before me, wishing I could shut out the sound of the whip slicing the air and the cries as it cut into the tender flesh of my friend. Ten times he must have raised the whip. Ten times it must have cut her before I heard him drop it. I opened my eyes and a cry escaped me as I beheld the bloodied mess of Gwen's back as she lay slumped over in the chair, neither crying nor struggling.

"Get this place cleared up," Skinner said and moved away as if his passion was finally sated. He walked outside, slamming the door behind him.

"Gwen, Gwen, I'm sorry, so sorry," I whispered as I dragged the straw pallet over to the chair before untying her and laying her on it as gently as I could, the tears washing down my face. I picked up the kettle and poured warm water into a bowl, tore my shift, knelt beside her and steadied my hand to bathe the ripped flesh. Gwen cried out and I stroked her head, and said it would be all right, all would be better in time, though I could not see how. When I had patted her dry I laid a clean shift over her and dragged the blanket from our bed, draping it over the pile of sacks I placed each side of her, so she could have a little comfort of it without the weight, finally throwing a few more logs on the fire to warm the room.

Minutes later Skinner came back. "You still here? You should both be at your duties."

"Gwen can't work," I shouted back at him. "Can you not see what you have done?"

He lunged out at me, grabbing my arms in a painful grip. "Then you have twice as much to do. Now out," and he pushed me towards the door, "and don't come back until you have done it all."

I scooped his tankard up beneath my shawl as I went - I would get warm milk for Gwen.

"One day you will pay for this Skinner," I muttered as I left the house.

Chapter 18

I worked unceasingly and without complaint, guilt driving me on; how could I complain of being cold, or tired, of calloused hands and bleeding feet when I saw my friend's suffering?

"You must heal, I can manage," I told her time and again. I thought of my daily exhaustion as my payment for her pain. Skinner's contempt for us now was absolute, we were broken and he knew it. The routine of the farm ruled our lives - the weeks flowed into one another and if it were not for Skinner's weekly trip into town the weeks would have passed without count. We assumed the day he went was a Saturday, at least we named it so, and it was our favourite day, the thought of which kept us going at the worst of times. On these days we gathered the ingredients and went to work in the bake-house, our haven of warmth and indeed of a little comfort, for we had a way of arranging the sacks of feed to make passable seats or even beds.

"He's gone," Gwen said with relief as we heard the clatter of the horse's hooves receding across the yard. We were locked in, but now that gave us more a feeling of safety than imprisonment. We busied ourselves preparing several loaves and rolls, then sat back.

"We could get the bath out," I suggested. "I'll put a couple of pots of water in the oven while it's heating up." The tin bath stood upright at the back of the bake-house behind sacks of feed, we had used it for the laundry but not dared to take a bath before, but this day it seemed more possible somehow.

"Here, I'll do it." Stretching caused Gwen pain, tearing at the scars, though she was mute on the matter. I began to haul the bath out but stopped when I knocked an old piece of cloth to the floor and found it had been covering a small cupboard.

"What's in there?" asked Gwen. My heart beat a little faster as I noticed it had air holes covered with fine muslin - a food cupboard, surely. I pulled it open and a laugh burst from my lips as I saw a small smoked ham and a cheese that had been left to ripen, both covered with muslin to protect them.

"Gwen!" She came to my side, leaning over me. We regarded this food with more delight than a king would a gift of gold plate.

"There's something else - here under the shelf."

"What is it?"

I pulled out a sack and reaching inside I found a couple of old sheets, threadbare and torn but clean, ready to be used as rags. As I examined my find a roll of some sort fell to the floor. "Pig skins!" I sat, amazed at the bounty before us.

Gwen bent her head to sniff at the meaty scent of the ham. "These are all ours, aren't they? Skinner doesn't know about them?"

I thought back. "No, Skinner doesn't know about this stuff. Remember our first night here, when we found the blankets neatly folded and the plates stacked? And the spring cabbages - who planted them? None of that was Skinner's doing, this is no more his farm than it is ours. Some poor family has been dispossessed without even time to carry away all their goods."

"So, they are ours?" Gwen asked again, afraid to rejoice too soon.

"Yes."

We left the cupboard door open and stole a glance at the contents not really believing our luck, our thoughts too many to be spoken.

"The water will be warm enough in a few minutes," I said. We raked out the red-hot ashes before pushing the paddle bearing the bread into the oven and sealing it. I carefully put the tray of burning coals on to the cooling shelf and placed more pots of water to heat up on them. Gwen undressed as I poured the water into the tub.

"How is it?" Gwen asked as she showed her back to me.

It had been a month since Gwen's whipping, the lines of impact still criss-crossed her back but she was young and healing well, though I wondered if the signs of that day would ever leave her.

"It's progressing well," I said. "I'll bathe it for you."

Gwen had been subdued since the day of her beating. We could no longer hide from the truth of our position, what it meant to be captives, to be powerless and friendless. When I compared her present state to when I first met her, plump and smiling, at Wilderness Hall, I wanted to cry. She was thin now, her hands rough and torn with labour, her cheeks had hollowed out and there were dark circles beneath her eyes. To be with her every day, to see the dullness of those eyes, her mouth fixed in a line of sad determination, was alone more punishment than I could bear.

I kneaded the next batch of bread while Gwen enjoyed her moments of relaxation. Weeks earlier we had washed the gowns rescued from the pigsty and dried them in the bakehouse. When Gwen had dried herself on a piece of one of the old sheets and dressed in a clean shift she set to work with her needle to mend the rips in the gowns or, where the damage was too bad, to fill the holes with bits of the white sheet, making them into neat diamond shapes. I added more hot water to the bath and gently lowered myself in. Bliss was the only word to describe it. I closed my eyes and imagined I was somewhere else, the kitchen of my family home, stretched out before the fire, with Hope and Jessie, wrapped in towels, mother rubbing our long auburn tresses and telling us to get near the fire, but to be careful not to burn ourselves. Hope! I had been called by that name for so long; it seemed I was truly her. Ruth was almost a stranger to me now. The thought shuddered through my body.

"Is the water cold?" Gwen asked.

"No, no, it's fine." It was not only in the physical sense that I was lost; here I was, split between Ruth and Hope, and more, a mother without a child. I no longer had any milk - it had dried up, unwanted. I climbed out of the tub, dried myself and dressed, then removed the bricks covering the small hole in the bake house wall and set to ladling out the bathwater.

"Let's hope all trace of it has gone by the time Skinner arrives back, it might show up as it's dry today," I said.

"I wish it was colder, then with any luck it would freeze over and he'd break his neck on the ice," Gwen replied.

I began rubbing together the flour and butter to make pies with some of the costard apples we had found stored in the rafters of the cowshed.

"If Sir Neville pays Skinner to keep us - you - here he certainly doesn't spend it on provisions, the flour and salt are running very low," Gwen observed, laying her needlework aside in order to stretch her fingers.

"Oh, this is no farm to speak of. If he spent some money on a couple of oxen the land could be ploughed properly instead of having us just scratch away at it."

"You sound as if it troubles you."

"No! Not for his benefit. Never! But being a farmer's daughter even though we only had a few fields - it pains me to see it so badly run... oh, what does it matter - he drinks all his money away," I finished. Gwen nodded in agreement: salt and flour were not Skinner's priorities. When he went wherever it was he went, he would come back drunk, stumbling in the dark, cursing and bumping into things in the yard, even forgetting to put Cassie back in her stable. Worse was when he failed to unlock the bake house door, or to return at all, leaving us incarcerated till the morning when the oven was long cold.

I hung our washed linen near the oven to dry and dragged the bath back to its place. Did Skinner guess we stole what bread we thought we could get away with? He no more spoke of it than did we; he cared not for anything other than his own comfort. A wonderful aroma caught us in its thrall as Gwen checked the bread, pulling it out with the rake.

"Smells good," I said.

"A little burnt on the bottom."

Gwen had been silent for a while, deep in thought. "This means we can try again," she announced. "We can build up our strength and try again."

"It's too dangerous," I replied.

"No, it will be all right this time, I've learnt my lesson, we must plan everything. And it starts with this," she indicated the food before us. "We will eat some, we'll steal every mouthful we can, until we are fit and strong, and we will take what remains with us for the journey. We will make no mistakes."

I compared the strong determination of her demeanour with the impetuous "Run" of a month earlier. It was a hard lesson she had learned; I did not celebrate her sudden maturity, but mourned the youthful spirit she had lost.

"And I know something else we could do," Gwen said, a spark lighting her eyes so I could see a glimpse of the old Gwen. "We can make ourselves shoes with the skins, pig skin shoes in place of these bits of rag and string. He must have sold the shoes we were wearing when we arrived." We hugged each other at the thought of shoes, our feet were raw, the pain from them keeping us awake at night until fatigue mercifully gave us slumber.

I removed the pies from the oven, one for tomorrow, and a small one for us to eat now, with the warm tawny apple meltingly soft beneath the golden crust. We ate in silence then I ceremoniously cut us each a slice from the cheese. It was the most marvellously luxurious meal we had ever eaten. We sat in the glowing light from the fire, relaxed and content, such times precious and rare. We fell asleep there seated on the floor leaning against the sacks of feed, our heads together. When I awoke, I sat motionless for a long time, absorbing the sheer happiness of the moment, before rising carefully and hiding the cheese and the ham back in the cupboard, making sure no trace was left of our illicit feast.

Over the following days, whenever Skinner was outside or sleeping in front of the fire following an evening spent drinking, Gwen would take out the pig skins from their hiding place beneath our bedding. She set about her task of fashioning them into shoes. It took her two weeks of secret patient work, her fingers sore and bleeding, but one day, when we were in the bake house collecting the loaves she produced them from beneath her skirts. "Shoes," she said holding them forth for me to see. "Now we can get away from here."

Chapter 19

Spring was in the air and our spirits could not but rise with the softening of the wind, the greening of the earth. The sows would litter very soon according to Skinner; pigs were the one thing he seemed to know about - "For obvious reasons," Gwen said. He told us the signs to watch out for so when we saw the sows start to build their nests we knew the births were imminent. He said one of us must spend the night in the sty for fear a sow might lie on her new born and kill them, but we preferred to be together in the huts with the sows rather than for one of us to sleep alone in the house with Skinner only a few feet away.

"Woe betides you if you lose any," Skinner said, "they should be extra valuable this year, what with the coronation coming up, everyone'll want a suckling pig for the great day."

Gwen and I repressed our excitement at hearing those words: a day of celebration meant an opportunity, an opportunity to escape while all the country was distracted.

The sows farrowed a few days apart and we spent many nights in the pigsty until the piglets were old enough to be separated from their mothers at night. They were plump, joyful little creatures with such sweet faces that as I watched them playing I thought of my son. He was three months old now and would have changed, changed beyond my recognition, I feared. Did he smile? Did he reach out his hand towards a waved object? Was he ever held close to a loving breast? I shed a quiet tear but resolved to put my thoughts of him aside - the pain was too terrible to endure. My energy must go into preparing for our escape, my first step to holding him in my arms once more.

The weather was warmer now and April showers fell as we worked in the fields collecting cabbages to add to the sows' feed of cornmeal and milk to ensure the piglets could be well suckled by their mothers. We dug the land for back-breaking hours ready for planting turnips, swedes, onions and potatoes while Skinner strutted about the farm or brushed Cassie in the yard till her coat shone. The piglets were fattening up nicely. Thinking of their departure I realised someone would have to come to the farm to collect them.

"So there will be clear tracks for us to follow once they have been collected," Gwen said as we hoed round the cabbages, displacing the eager weeds. She regarded my downcast face. "What's wrong?"

"Oh Gwen, planning it is one thing, but the nearer it comes the more…" I took a deep breath. "If it goes wrong I can't bear to think of the beating you would get. It broke my heart to see you so badly hurt."

"That's just what he's counting on. No, we must make our plans." She smiled and squeezed my hand in encouragement, as if my pain had been greater than hers.

We thought the hens were on our side the next day when we found the first eggs for some time. We slipped them into our pockets and did not tell Skinner for a week. We secretly cooked and ate some and hid others in the bake-house and changed them every few days for fresher ones. We boiled one occasionally to eat in the fields or while locked in baking the bread. We were putting on a little weight and felt stronger for the better food we were eating. With the eggs available we did not disturb the precious ham and cheese in the hidden cupboard, keeping it for our journey. The gowns we had rescued from the pigs were ready if somewhat loose on our work-worn frames.

"Wait!" Skinner shouted as Gwen and I crept out at dawn to milk the cow and feed the pigs. He was an ugly sight getting out of bed, dishevelled and stinking of drink. "The first lot of piglets will be leaving today." He staggered across the room towards us. "I don't want a peep out of the pair of you while the carter's here." Gwen was unable to hide the flash of expectation in her eyes. "Sorry to disappoint you, Gwen, but expect no help from him - he was the one who loaned me the dogs to track you down." He enjoyed the despair written on our faces as our hopes were battered down once again. "He has no sympathy with run-away workers sent here as punishment."

Skinner pushed us out towards the bake house. "What about the cows? They need to be milked," Gwen complained as the door was locked behind us.

"They can wait," Skinner growled. "And keep the shutters closed," he added, condemning us to near darkness.

I went to the far corner of the bake house and quietly removed the bricks that kept the vermin out from the hole.

"What?" Gwen asked.

I put a finger to my lips and waited till we heard Skinner's footsteps retreat across the yard. "We must listen, see what we can overhear, there may be information, something we can use, something to help."

"If we can hear above the whistling of the wind," Gwen whispered back. When we heard the sound of squeaking wagon wheels drawing up in the yard we squatted down by the hole, bending our heads to hear better.

"Welcome, Johnson," I clearly heard Skinner say, the wind bringing his words to us. I was momentarily shocked to hear how pleasant and assured he sounded. "Unload the corn sacks by the barn, will you? You can leave the flour, cheese and ale here, I'll see they're put away later."

"You having a party with all that ale or just celebrating the coronation? Not long now. They say in town the fountains will be flowing with wine. That's where I'll be heading."

"Maybe, not sure yet, I was thinking of marrying the youngest servant, it's time I had some young 'uns of my own."

We put our hands over our mouths to prevent our gasps escaping into the yard. Gwen shook her head, time and again; she closed her eyes and I saw a tear begin to trickle down her cheek.

"A double celebration," Skinner's visitor was saying. "You've been watching that old boar of yours - you said the sows were in heat again, all that rutting - it's making you horny." He laughed. "Good on you. She's a lucky girl, marrying the master, better than she deserves. The sooner you get her with kid the better, that'll stop her straying. I'll stand witness for you if you like."

"I may take up your offer," Skinner replied. "I'll help you load up the piglets; they're a good weight and should fetch a fair price. You can choose one for yourself for lending me your dogs, good trackers those two." We heard the thud of the sacks and the chink of the flagons as the two men unloaded the supplies. "Walk on," we heard Johnson call, and the wagon trundled on heading for the sties. The energy that kept us still and silent drained from our bodies as they left and we slumped down on to the bake-house floor. I saw all colour had deserted Gwen's face. I took her in my arms as we heard the piglets squealing as they were loaded up into the wagon.

"I feel like those piglets," Gwen said.

I took her face in my hands. "It won't happen."

"If he threatens to kill you or beat you until I agree, what then? He would have me tied to him and the farm for ever." She headed for the hole in the wall, bent down and was sick.

An hour later when Johnson had gone we were let out to carry the flour sacks into the bake house along with the seeds, corn and a few onion sets. We would have to mill the corn for the pigs and chickens adding to our chores but I saw a use for the old empty sacks and put them in the full piss pot to bleach them. I could make them into bags and use oddments of leather left over from our shoes to make handles. We had a lot to do if we were to escape, and escape we must, Gwen must never be forced to marry that evil man. At Wilderness Hall I had asked her to help me, to bring my baby to me, and in doing so had brought all this suffering and pain on her head. How could she not hate me? Yet the marvel was her only thought was ever how to deal with our plight, not my part of the responsibility. This time our escape would be successful - the alternative was unthinkable. Mercifully, the weather was better and the days longer. God bless the king and his celebration.

Every second day Johnson called to pick up the piglets and with money coming in Skinner ordered a hunk of beef and even killed a piglet which made a change from the never-ending rabbits, salted fish and the odd scrawny chicken. Fluffy yellow chicks seemed to be everywhere as nature took its course and birds overhead were busy carrying twigs to their half-built nests.

We listened from our usual prison on Johnson's third visit, straining to hear their words as he and Skinner went about their work. "Has all been arranged?" asked Johnson.

"It certainly has. The celebrations will still be going on but the vicar says there is no reason why the wedding shouldn't take place the day following the coronation. Oh, I shall be celebrating all right! You'll come to the church?"

"Of course, I'll stand by my best drinking companion on his wedding day. Let's load up the final batch of pigs. And I've brought you a bottle of wine as a gift, to toast the new king's health and your last few days as a free man."

"We must be prepared," I whispered to Gwen when the wagon had rolled away and Skinner gone indoors; she sat on the floor with her head on her knees and covered by her hands, as if to fend off a blow. "Everything must be ready, but the most important thing is to find out how many days we have, when is the coronation, tomorrow, the day after, or the one after that? We must get him to tell us without arousing his suspicion."

Gwen's silence unnerved me but when she lifted her face I found she had not been hiding from the truth of her situation but she had been thinking, planning, too. "Skinner will be careful, if he thinks he can... marry me," she whispered the words. I could see how she hated to have them come from her lips. "He will be extra vigilant, I must not seem too horrified when he tells me, I must fool him, or he will lock us both in till the…" she could not use the word 'wedding' "… till the day."

"I have found something." I hesitated. "I think it can help us."

That morning I made a beef and ale pie with wild garlic and mushrooms and at dinner Gwen refilled Skinner's tankard the instant he drained it. After his third pint he became talkative and even offered us both a small glass of wine.

"We drink to the king," he said, getting to his feet, pastry flakes falling from his beard.

"To the king," we chorused, and all innocently I added, "Today and every day."

"Indeed, but specially this day, tomorrow the king is to be crowned, and the day after you, my girl," Skinner stretched out an arm and pulled Gwen to his side, "you will be going into town with me and there we shall marry."

Tomorrow - coronation day, I thought. *We must act quickly if we are not to waste this opportunity.* When my eyes focused on Gwen's face I could see how she struggled against her revulsion as she looked at the man who would be her husband.

"I am to be your wife?"

"That you are." He put his mouth to Gwen's flushed cheek as she fought herself not to pull away. "And remember to come along willingly or Hope will be put in one of the out-houses and left there without food or water until you agree, but not before she gets a taste of my whip, and you will remember how that feels." He lifted Gwen's chin with his grimy hand, turning her face towards his. "Once she is locked up you will come to my bed willingly enough." I felt ill at the

151

truth of his words. "Would you rather walk up the aisle six months pregnant with the town's people jeering at you? Wife or whore - take your choice."

Gwen curved her back, standing as I had never seen her, proud and tall. "And I shall be mistress of this house?"

"You will, as my wife."

"And you could buy us a proper bed and a new mattress?" A carnal smile lit Skinner's face.

"If I can find one at the right price."

Gwen regarded him coyly. "And new clothes for the wedding?"

"You ask too much - but perhaps I could find something second-hand in town."

"And I shall have charge of Hope, she must do my bidding?"

"Oh, my girl," Skinner laughed, throwing back his head, showing his blackened teeth, "you will suit me well."

I moved away; Gwen's words made me feel uneasy, she seemed to enjoy them too much.

"Hope, get out and put the animals away for the night," Skinner shouted across the room at me. "We want some time alone, if you get my meaning."

"We can wait a few more hours as our wedding day is so close," Gwen said. "We must make sure all is in order on the farm." How could even a shadow of a doubt have entered my mind?

Skinner laughed and pushed her away from him. "Go, my girl," he said, and we ran and did not stop till we were out of sight on the far side of the cowshed. Gwen was shaking from head to foot.

"Do you think he believed me?" she asked. I nodded, but did not add I almost believed her myself. "Good, good, I'll see to the animals, you get ready for tomorrow."

We slept only fitfully, afraid of what the day would bring. This was our great chance and if it passed without success then our lives would - we dare not even think what our lives would be if we failed.

We rose while it was yet dark, tending to the animals who had been our good companions through this imprisonment. I paused a moment in the cowshed after milking to run my hand across Betsy's smooth raven-black head and gaze into those dark eyes one last time. I would miss her more than the busy, pecking, squabbling hens or the bright-eyed intelligent pigs; she reminded me gentleness existed beyond the boundaries of this place. I caught my attention wandering and quickly slapped her on her rump and urged her and Bonnie out into the field.

"She won't go!" Gwen had fed Cassie and led her out of her stable but she made no bid for freedom despite Gwen waving her arms and urging her away.

"She's a faithful animal, we cannot change her," I said. "Come, we must hurry."

Gwen and I made sure to make a fine noise as we prepared breakfast and Skinner rose from his bed with a grumble but saying it was well to be up early so he could get to town to join in the celebrations.

"Your breakfast is ready," I said, and he sat down at the table.

"You'll do your baking today," he said between mouthfuls, "so take what you need to the bake-house, afore I lock you in."

Gwen and I carried the butter and flour into the bake-house as we had been bid, but used our moments there to change into our clean work clothes, our hasty fingers stumbling over the fastenings. We dashed back to stand outside the door. I twisted my apron into an ugly knot as I battled to keep my hands from shaking. The sky was growing bright, a clear blue, and we stood, frozen to the spot, scarcely breathing, until the sound came we had waited for - a loud steady snore.

We exchanged a glance and went back into the house to see Skinner was asleep at the table, his breakfast dish empty, his porridge eaten; his poisoned porridge eaten. The laudanum should keep him out of it all day with any luck. I had found it in the cowshed along with other rudimentary remedies left by the previous owner.

Skinner was a tall man, and too heavy for us to carry, so we each took an arm and placed a hand beneath a shoulder and dragged him to the bake-house. We left him on the floor. I rushed back to the house and grabbed the keys off the hook. Gwen slammed the door shut and I locked it, the key clicking in the lock the sweetest sound we had heard for a long time.

Gwen ran to the cowshed where we had hidden our bags, one packed with our rescued clothes, the other holding food – hard-boiled eggs, a whole loaf of bread, some milk, the remaining ham and cheese. It would have been good to take Cassie but she may have been recognised and horse stealing was a hanging offence.

We hurried inside and helped ourselves to bread and butter, almost choking in our speed.

"When he wakes, he should have a bad head and he will still have to get out of the bake-house," I mumbled, my mouth full, "hopefully we have eight hours, perhaps ten."

As we closed the door of the farmhouse behind us we found ourselves embracing. "We must go," I said. "Your hair! Pull down your cap, your red hair could give us away." I pushed my own hair under my cap before we turned our backs on the farm that had imprisoned us for so long, starting to run with the joy of freedom, following the impressions of the wheels of the wagon left by all the recent visits.

The sun was rising, brilliant and golden as we found a defined path, and our excitement grew - we were on our way and God willing, we would never see this place again. After a few minutes we saw a farmhouse in the distance, not unlike the one we had left behind us. Did it belong to Johnson? He was the person we now had to fear. We kept our heads low as we sped on, thankful when we reached a row of trees, following which we found our feet coming to a rest on the side of a road. Our joy at finding the road was dimmed only by the thought we must decide which way to go, and upon this decision our future might well depend. "This way," I said, knowing we must not hesitate. We hastened along so anyone coming would not know where we had joined the road but stopped when we heard the rumble of a cart and voices, merry voices, and the strange sound of laughter. We waited till it came into sight, a farmer's cart pulled by two horses, overloaded with passengers. My heart was pounding beneath my shift, as if it wanted to burst through my ribs.

"Whoa, whoa." The horses stopped, glad for the break. "Where are you going, pretty maids?" the white-bearded driver called.

"To town," I whispered. I closed my eyes to listen to the reply.

"All on your own?"

This was not Johnson's voice. I took hold of Gwen's hand. "Father said we could go, our aunt will meet us there." I did not know where the words came from but I was grateful to hear them flow from my lips.

"Tis a long way to walk, hop on board – make room, make room." His whole family were there in the cart, from an elderly woman who could have been his wife, to sturdy workers and their wives, one with a baby in her arms, to young men and women of our own age, filled with vitality, and they all happily shuffled round and a hand stretched out to help me. I waved Gwen up first and followed, to find myself surrounded by smiling faces. It seemed I had walked from a nightmare into a dream. "There'll be mighty celebrating this day," the driver said, flicking his whip and the horses moving on. "Since Cromwell had Queensborough Castle razed the people in this part of Kent have hated him with strong resolve and are all for the king. Now, we won't stop till we get to the ferry."

"Ferry?"

"How else are you to get off the island?"

Chapter 20

"Whoa," called the farmer. He pulled hard on the reins bringing the heavy wagon to a rumbling halt on the slope leading down to the ferry. We were all jostled against each other, rocking to and fro. I found a pair of strong arms holding me steady for a moment and felt a tear form in my eye, so unused was I to any show of manly kindness. I noted his broad, weathered features and felt a familiarity with them - it could have been my father's face when younger - the face of a man who laboured, and loved. I saw the gentleness with which his worn hands lifted the baby from his wife's arms to allow her to stand and smooth the creases from her dress. A younger man, who might have been his brother, jumped to the ground and held out his hand to help us down. Gwen and I moved a little apart from the family, silent, surveying this scene as if it were from some play, so strange and wonderful did it seem. A fog had been lifted from our eyes: the sky was a brilliant, infinite blue; the narrow passage of water we must cross reflecting the colour; the land on the far side of the channel a green line on the horizon with the promise of towns and villages. Ours was not the first wagon to reach the ferry, there was another group climbing aboard the little sailing boat swaying gently at the water's edge. The elderly farmer and his wife had not descended from the cart but were saying goodbye to their family.

"Are you not crossing with us?" I asked.

"No, my dear, not us, we are too old for celebrations, we have seen too many things, the young 'uns will come back tomorrow and tell us all about it. Half of Sheppey seem to be out today. Perhaps we will see you again then."

"Thank you, but we will be staying with my aunt a while. We're grateful to you for allowing us to travel with you."

"My son will make sure you board safely, today must be the busiest on the ferry for many a long year. Do you have your penny ready for the ferryman?"

I felt my stomach lurch, I had no coins, only the gold cross and chain Margaret had given me, and I depended on getting a fair price for the chain if we were to have any chance of getting away from Skinner. I tried to smile. "Yes, and thank you again."

"I've never been on a boat," Gwen confided as we stood watching as the little craft pushed off from the jetty and started pulling away, a light breeze opening its sail.

"Nor have I."

"Is it safe?"

"It must be - people are using it."

The younger woman from the wagon came up to us. "I always enjoy a trip on the Harty ferry," she said with a smile, her eyes following the course of the boat across the water.

"Is it safe?" Gwen asked again.

"Of course it is, have you never gone this way to Faversham? Do you use King's Ferry?"

"Yes," I answered quickly, "King's Ferry."

"I've heard the king is very handsome," the girl continued, the name of the ferry leading her along a different path, "and the court is full of beautiful women," she put her hand to her lips as if divulging a secret, "in low cut gowns, they say."

158

"So I have heard too - times have changed."

"And will the fountain in Faversham really flow with wine?"

"We can but wait to see."

"I'm sure my brother will drink heartily from it if it does, and tell me not to."

"Brothers are all the same," Gwen put in.

"Well, if there is dancing this evening, I shall not be dancing with my brother, that is certain."

We laughed, and for us the laughter was because we had re-found the world where such trifles were of concern.

The girl put her hand in a pocket and withdrew two pennies. "I have my money to spend, and this is not for the ferry man, either, my brother has those coins."

"We have our money, too," Gwen said, opening her hand and showing three pennies covering her palm.

"Oh," I cried involuntarily.

The girl seemed a little cross at Gwen's greater wealth and soon left us alone.

"Gwen!" I said in joyful amazement once the girl was out of earshot.

"Did I not say?" she whispered, "I had a few pence from my last wages at the Hall. I kept the money in the straw of our pallet so Skinner wouldn't find it."

"Gwen, you have saved us, I thought I would have to sell my chain for us to get aboard."

"It will be well spent if we can put all that water between ourselves and Skinner."

We were quiet as we walked about, feeling our freedom with every step. I spied a church lying low in the landscape a little way off and felt it pulling me. I touched Gwen on the arm. "There's a church," I said.

"I'll wait here, you have a little time before the ferry returns." It seemed Gwen knew my very thoughts, we had been so much together.

"I will not be long," I said, "but I have to go, you understand?"

She nodded and I picked up my skirt and walked as quickly as I could up the slope past the ferryman's cottage and towards the small church. For months now my prayers had been no more than thoughts as I worked the land or fed the pigs or mumbled words as I lay in bed. I opened the door, slipped inside and fell to my knees. The last time I had entered a church it was to be married - I had gone through the ceremony but I was no married woman, it had been nothing more than a sham. I could not live my life as the property of such a man - having escaped Skinner I felt once more the chains that bound me to Sir Neville. But my child! I could pray for nothing but my child, I could bear any pain but the pain of this separation. Escaping from Skinner was but the first step towards my son and I still had far to go. God give me the strength to go on, I prayed - my son must know his mother's love.

Having found this place of peace, this place where I could gather my thoughts and feel the presence of my son, I was loath to leave but I knew it was not contemplation that was needed this day, but movement.

I hurried back to Gwen. "You prayed for your son?" she asked.

"Yes, I am sorry I left you here, I needed to be alone for a moment."

"I said my prayers too," she replied.

"What did you pray for?"

"That Skinner doesn't catch us."

We were anxious to go but there was no hurrying the ferry. "We must find our way to this Faversham," I said as we sat on a bench, watching fleets of birds dance over the waterway. "It sounds like a good-sized town and we may be able to get a coach from there going towards West Penton, we must see Margaret - she will help us."

"You trust this Margaret, then," Gwen said.

"Absolutely."

"But she saw you married to Sir Neville."

"Only because she thought that was what was best for me and my child."

"And her husband?"

"He is a good man, but I think we must try to see Margaret on her own if we can. I shall cheer the day I no longer feel I have to lie or deceive good people," I said, thinking of the farmer and the ease with which the lie about my aunt had come to my mind.

"When we are safe," Gwen replied.

"I think we should be able to be safe without that necessity."

We sat silently watching the ferry make its way back to us. "I wish it would hurry," I said, "we have gone such a little way and now time is passing and we are making no progress." The ferry seemed like a snail sliding its way towards us. "What if Skinner is waking up?" The thought hung over us, a cloud on our horizon.

The sun had risen quite high by the time the ferry was ready for us to board. We walked down the slope to the water's edge where little ripples lapped at the shore, their gentle sound soothing our troubled minds. We were helped aboard and were unnerved by the unsteady boards beneath our feet. Gwen sat close beside me and the farmer's family placed themselves around us. Sitting low in the water the expanse of the channel seemed to grow and we held hands for comfort.

The sail flapped like washing on a good drying day and we moved away from the land with nothing but the creaking boards between us and the cold, dark water beneath. I closed my eyes but that only intensified the rocking of the boat. When I opened them again I noticed how the others travelling with us seemed to be enjoying themselves, laughing, reaching out to allow their fingers to dip into the water. I took a deep breath and told myself to enjoy this freedom, the flowing estuary, the soft breeze, the warmth of the climbing sun. I smiled at Gwen who scowled back at me and crushed my fingers in her hand. Over my shoulder I watched as we moved away from the island we had not known to be an island - what a clever place to have sent us, I thought. But now it seemed no prison; it rolled away green and luscious under the sun.

"Do not worry, we will soon be ashore," the farmer's son said as he sat with his arm about his wife, whose only concern was with her sleeping infant.

"We are not good sailors," I replied, glancing towards Gwen who had become pale and seemed afraid to speak.

It was with delight we heard the bottom of the boat grate against the opposite beach. We were helped ashore by willing hands and Gwen moved away as quickly as she could.

"Good day to you all," I called to the farmer's scattered family as I followed her. "Thank your father again for us. Perhaps we shall see you in town."

Gwen rushed behind a tree and I heard her retching. She emerged a moment later, wiping her mouth. "I'm never going on a boat again," she said.

I smiled.

"What are you laughing at?"

"Finally, I've found something you are afraid of."

"Well, I'd do it again to get away from Skinner," she conceded.

"Everyone seems to be going this way," I said, "it must be the road to Faversham."

Some minutes later, when the road had emptied of people, we slipped behind a pair of embracing trees to change into our salvaged Wilderness Hall dresses and home-made shoes. "Am I all right?" Gwen asked, as I stood back from helping her.

"You are wonderful." She was almost my old Gwen back if I disregarded the gauntness of her body, the roughness of her hands. "Particularly when the shoes are hidden beneath your skirt." I donned my own gown and marvelled at how different a woman I had been when wearing it. Some of its past aura clung to me now and I stood a little straighter, with my head a little higher. We each drank of the milk we had brought with us and carried on.

The tide was out and on this side of the shore barges and boats of many kinds were stuck fast in the mud. We passed wharves, warehouses, and a gunpowder factory and then we were in the town, the houses along the street closing in, keeping us safe, it seemed, with their friendly facades. Eventually we reached the market square thronged by people determined to enjoy the coronation day. Flags decorated every building and the roar of noise took us by surprise: we were used to nothing but our own voices and the call of the birds. Beer and cider were already flowing freely, and freely they were being enjoyed. We overheard someone say there were to be fireworks that would light up the sky and shake the ground with their explosions. What a different era we were entering - celebration was on everyone's lips, when just a few years before, under Cromwell's Protectorate, it was an idea that should not enter anyone's mind.

"So how far to West Penton?" I asked of the air, seeing a signpost stating 48 miles to London, 18 miles to Maidstone.

The day was warming up and we found a spot to sit and eat some of the bread and cheese just as a fiddler standing beneath an overhanging bay-window began a lively tune and couples started to dance.

"Here, you have a drink." An unsteady hand waved a pitcher before us.

"We..." I began, but before we knew it we had mugs in our hands and the man was pouring in cider, the aroma of apples wafting up at us.

"The fumes are strong enough to make us light-headed," Gwen muttered.

"You must drink if I am not to take offence," the man said, hanging over us where we sat, his beard almost brushing against my face.

"To the king." I took a deep swallow and only just prevented myself spluttering it back in his face.

"Here, girls," a woman's voice called across to us, "this here fountain's full of wine. Try it - it'll put hair on your chest!" She raised her tankard, letting out a great gust of laughter.

We resisted the invitation and eased ourselves out of the square and headed to the inn. I approached a tall man sprawled across a chair by the chalk board showing the destination of the coach.

"West Penton?" he said, "you have a fair way to go but you're in luck. With so many people travelling for the coronation there is a coach tomorrow going to Ashford - it will set you in the right direction."

"Of course," I said, trying to sound as if I expected nothing less. I hesitated and he tapped the board. "The coach leaves for Ashford at nine of the clock if the driver is sober by then."

"How much will it cost?"

"Depends, inside or out?"

He noticed my hesitation.

"The cheapest seats are in the open top section at the back, they're three pence each." He gave us a sympathetic smile. "If you buy the tickets you can sleep in the main saloon here tonight - once the bar closes."

"I will need to sell my gold chain to pay for the tickets," I explained. "Where do you recommend I should go?"

"There's a jeweller's shop in the market square. He'll be closing early today, so best hurry along."

We had to push our way through the crowds and search for the shop we wanted, finding its low entrance on the far side of the square. I slipped the cross off the chain and we went inside. A man no taller than four foot came forward as we entered and held out his hand for the gold chain. He examined it, carrying out a few tests.

"One shilling," he said in a whiny voice.

"It's worth more than that," came a cry from Gwen. "The man at the inn said its worth one and a half shillings."

"Did he now? I will give you one shilling and tuppence, no more."

"And three pence," demanded Gwen picking up the chain and moving towards the door.

"All right, all right, one shilling and three pence," he said, counting out the money as Gwen handed over the chain.

As the door closed behind us Gwen smiled. "My mother would always bargain for everything," she said. "She had to with all us children to feed."

Back at the inn we booked our seats for the morrow; it was mid-afternoon and there was nothing more we could do before morning. We prayed Skinner was still in the bake house. Opening the bag containing the food we tucked into bread and ham. Then, leaving our bags with the landlord for safekeeping, we went off to lose ourselves in the crowd. The market stalls were doing good business and we spent one penny on a woollen hat to cover Gwen's red hair.

By early evening the dancing was at full tilt with half a dozen musicians fighting for an audience. Gwen suddenly left my side as she was pulled into the swirl of bodies and soon I was dragged into the heaving mass. Many a dancer was so unsteady he or she might have been aboard the Harty Ferry, I thought. We were passed from hand to hand, from arm to arm, dance after dance, but they were cheerful, carefree hands and arms and we felt surprisingly safe among them. Flares were lit across the square and fire beacons glowed in the distance as darkness drew on.

"Fireworks! Fireworks!" the cry went up, and we found ourselves swept up in the crowd making for the riverside, laughing and giggling as we found a space to watch the show. "You wait until you see the rockets," shouted a lad. "I work at the gunpowder factory, you won't believe the bang they make, it'll knock you off your feet."

Gwen clung to me as each of the fireworks shook the ground and lit the sky, momentarily making night into day, the town with its houses and churches appearing then disappearing again. We had never seen such magic. It was a night we would remember. Arms around each other's waists we set off back to the inn for a few hours' sleep on the floor. To any witness to our progress along the street it may have seemed we had had taken a little too much of the wine, but it was the freedom that was running through our veins, painting the smiles on our faces and breaking from our mouths in laughter. We settled down at the inn using our bags as pillows. The sound of merriment went on long into the night as we drifted off to sleep after what was for each of us, the first carefree evening in a long, long time.

Chapter 21

I woke abruptly to the sharp, shrill sound of a horn piercing my sleep. I did not understand: was Skinner calling us from the field, had I slept too late, was I in for a beating? "Ten minutes," came a cry.

"It's time to go," Gwen said quietly. I opened my eyes and took in the dark wooden floor, the heavy furniture, the open space of this room. "The coach is coming." Of course, we were on our way, we were free.

"Your hair!" I said as I rose. Gwen's hair flashed like well-polished copper as she moved across a beam of sunlight; she picked up her cap and quickly stuffed her hair out of sight. There must be nothing about us to make us memorable – we must merge into the crowds, disappear in the throng still excited by the coronation celebrations.

"There are parcels of bread and cheese over here on the table," Gwen called across as I gathered my belongings and my wits. "One farthing each, I have a ha'penny, shall I get two?"

"Yes, we'll need something on the journey." I hurried out into the cool morning air and crossed the square to the fountain, washed out the flagon that had contained the milk and filled it with fresh water, gathering a little into my hands to drink, then running my wet hands across my face. Gwen joined me and we beheld the chaos wrought by a night of unbridled celebration, though it could have been a massacre, with bodies strewn in shop doorways, arms and legs in uncomfortable attitudes, as the townspeople slept off the excesses of the night before.

We stood a little back as others gathered outside the inn to await the coach. Gwen put the bread and cheese in her bag containing our discarded farm clothes. "I still have three hard boiled eggs; do you have anything left?"

"A little bread," I replied, "and one slice of gammon." At the thought of food my stomach danced a merry jig, but I was used to hunger and ignoring its call. The coach came to a halt, its great wheels throwing dust into the morning air. We waited while those of more comfortable means were assisted inside.

"Here you go, up top," a voice growled in my ear and we were both unceremoniously heaved up on to the rear of the coach.

"It's so high!" Gwen was still looking all about her, absorbing the unusual vantage point when, with a crack of the whip and a cry of "On!" the coach jerked into movement and we each rocked in our swaying eyrie.

"There," I yelled, "the bar, hold on."

We held on till our knuckles were white, for as the coach left the town behind the roads became more uneven, throwing the two of us against each other when a wheel hit a pot-hole or particularly deep rut. We held on tightly to our shawls as the wind we had thought fresh and benign on leaving the inn whipped across our faces and cut into our thin clothing.

"How long?" Gwen asked urgently.

"We're heading for Ashford, it's twelve miles, so the driver said," I shouted back, the words coming out in bursts as we rocked from side to side. "We should be there by midday."

"Midday!" Gwen cried, "if we live that long! I think I would rather risk that boat again than fall from here and have my brains dashed out on a rock!"

I thought of my coach journey to Wilderness Hall with Sir Neville, on padded cushions, warmly wrapped against the weather. I preferred to take my chances with Gwen, I thought, for all the heaving of my stomach.

After a long climb the coach pulled in to Challock to allow the horses to be watered; we loosened our aching fingers from the bar and were helped down, finding our shoulders and backs ached as we walked slowly across to a bench on the green.

"I think I'll stand," Gwen said, handing me one of the packs of bread and cheese.

"Come on, let's share a tankard of mulled wine, it'll warm us up."

'I'll go," Gwen said, "stretch my legs."

"Travelling alone, my dear?" asked an elderly woman who had taken the journey inside the coach. "How far do you have to go?"

"My sister and I are continuing to Ashford," I replied.

"And you will be met there?" I hated to avoid her kindly questions, but at that moment Gwen appeared with the mulled wine, and I quickly added "Yes, of course - oh, there she is," and moved away.

"Was she asking questions?" Gwen whispered.

"Yes, she means nothing by it, but the less we say the better."

"Skinner must be on his way by now, mustn't he?"

"He doesn't know which way we've gone."

"But he may guess, and he'll be quicker on horseback."

"We can but go as quickly as we may, we can do nothing more." *Would he guess we were heading for West Penton?* "He doesn't know we have money so he'll be searching for us walking the lanes or footpaths and make his enquires accordingly." I sounded more confident than I felt and hid my worries as we clambered on board, grateful to be moving again. How slowly the miles were passing. In my own mind I could not but help feel Skinner chasing up behind us on Cassie's strong back. Hopefully with so many travellers on the road for the holiday we had been able to pass unremarked but two young women travelling alone were seemingly always a cause for comment.

The chilly breeze had grown stronger when we finally reached our destination of Ashford, busy with the noon-time crowds, the royal bunting fluttering wildly in the wind. "Do we have far to go?" Gwen asked and I knew I must disappoint her with my answer.

"Yes, far I fear, though I cannot say how far or even in which direction." We wandered through the busy market wishing we had money to buy sweetmeats and fresh bread, the scent of which mingled appealingly between the stalls but knew we must take care of the pennies we had left.

"There, there." I spied a signpost. I could not restrain the smile that came to my lips when I saw the name West Penton. I was going home. "Eleven miles," I said, "we can do that before dark if we hurry." We followed the direction of the sign out of the narrow streets of the town and into the quiet fields. We put an hour's walk between ourselves and Ashford before we stopped on a grassy bank to eat the eggs and half of the slice of gammon, resting our backs against the broad trunk of an elm whose leaves trembled on the verge of opening.

"Do you not feel it would be wonderful just to stop here?" Gwen asked me. "If only we weren't being chased."

My stomach lurched at Gwen's words, for chased we were, by an implacable enemy who could be around the next bend in the road. "If we can get safely to my friend Margaret I am sure all will be well," I said, to comfort myself as well as Gwen.

We did not stop again until we reached a few cottages huddled close to a bridge over a swiftly flowing stream. Moving out of sight we went a way along the bank treading among the scattered primroses and sat down at the water's edge, drinking the cool fresh water to ease our parched throats. Gwen leant over and slipped her feet out of her shoes, dangling them so they were brushed by the hurrying stream.

"I know, we must go," she said, "but allow me just one…" Alert to every sound she fell silent as we heard the rumble of a cart. We grabbed our belongings and made our way towards the road but took cover behind a tree until we could make out an elderly man with a small wagon loaded with bulging sacks. He was going our way. Gwen nodded at me and we ran to the bridge.

"Steady, Marjorie." The man pulled at the reins as we smiled to hear the name. "What's this, Marjorie, two young ladies on the road, do you think they would like to sit on our cargo to rest their feet?" It appeared Marjorie gave her consent for the man reached out a hand to help us up.

"We're going to Sandhurst," I said, ever cautious, not wishing to give away our true destination.

"Then I can take you as far as High Halden," he said removing an empty pipe from a mouth well-hidden beneath a white beard. "It's on your way." We sat on top of the lumpy

172

sacks, and the cry came "On, Marjorie, on," and we rolled along with only the thought that Skinner could be on this road and we were all too visible on our perch, to keep us from utter contentment.

The cart pulled up outside the Chequers Inn, Marjorie raising her head and braying, recognising her home. "This is the end of my journey," the old man said. "I am going into the village but you should stay on this path, go left at the cross roads and follow the sign. It's a fair way to go. Be careful and a good journey to you both."

"Thank you for helping us on our way," Gwen called after him.

"'Twas all Marjorie's doing," he muttered as the cart moved off.

"I like Marjorie," Gwen said, laughing as we crossed the road to the inn. "Oh, I must use the privy." Gwen darted towards the back of the building while I waited outside, thinking another glass of mulled wine would refresh us for the remainder of our journey. The innkeeper came to the door, scanned the empty street and walked back inside without seeing me.

"You would not believe how rude some people can be," I heard him say.

"Who was that then?" a woman's voice replied from within.

"The man who just left, the one who wolfed down your food like he hadn't been fed for a week. He demanded I put up a poster about two young runaways, demanded I tell you, me, in my own inn. Civility pays, that's a lesson he's yet to learn. I said it would cost him a penny and he threw the money at me and walked out."

"So where's the poster?" the woman queried.

"Tossed it after him!"

I edged away from the door feeling sick. The poster, out here somewhere. I felt for the direction of the wind and began searching the bushes on the far side of the inn. There it was, torn in two. I grabbed at it and ran to the back of the building.

"There you..." Gwen began, but I put my finger to my lips and indicated she should follow me, keeping behind the trees until the inn was out of sight.

"He's here," I cried, "just left - Skinner - here." I was too shaken to make much sense but held out the torn poster.

"What does it say?"

"'Reward five sovereigns,'" I read. "'Escaped Thieves' and then our names, 'Gwen Dixon and Hope Courtney, dressed in brown woollen skirts, the shorter one with red hair'." Gwen's hand went automatically to her cap. "'It is forbidden to help them. If sighted the local magistrate should be informed to hold them until their jailer, E Skinner Esquire, can take possession of them.'"

"Jailer!" Gwen said with a shudder as she rammed the torn halves into her bag to prevent anyone else seeing them. "Possession!" The very words seemed to put chains about our feet. "And Skinner 'Esquire' indeed."

"Margaret," I said.

"What?"

"Has he been to see Matthew or is he on his way there now? Is he sitting in Matthew's study this very minute? What lies has he told?"

Chapter 22

"We must get off the road, follow it as best we can through the fields, listen out for horses' hooves." The words tumbled out of me in fear. "The only reason he would be on this road is to visit West Penton. But is he on his way there, or coming back?" I gathered my shawl over my head; the warmth of the day seemed to have disappeared.

We walked on, using the well-trodden footpaths across the fields, away from the highway and out of Skinner's sight, always watching, always on guard.

I felt a tug at my heart as we found ourselves at a crossroads. I knew this road, there was a lane a mile ahead leading to our farm. No more our farm, no more us, just me.

"Why are you crying?" Gwen asked, reaching out her hand towards me.

But I could not say and did not say, but muttered "Not far now," and took to the path again, Gwen following in my footsteps.

As we approached the first houses on the edge of the village Gwen caught up with me. "What should we do? There will be posters all over the town."

"Not here, this is one place he won't dare put up a poster."

"Why ever not?"

"If he wants Matthew and Margaret to believe some story of illness, of me being unfit to care for my child, there can't be posters in the town naming me as a thief."

"Oh, of course, do you think he is clever enough to realise that?"

"I fear he is, though I would not call him clever, only cunning. I think we should wait somewhere, out of sight, until dusk." I searched my memory. "This way." I led Gwen to a crumbling barn on the edge of Farmer Bright's land and we slipped inside. "I think we are in more danger of the place falling on our heads than anyone coming in," I said.

When the rain began to fall and dusk creep its way down the hillside we left our hiding place and moved carefully along the main street. I knew every inch, every bush and tree, every garden gate, every house. I pulled my shawl forward to hide my face. "You must speak for me here, Gwen, I will be recognised."

The church's squat tower sat as a pale outline against the darkness. The vicarage seemed lit by a single candle and moth-like I felt its pull upon my heart. I had to stifle a cry of dismay as two men stopped by the gate as they met in the street.

"Into the church, quickly," I whispered to Gwen. "We have to wait till they've gone."

Gwen and I knelt in silence in the darkening church. I could just make out the Courtney stone and my thoughts became simple words: *I have to tell you I have a son - and this is Gwen, my friend.*

Opening my eyes from a moment of peace I could see with a shudder my wedding day re-enacted before the altar, Matthew in his clerical clothes, Sir Neville in all his finery, showing how far above me he was in the stations of life. Wedding! It had been no wedding - nothing but a sacrifice. I knelt but my silent prayer was interrupted by a voice I recognised - Aggie! The woman who had blamed me for surviving the fire at the farm, who had called me unspeakable names. If there was one person who would enjoy my present situation, it was Aggie. She was talking to another woman at the back of the church. "I know her," I whispered to Gwen, remaining on my knees. "Ask her if the vicar will be taking evensong tonight."

"Not the vicar himself, he's away in Canterbury," Aggie replied to Gwen's question.

Away! I was afraid Aggie would hear my sharp intake of breath.

"Helping he is as the Archbishop's in London for the coronation. The curate from Banton is standing in for him."

Away! The word echoed in my head. Now what could we do, with Skinner chasing us and no-where to stay, and with but a few pennies between ourselves and starvation? Who else could we turn to? The kindly face of Major Lawson flashed into my mind but I knew not where to find him, he could have been sent anywhere in the country. We had been lucky to get this far but I suddenly knew how tired I was; I felt the weariness of every step I had walked, every battle I had been forced to fight, fight and lose, from the terrible day that still haunted my dreams to this one. Perhaps Gwen should go on alone, she had more spirit in her and they were searching for two girls not one, alone she would be safer, and she was not known here. If she could but colour her beautiful hair, perhaps she could get work on a farm, anything until the hunt was over. I could allow them to find me, but away, away from here to distract attention from Gwen. All those thoughts as I took that deep breath of despair.

"Oh, I was hoping to speak to him," Gwen was saying.

"Well, the vicar's wife's at home, she should be able to tell you when he's back."

I covered my face with my hands and prayed a new prayer of thanks.

"You are a stranger here, are you not? I know everyone hereabouts." I recognised the accusatory tone in her voice.

"My mother and I are on our way to Sandhurst."

A smile crossed my lips at Gwen's description of me.

"Are you wanting somewhere to stay?" Aggie's voice was eager now. "I could recommend you to the inn on the other side of the village or some other suitable lodging."

Oh, Aggie, I thought, almost with fondness, the fondness of the familiar, whether it be good or ill, *still trying to push your way into other people's affairs.*

"Thank you but no," Gwen said and I was amazed at the steadiness of her words. "My mother and I will be on our way shortly, to my aunt's."

I could hear Aggie's breathing as she stood at the end of the pew and I sensed she was waiting for me to raise my head, to engage in conversation, but Gwen quickly added "My mother is very sick."

"Must be getting on my way," Aggie replied, quickly forsaking further prying, "and so should you, it will soon be dark. Come along, Alice," she called, and I kept my head bowed until I heard the click of two pairs of clogs on the flagstones as Aggie and her companion left, the church door closing behind them.

"I'll go alone," Gwen said as she sat back down beside me.
"No!"

"Yes, listen, I'm sure Skinner's not there, but if this Margaret has another visitor - it could be dangerous for you."

"No."

"But I can simply say I want to speak to her of some private matter and wait until the visitor has gone. When it is safe I'll come to get you."

"But…"

"But you know I'm right."

She had thought it through and she was right, though I hated the idea. "Be careful," I warned Gwen a few minutes later as she prepared to make her way to the vicarage. "Just be careful." Gwen pulled open the heavy church door and slipped out into the night. After a couple of minutes walking up and down the aisle I followed her out into the shadow of the porch. It seemed to me I was waiting far too long for there to be a good outcome - had Gwen been caught in a trap? If so I must join her as she had joined me in my imprisonment. These anxious thoughts were gripping me when I saw the curtain move and a face appear at the vicarage window, lit by a flickering flame. Margaret! I picked up my skirts and held myself tight in order to resist the instinct to run towards the house - I had so sorely missed that kindly face. I crossed the few feet of garden and pushed at the front door, it swung open and Margaret stood before me, her arms outstretched. I had come home – the nearest I had to a home. Tears splashed down my face as I clasped her tightly, afraid of letting go.

"Come, sit." Margaret drew me into the familiar parlour where a small fire crackled in the grate. How many times had I lit that fire, swept this floor? "I can feel how thin you are," she continued. "You have been unwell - I have heard."

Those last three words sent a chill through my body; Gwen's expression told me more of what I feared.

"He's been here, then?" I managed to whisper through dry lips.

"Yes." Margaret stood a little way off, putting distance between the two of us. "I have been told of all the unfortunate circumstances which have befallen you since we were last together. But," she glanced at Gwen, "I do not know whether your young friend has acted in your best interests in bringing you here." She moved towards me and put her hands over mine. "I believe you are still in need of care and protection, the care and protection only Sir Neville's physician can provide."

"Physician! Do I, do we," I pointed at Gwen, "do we look as if we're being cared for?" I held out my torn hands, my thin arms. "Protection? The protection we need is *from* Sir Neville, he is our enemy, our persecutor, him and Skinner."

"Please don't upset yourself, Hope dear. You know I will do all I can to help you, whatever your difficulties but first I must understand." She regarded me as if seeing a stranger. "You see, when we had not heard from you about the baby and I feared all may not be well, we took advantage of a visit Matthew had to undertake to the area to make a call upon you. It must have been five or six weeks ago, yes, six weeks ago. Sir Neville made us welcome at Wilderness Hall and explained what a difficult time you had after the birth, how you were acting wildly, hallucinating," she dropped her voice, "violent." She was silent a moment. "For the baby's sake, he said you had to be sent away, he knew you would never forgive yourself if you harmed little Jacob." Her eyes met mine and I winced to think Margaret believed that of me. "He

180

said he had not written to us as he hoped you would be better soon and he would not have to pass on such bad news. He told us the doctor had expressly said you were to have no visitors. We saw the baby, though," she added, "such a bonny child and well cared for; you need have no concerns for his welfare."

"You have seen my son?"

"As I said, he is well. He has your eyes."

I smiled at that last comment. And he was well - tears of relief ran down my face. "Thank you, thank you, Margaret. My prayers are answered, now all I need is to see him again, to be with him, to have him as my own."

"Do you think you are well enough? Matthew and I have prayed every day for your recovery but what I have heard, your appearance here in these circumstances, it gives me much concern. I wish Matthew was here, he would know what to do."

"He would know whether to believe me or not, is that it, Margaret? Do *you* not know?"

"I know I wish to believe you with all my heart."

I tried to hold the reins on my emotion. "Margaret, you have no idea what a cunning man I married. Did you not think it strange my child is called Jacob, the name of my rapist? I would never have agreed to that."

I could see the resistance in her eyes. "But I learnt you weren't at the christening, you were too ill at the time."

"Drugged, to make it seem that way!" I cried. "Sir Neville married me to take my child from me, nothing more." I was desperate to make her believe me. I had never thought Margaret could turn against me. If she deserted me, I was lost.

"It was his son Jacob who raped me and he wanted the baby. He believes the child is his grandson."

A deep frown creased Margaret's brow. "If what you tell me is true, then it is surely wicked, but…"

"If?" I felt such pain at the word I could not but reiterate it.

"I do not want to seem to doubt you but you have been ill. Why do you think he is your attacker's father, did he tell you so?"

"Oh no, not him. I found a portrait of his son, of Jacob, and then it all made sense."

"Could it not have been one of your hallucinations, you have been through so much."

"No, no it wasn't. Gwen knew his son, that he was called Jacob and never returned home."

"But you were sent away to be nursed, are you saying the doctor went along with Sir Neville's concocted story?"

"There was no doctor!" I allowed the implication of my words to reach her. "Lies, it's all lies. Gwen," I reached out my hand to my friend, "Gwen can verify every word of my story. She was my maid at Wilderness Hall when the baby was born and because she saw all that was happening she was exiled with me. For my sake she has suffered. We have been held prisoner on the Isles of Sheppey, on a pig farm and made to work like slaves, by that vile man Skinner who was paid by Sir Neville to keep us there. Skinner was one of the men who murdered my family. Did you not recognise him from the description I gave Major Lawson? Don't you believe me?"

"I want to but Skinner came to see me this morning saying you and another girl," she glanced across at Gwen, "had escaped from the doctor's premises where the mad are treated, an asylum I think he called it, and I should be careful if you came to me. He said your head was full of nightmares and he was sent to take you both back to the asylum before you harmed someone or indeed yourself." I regarded her in despair but she avoided my eyes. I could see Gwen was close to tears. How many times had I told her we needed to get to Margaret, Margaret who was my friend, Margaret who would help us, Margaret who would be our salvation. "Gwen, Gwen where is your bag? If you cannot believe me, perhaps you can believe this." I withdrew the torn pieces of the reward poster from Gwen's bag and handed them to Margaret. I watched her face as she read the notice.

She let the two pieces of the poster fall to the floor with a cry. "Oh, how could I not have trusted you? I am so sorry Hope, forgive me."

"I cannot blame you, but I swear on my child's life every word I've told you is true. But now, I need your advice and your help if I am to get my child back."

Chapter 23

"You must be hungry," Margaret said. "We'll eat and then we shall make our plans. Are you sure no-one saw you come here?"

"We were careful."

"You two make the bed while I prepare the dinner," Margaret continued. "Sleep in your old room again tonight."

Everything in this house was dear to me, it had been my refuge before, it was my refuge again. The pewter pot on the side table was full of spring flowers and I knew the pleasure Margaret must have felt at picking them as she walked by the river. The four months since I had been here, so long and painful in the living, dissolved as I ran my hand over the settle by the fire where I had been placed the day when the river had seemed to be my only possible fate. My life had swung so violently between utter cruelty and wonderful kindness and I could feel that kindness enveloping me again.

"I need time to think," Margaret said almost to herself as she made her way into the kitchen.

"Gwen," I held out my hand to her. "Come and see my room." The sensation of sisterhood, of sharing with pleasure, took me back to my home, my family. My breath caught in my throat.

"Are you all right?" Gwen asked.

"Happy memories."

I led Gwen upstairs but stopped as I entered my bedroom as I pictured the night when my voice had returned to me and the night I had slept here before my marriage, and the one after. These four white walls had held me safe through so many tribulations.

"Is the linen in that chest?" Gwen asked, nodding towards the old carved chest in the corner, and I nodded, pleased to be distracted. Downstairs again Gwen went into the kitchen to help Margaret while I laid the table. We ate cold roast beef with bread and butter, and spoke only of lighter things - the coronation, of Matthew's trip to Canterbury, as if we did not have the stomach to digest two things at once.

The meal finished we carried our goblets of wine into the parlour. The fire burned brightly as the rain pounded against the window. Margaret took my hand as we sat next to each other. "As I see it," she said, "you will need to try to obtain an annulment of your marriage."

"A what?"

"An annulment, it's a legal declaration that your marriage never existed."

"But I *was* married."

"But you never knew your husband, you understand? You never slept with him."

"Oh, I see, so I am not married?"

"At the moment you are but if we can prove in court you never slept with Sir Neville then your marriage could be annulled, which means it is as if it never took place; you were never man and wife."

"We were never man and wife, never, I swear it."

"The court will need evidence, not just your word, especially as Sir Neville is sure to declare the opposite and he would be the one believed."

"Why him, why is his word better than mine?"

"He is a man, that is enough, you have no chance unless you can produce evidence."

Gwen moved closer to me. "I can swear from the time you came to Wilderness Hall you never shared his bed," she said.

"And Matthew and I can vouch for the time you were under our protection up until your marriage, indeed until the following day when you left this house. But that leaves the journey, the days you spent on the road on your way to Wilderness Hall."

"But we did not share a room – Sir Neville had arranged a separate room for me, mine was downstairs and his above. Does this mean I can be free of him?"

"It will not be easy but first tell me about the inn, where was it?"

"I can't say. I paid no attention." The excitement fled from me, "Oh, Margaret, I do not know!"

"I believe I can help," Gwen broke in as she saw the panic on my face. "There was talk at the Hall after your arrival. I was in the kitchen the following morning when the coachman, the new one, said he had never driven that road before, he was complaining, saying how awful it was compared to London, he said you stopped at the White Horse and the inn was as bad as the road."

"And I was given a key to lock my door," I added joyously.

"Good, that is excellent; we should be able to get confirmation." Margaret stood resting her hand on the mantle shelf as I had seen Matthew often do. "I shall have to lay out the facts of your life before and after the raid on your family's farm, that Sir Neville told Matthew he wanted you only as a companion and to manage Wilderness Hall to make it more of a home. I shall testify the contents of the letter are true and my husband will verify the facts if need be when he comes back from Canterbury."

"Do you think the letter will be sufficient for the authorities?"

"I hope so, however Sir Neville is well regarded in society and his word will be given more weight than your own but I doubt he will want his dirty linen washed in public. However, our first problem is to get you both safely to a lawyer. Skinner is out there and he is dangerous, he knows you can accuse him of murder and of the wrongful imprisonment of Gwen."

"What of my incarceration?"

"Your own captivity would not count, your husband is within the law to put you away any where he chooses."

I shook my head in disbelief. "Surely it cannot be correct - that men should have such rights over us."

"That has always been the way as you must know - another burden for womankind."

"I did not know I was living in such a cruel world," I said. "I saw none of this as I grew up, my father would never do anything to make my mother unhappy, let alone harm her."

"You could easily live your life and never know the way of the world," Margaret explained. "Good men, men who truly love their wives and their families, never have recourse to such measures but unfortunately the law is there to support the selfish and the cruel."

Gwen and I were silent a minute while Margaret's words dug their way into our minds - that the world should be so biased against us.

"There is something I must tell you, Hope, before you make the decision on what you should do. If you are successful in obtaining an annulment it will mean your son is likely to be branded a bastard. Your protests that the child is Henry's not Jacob's may not be believed and is impossible to prove. Are you willing to pay that price?"

"Rather than have him named as Sir Neville's son, yes – yes."

"You will be taking his inheritance away from him."

"So be it - I cannot be married to that man."

"If you are determined then I shall write the letter adding the facts which prove Sir Neville never had carnal knowledge of your body, that you are not his wife in law and your son is not his child."

"Where do we have to take the letter?' Gwen asked.

"Gwen, there is no need for you…"

"Do you not want me to come with you?"

"Of course I do, of course I do, but you are free now, this is my battle."

"But it is my battle, too."

"Hope must go on to pursue her case in law," Margaret put in, "but it is not necessary for you to put yourself in further peril. My brother is a shop-keeper two counties hence, I know he would take you in. You will be far from Sir Neville's grasp."

"I would love to have you by my side but you will be safer if you are away from me," I added.

"And you will be safer if I am with you, we can both keep an eye out for Skinner, we have defeated him before and we can do so again." Gwen hesitated, her voice breaking a little as she continued. "And I have the right to see him pay for what he has done to me."

"Indeed you do, but you are too kind to me, Gwen."

"You told me long ago, when we were first at the farm, that our lives and our fates were entwined – I can never be really free unless you are also."

We embraced and I knew with a shock how desolate, how unbearably alone, I would have felt without her.

"There is one more thing," Margaret said, "I am sorry, but I think you should leave tomorrow." I felt myself wince at the thought of having to go from this place so soon. "It is too dangerous for you to stay, Skinner could return or someone see you. This, after all, is the most obvious place for you to come for help. Skinner knew that, which is why he came here this morning. You must be gone as soon as you can - and we have much to prepare."

"What will we need?" Gwen asked of Margaret.

"Clothes, new clothes. I think I can help there - and a disguise for your lovely but remarkable hair, Gwen, and of course you will need money to travel and stay overnight."

"What we need is your grandfather's money tree," Gwen said.

"Money tree?"

"Oh!" Gwen's hand flew to her mouth. "I should not have said that, I'm sorry."

"No, tell me."

"It was when you delirious - after the birth." Gwen lowered her voice. "You called out time and again - no, I cannot say."

"Please."

"'They hanged the boy', you kept saying, and your name and your husband's. 'Hope! Henry!' and 'Jessie, Jessie, hide in the money tree - hide!'"

"I did not know," I whispered.

"I didn't mention it, all thoughts of your family distressed you so."

I fell back into remembering. "The money tree, that's what we heard grandfather call it once. We were at grandfather's farm, only small girls at the time. He saw…" the words caught in my throat, "he saw Ruth and me watching as he buried a box. He said if you fed the tree some money the fairies would make it grow but we mustn't tell anyone or it wouldn't work. We thought it so funny and just one of his stories. It was never mentioned again."

"The disturbance of your mind must have brought the memory back to you," Margaret said with a tender smile.

"But… it could be true. Father buried money and other valuable items at our home in Kingsdown, even wine, in case the soldiers came. The war had made father cautious," I added.

"And probably your grandfather too," Margaret said.

"If it were true there could be the money we need for all we must do to fight Sir Neville for my son."

"But do you know which tree?" Gwen asked.

"The great oak – it was the great oak tree. But Oliver Whitby lives there now. Though - the tree is outside the farm, right beside the road."

"Let me think, let me think," Margaret said, sitting herself down on Matthew's big leather chair. Gwen and I stood quietly by until Margaret stood up with a start. "I believe I have an idea, but now," she said with a change of tone, "we must get busy if we are to arrange everything in time for you to leave tomorrow. I think we should all go upstairs, away from any prying eyes."

"The plan?" I asked.

"I am still working it out," Margaret replied, "but upstairs now."

A few minutes later Margaret came into the bedroom carrying three gowns over her arm. "You will recognise these, Hope," she said as she laid them on the bed. There was the black velvet dress I thought I would need working at Wilderness Hall and two summer gowns given to us by Sir Neville. "I think they can be made to fit the pair of you," she said holding them up. "The black dress we will leave as it is, wait just a moment and you will see why," and she left the room coming back with an old cushion and a narrow length of material. "If we are to smuggle you out of here without Skinner finding out, then what better than as a pregnant widow still in mourning, I have a black veil, and this," she caught my eye as she tied the cushion in front her, "if it does not bring back too many memories."

I shook my head. "If it gets us out of here..." I tried on the gown and cut and pinned the hem of one for Gwen, Lady Neville had obviously been a very tall woman. Margaret finished stitching the strap to the cushion for me to tie about my waist under the black dress. Margaret clicked her tongue. "Even with the lacing pulled in tight the gown is still loose, a couple of darts are needed here and here. Hand me my pins, please. Now what do you think Gwen? Would you recognise Hope under that veil?"

Gwen opened her mouth to reply but was silenced by a loud knock at the door. Margaret put her finger to her lips and hurried down the stairs. I held a pale Gwen in my arms in the doorway as we heard Margaret cross the hall. I peered down and watched as she ran her hand over her hair and neck and took a deep breath before pulling the door open. I moved smartly back into the bedroom. "Good evening curate, how may I help you?"

Gwen and I relaxed and tiptoed over to the bed. Margaret was right, we were too vulnerable here and had to leave.

"Just the curate," Margaret said as she re-entered the bedroom. "Now we must concentrate on our plans for tomorrow. Before dawn Gwen and I will go to your farm, Hope, fear not, I do not expect you to go there, in fact you should not, Gwen is not known and I am often seen taking provisions to sick parishioners. We shall go to your oak tree and see if there is indeed some money to be found there for your journey."

"But you will be seen," I protested.

"Leave that to me," Margaret reassured me.

"And it may be nonsense," I added.

"At least we'll know and, if we find nothing, then I am sure there will be some other solution to our problem. Gwen, in that chest in the corner you will find cloaks and a black wig, try them on, they were donated for the poor by Lady Wallace, though what need she thought there was for a wig I cannot imagine."

Gwen fished the wig from the box with a giggle and rammed it on her head. "I can't wear this," she cried.

"It'll look better if you turn it round, you've got it on back to front."

"It's still ridiculous," Gwen argued.

"Just wear it while you're here in the village, everywhere else your hat or the hood will do," I said, holding up one of the cloaks, "but not here – Skinner will be hunting for any sighting of us, it's worth looking ridiculous to be safe."

"You're not wearing it," Gwen replied, nonetheless putting it aside with her belongings.

"I think I know what it would be like to have daughters now," Margaret commented, "but we should not waste time, we must hurry to get everything ready. As soon as we have adjusted the clothes to our satisfaction you two must get off to bed, I can see how tired you are, and you will have another long day's travelling tomorrow. I shall find the quill and ink and write the letter." A little later I kissed Margaret good night as I had done so many times before and Gwen and I climbed into bed. Gwen was asleep in no time but my mind was in turmoil and sleep was eluding me until sheer exhaustion took over and my eyes closed at last.

I woke to find the house empty though the sun was still low on the horizon. I washed and dressed and waited for Margaret and Gwen. In truth, I was relieved not to have to go to my old home, the idea terrified me. I had put all thoughts of the farm out of my mind - it was the only way I could get through living every day. There was nothing for me to do as I waited but worry: where was Skinner now? Would he return to the vicarage to see if we had arrived? My restlessness became urgent steps as I paced up and down in my room. What if Skinner was still in the area and had recognised Gwen even with her black wig? I heard a creak as the kitchen door opened. I covered my mouth with my hand to quiet my breath, my heart beating faster than I could bear. Then I heard my name called softly and I ran down the stairs.

"Hope, there you are. Come here and see what we've found."

The curtains were still drawn as I entered the room, the dining table lit by a single stout candle. There, on the corner of the table, was the worn black brick of the family bible. I lifted the old leather cover with shaking hands. Here were the names of my family, our history. The handwriting had changed over the years and the ink of the earliest entries had faded a little. They were all present, generations of the Courtney family, their baptisms, marriages and deaths - grandfather and his three brothers, my grandmother, Mary, my parents' marriage, the baptismal dates of myself and my two sisters. "There I am," I whispered, and my finger reached out to touch the name Ruth but with a stifled sob I forced myself to slide my finger forward until it rested on the name Hope.

"Yes," Margaret said, "and beneath it, here, the date of your marriage to Henry. Your son should be added."

"And so many deaths."

Margaret gave me a moment to recover myself as I read the names of my lost family but then she placed a roll of parchment before me.

"It's the deeds to the farm," she said, "you must read them when you are away from here, and take them to a lawyer, he will be able to advise you if your son has any claim on the property."

"Margaret," I began, "will you keep the deeds and the bible safe for me? There will be time later to pursue those matters once I have my son back. If anything should happen to me - if Skinner cannot take me back to Sheppey he may think it is better if I am dead - it will be a mercy to know you are holding these documents so my son may see them one day."

I could see the distress on Margaret's face but she replied, "Of course."

"I think there are coins in here," Gwen said, handing me a small, well-worn leather pouch. I loosened the threads that closed it, tipped it up and there was the flash of gold and silver on the table.

I picked up a handful of golden sovereigns and silver shillings. There was a small gold ring and a chain. "So much," I said.

"There should be no problem now getting you both to Maidstone and finding a church lawyer to help with your case. I will sew the sovereigns into the hems of your skirts for safe keeping."

There was far more money spread out on the table than I had ever seen before. How hard father had worked for it, and grandfather too, along with his brothers. They did not seek to spend it, but to hold it safe, for future events they could not envisage. I hoped they would approve the use I would be making of it. I took the gold cross out of my pocket and threaded the chain through it and asked Gwen to fasten it for me.

"Back where it belongs," said Gwen, patting my shoulder.

"I had to sell your gold chain, Margaret, to pay for our journey. I'm sorry, but now at least I can wear your cross again."

"I am happy it was of so much use to you, now you should see this," Margaret said, "it's a map Matthew uses for parish business." She unrolled the map and ran her hand across it. "Here, I think you should take the road leading to Sandhurst village but on reaching Rolverden take the path to Hartley and then the highway to Maidstone passing through Cranbrook.

Maidstone is a further fourteen miles from there. It is not the shortest route but I fancy Skinner will be on the main thoroughfare. But now come into the kitchen, I must prepare something for you to eat."

"Mushrooms?" Gwen queried.

"You may be right."

"Why so many smiles?" I asked, seeing the glance that passed between my friends.

"We decided to use picking mushrooms as our excuse to be out so early if anyone was to ask," Gwen explained while Margaret busied herself. "It was before dawn when we left, Margaret had found a short-handled spade I could hide under my cloak, I carried that while she had a basket half-full of mushrooms. She kept watch while I did the digging, watching for candlelight coming from the house; we guessed the box would be on the side of the tree away from the road. Luckily it wasn't buried more than six inches deep. There was just one moment…"

"A rider came by," Margaret said, adding three eggs to the sizzling pan. "And we had to hide, just as well that oak tree of yours is so huge. We reburied the box when we had taken the purse and papers out, it was too big to carry back."

I regarded my friends, the heightened colour in their cheeks, the ready smiles on their lips. "I think you two have enjoyed your adventure," I said.

As we sat in the kitchen having breakfast, thankful it was not a day when Aggie worked at the vicarage, Margaret told us where we should go when we got to Maidstone and the name of the office to visit. "You must take my letter to the lawyer who deals with religious cases, he will review your situation and suggest who best would help you later at the

196

hearing. I shall write it all down for you." I found it difficult to eat the food Margaret had prepared for us; my heart was full of sadness at having to leave my friend again. "I will come part of the way with you, just to see you safely out of the village," Margaret said, and I knew how afraid she was for us.

After breakfast we packed our things and each of us departed the house separately. The cushion beneath my dress seemed oddly comforting as if my son was accompanying me and in some way, I could not say how, protecting me. I met up with Gwen and Margaret outside the village and we walked on together until we reached Rolverden. There, the tears I could no longer deny flowed uncontrollably.

"Now why the tears? We won't be apart for long, darling girl." Margaret hugged me close. "Have faith, you have come so far, I know you will succeed in your next task. Now be off the pair of you and God speed."

I looked back until Margaret disappeared from sight. Gwen took my hand and squeezed it. I wiped my eyes with my sleeve as we hurried on, myself driven by the thought I was taking another step towards my son and away from Sir Neville, and Gwen, driven by nothing other than pure friendship.

Chapter 24

An hour after dark a lone horseman rode into West Penton; he shivered a little as he dismounted and stretched his weary limbs before making his way into the inn, stopping briefly to brush the dust from his breeches. He threw his saddlebag over his shoulder and removed his wide brimmed hat, running his hand along its large feather to remove any dust. He shook his long brown hair and his quick eyes took in the scene before him. The inn was a two-storey building and offered a welcome sight to the traveller; it seemed respectable enough and he saw there was good stabling for Gideon, his one companion these many months. He was as concerned about his horse's comfort as his own.

He pushed at the door and bent his head to pass into the low-ceilinged room noting the silence that fell as he entered. He was an unusual sight among the farmers in their loose shirts and open doublets.

The landlord, as squat and square as a hayrick, scrutinized him for a moment, taking in every detail of the younger man before asking, "May I help you, sir?"

The weariness seemed to depart the visitor. "A room if you please, the beds are clean? No bedbugs?"

If his elegant but well-used clothes had not been sufficient, it was obvious from his commanding tone that this was a gentleman of means and in all probability an army officer. The inn-keeper answered with equal pride. "Sir, if your room is not clean you need not pay."

"Fair enough," the visitor said. He noticed the worn faces in the room regarded him with undisguised interest, their ale untouched as if waiting for the command to continue with their evening's recreation. The man acknowledged the gathering with a nod of his head and the buzz of conversation resumed in the room. "It is late I know but is there a chance of some supper?"

"Of course, if eggs and bacon would suffice."

"That will be most welcome, and a tankard of your finest ale. Oh, and can someone take care of my horse? We have had a long ride this day and he is deserving of your best oats."

The inn-keeper clicked his fingers and a wisp of a boy of twelve or so ran out to do his master's bidding. "Your name sir?" the man asked.

"Sir Edward Ashton-Somerville."

"I will have a fire lit in your room, sir," the landlord said with a smile as he could see the promise of a rise in his takings. "Will you have your meal downstairs while preparations are made?"

"Certainly. Have my bag taken up, will you?" Sir Edward did not wait for a reply but strode towards a small table close to the fire and aware of some presence other than the farmers seated at the roughly hewn tables and chairs, he tilted his head to see the head of a handsome stag with magnificent antlers staring down at him from the wall. He smiled and lifted his tankard in mock salute to the animal. The meal was served by a middle-aged woman flushed from cooking and was soon devoured. The landlord brought over a second tankard of ale. "Your horse has been taken care of and your room is ready, sir - our best room, of course, quiet, with a large and comfortable bed - at the top of the stairs." He placed the key on the table. "Your bag has been placed in your room."

Sir Edward listened patiently to all the niceties of the landlord waiting for the question that would surely follow.

"If you don't mind me asking, sir, what brought you to our village tonight?"

"I have an errand, some family business."

It was obvious the landlord had more questions ready to ask but found his manners and moved to join his other guests. Sir Edward picked up the key, his cloak and hat and made his way up the narrow staircase. His eyes appraised the room and he nodded in approval. He was used to both far better and far worse. In the army he'd slept in many a ditch with a stone for a pillow; a fire and a soft place to lay his head was as much as he wished for - anything more he considered a luxury.

He laid out a clean shirt for the morrow, throwing the other aside to be laundered. He stripped and washed in front of the blazing fire, the firelight burnishing his lithe naked body and the long scar on his left leg. He climbed into bed allowing his weary muscles to relax at last and was soon asleep.

The early morning sounds of floors being swept, grates cleared and fires lit roused Sir Edward from his slumbers. He was anxious to get on with his mission - there was one last duty to be performed, then he would be a free man, responsibilities discharged, and life could resume a quieter course. He wondered if he could tire of it, tire of contentment; he did not believe so, he had seen too much of life's disturbances to dismiss peace as tedium.

He sat by the new fire which was still struggling to burn and was served a breakfast of sausages, blood pudding and bread still hot from the oven. "I was going to ask you to point me in the direction of…" Sir Edward began.

With a crash the door was flung open and a cold draft of air almost extinguished the fire.

"You!" a rough voice called and the landlord turned towards the black-clad intruder, as unkempt as he was uncivil.

"What?" the landlord cried.

"Are there two young women staying here?" the voice continued, "or passed by?"

The landlord stood his ground but found the man now standing over him.

"And why should my friend here answer a question so rudely put?" Sir Edward asked, rising from his chair.

The visitor retreated a step and his voice became quieter. "I am looking for my cousins, two young ladies travelling alone, I believe they are coming this way."

"Well, I am the only guest here," Sir Edward replied in an even tone, "and I am not your cousin."

The inn-keeper squared his shoulders now he had his guest supporting him and neither man spoke a further word, waiting for the visitor to feel his dismissal. With a twist of his lip the man let out a grunt of anger and departed. Sir Edward resumed his seat and pierced the sausage remaining on his platter. "If his cousins are indeed young ladies, I can only hope they continue to elude him, it would be preferable to be lost than found by such a man."

"We do not see many of his ilk," the landlord said apologetically, as if bearing some responsibility for every person who stepped over his threshold.

His breakfast plate cleared, his tankard emptied, Sir Edward rose, picking up his hat as he left. He strode outside to the stable and smiled as he saw Gideon standing ready, his dappled coat shining. The stable boy was holding the bridle with one hand and stroking the horse's muzzle with the other.

"I see you like my horse."

The boy's face was lit with enthusiasm, "Oh yes, sir, he's a real beauty."

Sir Edward withdrew a penny from his pocket and flipped it into the air, the boy catching it with a quick grabbing gesture of his grubby hands. "Lead him outside, will you?"

"What's his name, sir?"

"Gideon."

"How did he get that name? There's an old man in the village called that."

"When I bought him, his owner said he would always gallop on, 'Come on then, gallop on,' I would say, and with time 'Gallop on' became Gideon." Sir Edward spoke quietly, his hand absently stroking the horse's flank. "A good horse is worth more than gold - he is your friend, your companion, and oft-times your saviour." With a pat on Gideon's rump he stepped on to the mounting block and sitting astride his horse donned his hat and asked, "Hamblemere Farm - which way?"

"Through the village and two miles on, where the great oak stands by the road, you can't miss it."

The tree was as unmissable as he had been told, it stood just a few feet from the lane, its weathered bark deeply cut, the branches spreading out above bursting with the new life of spring. As Gideon trotted into the yard Sir Edward heard a sound, a low growl, and saw a small girl with a tangle of brown hair standing before him with her hand resting on the head of a wire-haired mongrel. He steadied his horse and smiled down. "Are your parents at home?" he asked.

He heard a step beside him. "Parents and brothers out, everyone 'cepting us two." A lad of fifteen or so appeared and stood in front of his sister. Sir Edward frowned, puzzled.

"This is Hamblemere Farm, is it not?"

"Yes." The lad seemed reluctant to say more.

Sir Edward tried to reconcile these children with the family of which Henry had spoken. "Is Henry here?" He saw the confusion on the boy's face, "Henry Ashton, is he here?"

"Who? This is my father's farm, Oliver Whitby."

"No, no," Sir Edward said, "show me to the farmhouse, will you?" The boy pointed to a low wooden building. "But that's more of a barn."

"It's where we live."

"But the farmhouse - the main farmhouse."

The boy turned and Sir Edward followed his gaze towards a blackened chimney stack, the remains of an oven and some foundation stones at the far end of the yard. Jumping down from his horse he crossed to the stones marking out the shape of rooms and doorways, the stones blackened in places, showing the signs of the fire that had raged there, consuming the building.

"When was the fire?" he demanded of the boy.

"Before we came here - last spring."

"And where are they? The family who lived here?"

"Dead, sir, all dead."

"It cannot be!" Sir Edward staggered backwards, shaking his head. "It cannot be," he repeated in a whisper as he climbed on to Gideon's back. He fled the farm, his eyes blurred with tears. He had thought the shock of sudden violent death would touch him no more now the king was crowned, the nation unified, but this, "Dead, all dead" had shaken the very fibre of his being. The words echoed in his brain; could the boy be mistaken? Could his brother be dead with his bride and all her family? But how? Accident or violence? If the latter he would be avenged.

He jumped from his horse when he reached the inn and ran inside. "Hamblemere Farm," he shouted, interrupting the landlord as he counted his takings from the previous day. "What happened?"

"Oh, that was a bad do, sir, was that where you were bound? I could have told you if I had known."

"Tell me now."

"A raid sir, angry renegade soldiers - a year past, hunting for booty on their way home, thought to find easy pickings. The family was put to the sword, the house burned down – belongs to some distant relative now, so I've heard."

"All dead?" Sir Edward mumbled.

"Not all, sir, there was a survivor, a girl, taken in at the vicarage she was."

Sir Edward moved to the door. "And the vicarage is…"

"Opposite the church, sir, though…" but he was gone.

Reaching the church Sir Edward pushed open the door so quickly it almost flew back in his face. He had hoped to find the vicar within but the place was empty. Instead, he said a silent prayer for strength, calming himself for what was to come. He hurried across the road to the vicarage but got no reply to his knocking at the front door. Seeing a side entrance to the garden he made his way along the path to the rear where a woman of middle years was struggling against the wind to gather in the washing. Stepping forward Sir Edward took the flapping ends of a sheet. "I wish to see the vicar," he announced.

Panic crossed the woman's face and she dropped the clothes pegs she was holding.

"I'm sorry, I startled you," he apologised. "When no-one answered the door, I presumed to come to the back. I am Sir Edward Ashton-Somerville, at your service."

The woman gave a small dip of a curtsy, her face drained of colour.

"Are you all right?" he asked, putting out his hand to steady her.

She nodded. "Yes, thank you, sir," she replied in a shaking voice. "The vicar, my husband, is away at Canterbury, but Ashton, you say?"

"Indeed."

"You had best come in, sir," she said. "We have much to speak of. I trust you will not mind entering through the kitchen." She placed the dried linen on the kitchen table and led him into the parlour. She indicated Matthew's leather chair for him and sat herself down facing him.

"I was told," Sir Edward began, hesitated, then continued, "I went to Hamblemere Farm…" His voice broke with the pain of what he had seen. "Please say it's not true." Margaret leaned forward, unshed tears gleaming in her eyes. "I heard there was a survivor," he blurted out, unable to hold his impatience any longer.

"Hope," Margaret said, "Hope survived."

A tearful smile sprung to Sir Edward's lips. "My brother's wife."

"Henry Ashton was your brother?"

"Yes, a dear brother, though a brother by the marriage of my mother to his father as you may assume from my name. No doubt Hope has spoken of my family. Henry is," he paused, "*was* ten years my junior and his youth had saved him from the horror of violence, or so I thought until this morning when I found all my assumptions were as nought."

"It is the most terrible shock you have had, sir," Margaret said as Sir Edward's hands covered his tear-strewn face and he allowed himself to grieve. She left the room and appeared a moment later with a small glass in one hand and a bottle in the other. She poured a goodly portion of brandy into the glass. After a minute or two Sir Edward roughly wiped his eyes and gratefully accepted the drink - it disappeared in one gulp. "I am sorry," he said, "I have been a soldier too long, you will find me a little rough around the edges."

"Do not excuse yourself, Sir Edward, I find nothing amiss, only genuine affection between brothers long separated. It is good to see, even if that affection brings pain in its wake."

Sir Edward sat silent for a moment. "Henry's choice of wife was something of a surprise to us all but I could not understand his father's decision to cut his son out of his life - surely it would be preferable to endure the presence of your son's wife than the absence of your son." The words poured from Sir Edward following the tangled train of his thoughts. "If his father had been more charitable Henry would have been saved from that terrible fate and Ashton would not have lost his heir."

"If we did but know where the path we take may lead us," Margaret said with a sigh.

"I will offer his wife a home. I came to give Henry news, sad news, though it pales before what I have now heard, but the news his father died last August. He told me he had become reconciled to Henry's marriage and wished to see him again but he died before he communicated that wish to his son, not knowing it was already too late." As Sir Edward wiped away fresh tears Margaret poured him another drink. "It was my wish to tell Henry myself but I have been much abroad and busy with my duties. Several times I had to postpone my visit. Eventually I wrote to him but received no reply." He broke off to swallow more of the brandy. "You have not said, where is Henry's wife? I heard you took her in."

"She is not here," Margaret replied.

"Where did she go?"

"If you will allow me, sir, it is a long story." Margaret sat down, her hands gripping each other as if to steady herself as she told the long and terrible story of the happenings at Hamblemere Farm and their aftermath. "Hope was silent for so long, Sir Edward," she concluded some minutes later, "I feared we would never hear her voice, but when she spoke at last, it was to tell us she was with child."

"God save us!"

"She believes the child to be Henry's, not her attacker's," Margaret added quickly. "I believe it was only the thought of her child that gave her the strength to continue."

"And the child - was it safely delivered?"

"It was."

"And is it a son?"

"It is - born in January."

The pain on Sir Edward's face disappeared for a moment. "Then not all is lost, I have a nephew to cherish as well as a sister and another Ashton will take his place at Linton House."

"Not so, I fear." Margaret said. "Hope believed she had nothing - no family, no home, not a penny to her name, so - so she agreed to marry a man who promised to take care of her and protect the baby by giving it his name."

"But once her son was born he would surely inherit her family's farm, she could have lived there and the place would have brought her in a living of sorts."

"She was told there was a male claimant, a relative on her father's side, Sir Neville assured us, my husband and myself, that the claim was genuine and it would be useless for Hope to challenge it. The man, Oliver Whitby, moved to the farm in the summer."

"This Sir Neville, he confirmed the matter?"

"He did. He was a visitor here; it was he who married Hope - Sir Neville Lattimer."

"Sir Neville Lattimer you say, I know him, we dined together in October. I had fought with his son Robert and we spent an evening together talking of him and the battle in which he died a dozen years ago. But... but he knew Henry's father had died, we spoke of it. Why did he not tell Hope?"

"I did not think there could be a further calumny on the head of Sir Neville," Margaret cried. "Hope would not have felt so alone if she had known her husband's family had forgiven the marriage, and we would not..." Margaret could barely utter the words, "Matthew and I would not have encouraged Hope to marry Sir Neville - we were so wrong." Margaret's voice shook with despair. "Hope married Sir Neville at Christmas, thinking she was doing the best for her baby - a home, a husband…"

"Forgive me, but why would Sir Neville be so keen to marry Hope, I mean, a widow, a penniless pregnant widow."

"You make me feel so foolish as you cut to the point of the issue. My husband and I became caught up in the lies, the deceit. Sir Neville deliberately tricked Hope into marrying him as he wanted the child."

"But why?"

Anguish was writ large on Margaret's face. "Because he believes the child to be his grandson and his only heir. It was his son Jacob who raped Hope."

Sir Edward's face twisted in anger and pain. "It is a long time since I had a day as sorrowful as this," he said, glancing up at Margaret. "Some years ago my troop was caught in an ambush..." He fell silent and shook his head. "Jacob Lattimer, his father said he'd died, dead in a skirmish."

"No, Sir Edward. Hope defended herself. She killed him with a pitchfork."

"I salute her. Then, perhaps I know why Henry married such a woman, he would have been as proud of her as I am. Where is she now? I suppose she and her son are with Sir Neville. We must find a way of bringing her and the child back into our family."

"The boy was born after the marriage, he is recognised in law as Sir Neville's son."

"Not by me."

"I believe even if Sir Neville were to be convinced the child was not his grandson he would not give him up, it would be his revenge for what Hope did to his son."

"We shall see. I will go to Wilderness Hall." Sir Edward said, rising to his feet.

Margaret put out a restraining hand. "She is no longer there."

"Where are they, then? Hope and her son?"

"Jacob is there."

"Jacob?"

"Sir Neville named the babe for both his late sons - Jacob Robert Lattimer."

"Ah, Robert was a good man - this would not have happened if he had not been killed, he would never have allowed his father to behave in such a way."

"A death is no simple thing - it changes everyone it touches."

"So where is my sister?"

"She was on one of the Isles of Sheppey, but escaped."

"Escaped?"

"Once the child was born Sir Neville incarcerated her on Sheppey with her devoted maid, Gwen. They were kept like prisoners on a pig farm. A man called Skinner was their jailer, one of the raiders at the farm, one of her family's murderers, who'd evaded capture. But Hope and Gwen escaped the day of the coronation, and came here seeking my help."

"So where are they now? No longer here?"

"No, no, it was too dangerous for them to stay but overnight. I had a visit from Skinner before Hope's arrival here and he returned this morning, crashing into my home uninvited, demanding to know if they were here."

"I believe I saw this man - Skinner, did you say? A dark, surly man with a scar? He came to the inn, said he was seeking his cousins."

"He was lying, he is after them."

"So, what did you say to him?"

"I said, 'I told you before I had not seen them.' It was the truth when I told him so and I merely repeated it - it was not quite a lie, was it? It was deception, but not a falsehood, though it is heavy on my conscience."

"You were clever, you could not give the girls away."

"That was not all," Margaret confessed, "I mentioned Hope still had friends in Kingsdown, hoping to point him in that direction."

"But they have not gone there?"

"No, to Maidstone, to see an ecclesiastical lawyer about an annulment."

"You did well."

"But I deceived with the truth, I must pray for forgiveness. I am afraid for them, on the road, alone, I can give them no protection."

"But I can," Sir Edward said.

"I pray you can, Sir Edward, but first - you will want to see the last resting place of your brother and the other members of the Courtney family - what remained of them - Hope's father and mother, her younger sisters Ruth and Jessie."

"Ah, you must forgive me, my mind is much confused. Please take me - show me where, and then I must find this Oliver Whitby."

Chapter 25

As Sir Edward rode out of West Penton his head was abuzz with all Margaret had told him. If Hope could get the annulment of her marriage then Henry's child could take his lawful place as an Ashton and Hope would be accepted into the family as Henry's widow. If only it could have been otherwise. Though he had rarely seen his brother of late he sorely missed the prospect of resuming his role as elder brother, to give advice and watch with good grace when it was ignored.

He saw the great oak of Hamblemere Farm stretching its branches against the sky; how differently he regarded it now as the sun began to lower itself towards the horizon, now it was 'the money tree' where Margaret had told him she and Gwen had found the deeds to the farm and the family bible. Perhaps Whitby had returned, Sir Edward thought as he guided Gideon's footsteps along the path for the second time that day, his mood so altered the farm seemed to be a completely different place.

"Father, father, he's back." He saw the boy standing, glaring at him. A big man with a mop of grey hair emerged from the barn with two young men, obviously, the brothers of the boy he had spoken to. With a gesture, Whitby told his sons to stand back and he moved forward and held the horse's head while Sir Edward dismounted. "You called this morning when I was at the market in Sandhurst, I believe, sir."

"Indeed. I am Sir Edward Ashton-Somerville."

"Please come inside so we may talk."

Whitby led the way towards the new farmhouse fashioned from the old barn. Sir Edward found his eyes straying to the ring of scorched earth where his brother had died. Inside the house, Whitby indicated a plain wooden chair but Sir Edward did not sit. "How may I help you?" Whitby asked with a tremor in his voice.

"I want to know how in God's holy name you come to be here."

Whitby fell onto a chair, sweat breaking out on his forehead.

"It was Sir Neville."

"What has this farm to do with Sir Neville Lattimer. It belonged to the Courtney family, they were living here until they were slaughtered." His eyes glanced towards the window and the ruins beyond.

Whitby hung his head, keeping his eyes on the floor. "I have been dreading someone coming to check up on my claim to the farm and have not had a decent night's sleep since moving here, as God is my witness." There was a sincerity in his words and attitude that made Sir Edward listen to his story in silence. "I rented a farm from Sir Neville and my father before me, a pig farm, far from here. One day Sir Neville came to see me, telling me he had good news, he had discovered I was due an inheritance. I could hardly believe it, there has never been much money in the Whitby family as far as I knew, but he said there was a farm where all the family had been killed in a raid and he had looked into the matter for a friend, a Major Lawson, and found I was the nearest male relative. He showed me a pile of papers, but of course I could not read them, as he well knew. His family had known mine for many years, so I had no reason to doubt him. He said we must leave our farm immediately or we could lose our claim, so we left, only taking with us a single cartload of belongings, leaving much behind. We came here and found the ruins as you see them and had to make our home in this barn, though it is comfortable enough now, my wife has seen to that."

"My brother Henry Ashton was one of those murdered here but his wife lives still as does their son."

"I learned of that only later, that the poor wench had been spared. I spoke to Sir Neville when he next came to see me, I said perhaps she could come to live here, I knew it was the least I could do, but he said I was to do no such thing. I must never even speak to her. He said it had all been a mistake, my grandfather had been born the wrong side of the blanket if you know what I mean, and I had no right to the farm and could be taken to prison for making a false claim. I could stay here and stay silent or it was destitution for us, he said. I had nowhere else to go. And then he said I should not worry about the girl, he would see she had a home. I was so surprised when I found out later he had married her but thanked the Lord she would be all right."

Sir Edward regarded the man before him, another victim of Sir Neville's evil plans and saw no point in making him feel more wretched than he did already. "I sent letters addressed to Henry Ashton, do you have them?"

"There were letters, Sir Neville took them away with him."

"I bet he did, he had to cover his tracks."

Whitby lifted his head. "Will I be evicted, sir?"

"I will not tell Sir Neville what you have told me, try not to worry, it may yet work out."

"I cannot but worry, sir, four children I have, and no home but this."

"I shall see what I can do for you. I am not without influence."

"Thank you, Sir Edward. May I ask you to stay an hour?"

"No, I must be on my way."

Sir Edward mounted his horse in the yard, the boys regarding him with some show of resentment, only the little girl was oblivious to the import of what had happened as she chased the dog, squealing with laughter. Sir Edward made ready to go but hesitated. "That pig farm of yours, where was it?"

"The Isle of Harty, sir, Sheppey."

Chapter 26

"Well, that's it!" Gwen exclaimed as a smart breeze took possession of the day. "My head is boiled and now this thing is bouncing up and down." Gwen grabbed at her black wig and tossed it into a field. "Let the crows have it." She shook her head, her hair cascading over her shoulders.

"You'd better pull your hat on," I said.

"Give me a moment," she replied.

I could not prevent a smile from breaking out on my face as we walked on to see Gwen thus striding along – free, so free.

"Wait, wait." I stopped, threw off my veil and extricated the cushion from beneath my dress: it seemed more a lie than a disguise. "And I'll get out of this black dress as soon as I can," I said.

"And these shoes," Gwen added.

"They've served us well." Despite the blisters, I felt I must defend the shoes Gwen had spent so much time and effort making.

"And for long enough," Gwen said with some feeling.

Thus, the first thing we did when we arrived in Maidstone late in the day was to buy shoes from a stall in the High Street. We bought decent second-hand pairs for outdoors and soft slip-ons for indoors, as pleased to discard our homemade ones with their unyielding edges and frayed stitching as we had been when we first put them on.

"Can you tell us where we may find the Royal Albion Inn?" I asked stall holder.

"'Tis on Faith Street - it'll take you five minutes, what with the crowds." He waved his hand this way and that and we attempted to remember his mumbled instructions. Comfort. Safety. Please, God, we would find them both.

The day had been very long, it seemed an age since we had said goodbye to Margaret. Darkness was gathering between the stalls and the market men were clearing their pitches as we pushed open the door of the inn.

"What can I do for you?" asked the man at the counter, eyeing us with obvious curiosity.

"We are hoping for a room for a few nights."

"I'm sorry mistress, we have but two rooms and they are taken."

"Please sir," I said. "We are friends of the vicar at West Penton, his wife suggested we come here. We are mighty tired. Is there nowhere?"

He sighed. "Nothing but the dusty attic and we only use that for the occasional carrier passing through."

"But it will be fine," Gwen interjected, "it will suit us well."

"We will pay the going rate, of course," I said.

The man shrugged his wide shoulders and reaching up, took a key from a hook and slid it across the desk to us. "The last flight of stairs is steep, so have a care."

"And if we could have something to eat?" I added.

Once through the low doorway we found the room to be a good size, hot and dusty as the landlord had said, and we had to take care not to hit our heads on the sloping roof, but we let out a sigh of contentment as we closed the door behind us and fell on to the bed.

I poured water from the jug into the tin basin and placed it on the floor. I removed my stockings and wiggled my toes as I placed my sore feet into the cool water, allowing myself to think of nothing but this moment. I heard a knock at the door and Gwen went to collect dishes of stew from the maid. She brought them over and sat beside me. We shared the hunk of bread. Bliss.

Despite the noise from the street below Gwen and I were asleep before the mice finished scurrying about beneath our bed in their hunt for crumbs.

The door to the gatehouse of the Archbishop's Palace was open when we arrived there the next morning and a man was sitting in the anti-chamber constantly moving his hat around in his hands.

We took our place on the bench to wait. I was tense and shared the man's anxiety as I began to feel a little faint, my skin clammy. So much depended on this review of my situation.

The door opened and an elderly woman with a walking stick came forth. The man rose and went over to her. The Reverend Wilkins, in his black gown and cap, with its long sides covering his ears, gestured for us to enter. The room was small, every inch of it littered with books and papers. Bookshelves covered the walls and those volumes that could find no home there were gathered in piles across the floor. The large desk was strewn with papers and scrolls. Gwen and I stood still, overwhelmed - the only sound was the brushing of the branch of a tree against the mullioned window - lit by the sun it was a flash of tender green in the sober room. The scholar was as silent as his chamber; wordlessly he brought a second chair to his desk and indicated we should sit.

"You came alone?" I nodded. "How may I help you?" His voice scarcely interrupted the silence.

"I have come to seek your advice as a lawyer," I began, my voice hardly above a whisper. "The vicar's wife at West Penton sent us and gave me this letter for you." My hand shook as I passed it over.

Neither Gwen nor I spoke nor could we raise our eyes from our laps as we waited, listening to the short quick breaths of the elderly man before us and to the branch scratching at the window.

"You are Lady Lattimer, wife of Sir Neville?" the gentle voice asked.

I raised my eyes and nodded as if in acceptance of some shameful allegation.

"If you want my advice to be confidential you must pay me a fee as your personal lawyer, any sum will do."

I had not offered him a fee - how could I have been so forgetful? He saw my confusion as I delved into my bag. "How, I mean, how much?"

"Any coin will suffice." I handed over a shilling, the first coin I came across in my purse. "Thank you." He placed it in a drawer without a glance. "You are now officially my client. This missive," the back of his hand touched the letter, "informs me you wish your marriage to Sir Neville to be annulled."

I found I could hardly breathe; my eyes were stinging. "I cannot be with him, he tricked me, tricked me into marrying him, it was my child he wanted, not me." I prepared to tell my tale, praying to be believed, desperate for it to be over. "Sir Neville is under the mistaken illusion my child is his grandson." A single sob shook my body.

"Now calm yourself and tell me all."

When I had finished my story, he got up and paced the room for a few minutes. Gwen and I were still and silent, the only sound the insistent branch tapping at the window. "This is a most unusual case, in all my years I have never heard another such." Did that mean he believed me, or he did not?

"Tell me, did you go willingly into this marriage?"

"At the time, but then I did not know…"

"Ah, but one never knows. That is why the marriage ceremony asks you to affirm you take this man for better or worse, it is accepted that not all is known."

"But he did not tell me the truth."

"Truth is often a casualty in courtship."

"But," I began, but the reverend had not finished his thought.

"In courtship," he continued, "we show only that part of ourselves we wish the other to see."

I felt Gwen's hand take mine as the tapping at the window echoed in my head.

"It is extremely rare for an annulment to be granted, or a divorce for that matter, and it would need to go before Parliament." The reverend stopped speaking when he heard me gasp.

"Must I tell my sorry tale before all those people, the greatest in the land?"

"You will be giving up your son's right to inherit Sir Neville's not inconsiderable estates. Some might say you were buying your freedom at the price of your son's inheritance."

"But…" The old man held up his creased hand.

"Let me finish my deliberation. I can understand why you would not have considered marrying Sir Neville had you known it was his son who helped murder your family and who violated your body. It was a grave deception. With the child making him a blood connection, or so he believed, he would have had to apply for a dispensation and this he did not do. The marriage not having been consummated also goes in your favour of course."

"I care for nothing but my son." The branch tapped the window as a tear slid down my face. "He has kept my baby away from me since hours after his birth, I have barely held him in my arms. Sir Neville made me a prisoner and kidnapped Gwen. How could I leave my baby in the hands of such a man?"

"I shall write a letter of introduction for you," the lawyer declared with sudden decision. "Your greatest problem will be getting people to listen to you; forgive me pointing out you are but a farmer's daughter and Sir Neville is an aristocrat. He has the money to hire the best lawyers and the influence to have rumours spread about you. The story will be told in such a way you become the villain of the piece, an ingrate blackening the name of the gentleman who took pity on you and gave you a home. People may well believe the tale that you are mad; you will need to be very strong."

"So what should I do?"

"You will need money to fight your case."

"I have some money."

"Guard it carefully, also, this letter and the one I shall prepare for you addressed to John Nichols, a good lawyer you will find at the Inns of Court in London who will help you all he can. It may take many years, are you prepared for that?"

"Years! But what of my son? I will be a stranger to him."

"I can but tell you how things are, not how you might wish them to be. If you are not prepared for a long struggle perhaps this is a fight you should not start."

Reprimanded, I nodded. "I will do whatever is needed, for as long as it is needed."

"See the lawyer, I believe his advice will serve you well. Come back in an hour and I shall have the letter ready for you."

As I made to get out my purse he shook his head. "No, thank you. You have paid me enough."

I had had the foolish belief I had merely to talk with the theologian lawyer and all would be settled, a path would be set before me that I simply had to travel and I would arrive at my destination - the annulment of my marriage and the return of my son. But I was as far away as ever, my son receding before me as ever more hurdles were placed in my path. Now there was another learned man to see, another interview, leading where? To more disappointment? I wiped my hands across my face: I knew I would not be able to continue unless I could shake my mind free of all the woeful thoughts crowding in upon me.

"Shall we sit here awhile?" I asked as we made our way beside the river. The words died on my lips. I pointed to the far bank. "There!" I cried. Gwen's gaze followed my hand. "Is it Cassie?" I could see the alarm in Gwen's eyes as they narrowed and scanned the black and white horse on a distant pathway.

"It's all right," she said, her face relaxing. "See, both her ears are white, Cassie has only one white ear." I nodded. We wandered away to wait elsewhere for the letter, our peace disturbed by the spectre of Skinner.

As we entered the inn where we were staying after collecting the document from the Reverend Wilkins the landlord called us over. "A man has been asking if two young women are staying here, he had obviously been riding hard. I told him you were out at present. He left some ten minutes ago, saying he would soon be back."

I braced myself to speak. "Oh, a visitor, thank you." My voice quivered as I tried to hold myself in check. "As it happens our business has concluded so let me settle up with you now as we must be leaving shortly - for Canterbury," I added.

"And what of your visitor?"

"We will see him first, of course." I was surprised how calm my voice sounded despite the turmoil I felt within. While I handed over the few shillings required Gwen ran up to our room. On entering I found her frantically throwing everything into our bags; I closed the door behind me and tried to gather my thoughts. We heard steps, a creaking of the floorboards outside the room and moved into the recess each side of the doorway, petrified, barely daring to breathe. The brisk knock at the door released us. Gwen lunged for the china jug on the washstand and as the man bent to step into the room she swung her outstretched arm and smashed the jug down on to his head with a mighty blow and he crumpled to the floor. As I stepped over him I knew from a fleeting glimpse that whoever he was, he wasn't Skinner. I grabbed Gwen's hand and pulled her away shoving her bag at her and bundled her out of the room. We practically fell down the stairs. I threw the key on to the desk grateful the landlord was not there and we hurried out of the door.

Chapter 27

"Have I killed him?" Gwen asked, grabbing my arm. I had never seen her so afraid.

"You hit him with a jug, that wouldn't kill him." A silent prayer rose from me that I was right.

"Who was he?"

"I don't know."

"But he was a gentleman."

We found our footsteps had taken us towards the river and there was no need to discuss our progress from there: a barge sat at the water's edge facing down the river. Its sail was being hoisted, the strong breeze filling it.

We picked up our skirts and ran.

"Boats!" Gwen exclaimed. "I hate boats."

The group of working men playing cards on an old chest paid us no attention as we found a seat on the barge next to a farmer keeping guard over half a dozen bewildered sheep. The chill breeze pushed the craft along through the heart of the town and away, between the wooded riverbanks, giving us the invisibility we sorely needed.

"The man at the inn, he must be a friend of Skinner's, mustn't he?"

I could see Gwen's conscience must be appeased before she could rest. "No one is looking for us with good intent," I said. I put my arm around her and felt her shoulders relax a little and a faint smile crossed her face. It was gone in an instant.

"I feel sick," she said.

The strong wind caused constant unpleasant waves on the river and more than once Gwen had to lean over the side to be sick as woods, pastures, orchards, villages, drifted by. When she seemed recovered a little I suggested she lay her head upon my shoulder to rest. Hours came and went as gently as the scenery. The workmen departed at Snodland as sacks of lime were brought on board.

"Won't be long now," one of the sailors said as he passed. "Rochester's not so far ahead."

I nodded my thanks as the barge pulled away into midstream once more. I was watching the activity on the docking stage when my eye was caught by a movement: a horseman on the lane going towards Maidstone. This time there was no mistaking the horse, or the rider. I lowered my head and bent my shoulders to become one dark mass with Gwen's form and did not open my eyes again until a young boatman stood before me offering us the use of an old cow skin against the threatening rain.

The great castle at Rochester stood square and grey against the evening sky, its size and age sending a surge of my own weakness and the impossibility of my mission through me. I shuddered.

"Are you all right?" Gwen asked.

"Of course." I gathered my wits, thinking of the shelter we needed for the night, though the image of Skinner on horseback was gnawing at my brain: he was travelling in the opposite direction to ourselves, but for how long?

We alighted, grateful to have the rolling deck replaced by the solid earth.

"Want a friend?" a voice called across to us, a burst of laughter following the words. I could not prevent my gaze from falling on the group of sailors standing at the water's edge. "'Cos we're very friendly." More laughter. Gwen and I hurried away, hearing the catcalls chase us along the road.

"We must find somewhere for the night," I said as we walked towards the High Street. I pushed at the door of the first inn we came to but the sound of laughter and coarse language bouncing between the walls and stairs sent us back outside. The next inn brought forth the same sound and the same sight: sailors, their faces flushed with drink, their hands reaching for any female form within an arm's length.

"We'll have to get away," I said, "it isn't safe for us here."

"Indeed, it is not," a male voice called out to us and we looked back to face a middle-aged couple, arm in arm, walking behind us.

The woman came towards us smiling, pulling her silk shawl more closely over her plump shoulders. "Are you lost, may I ask?"

"We need a suitable inn in which to pass the night," I replied.

"You have not chosen a good evening for that." The man stepped forward, as tall and straight as his wife was circular. "There are many ships in Chatham Dockyard tonight and the sailors are, what shall we say, making up for lost time at every tavern and inn for miles around."

"But we cannot leave these young ladies on the streets all night," the woman said, her brow creased with concern. She moved closer and took Gwen's hand in hers while addressing the man behind her. "Surely husband, we must invite these young travellers to come home with us."

The man smiled. "You are right my love. It is our duty to see no harm comes to them."

"Oh," I mumbled, "we cannot… we cannot accept," but I could not think what alternative we had, darkness was draping itself over the city and the sailors' raucous calls seemed to come from all directions.

The woman dropped Gwen's hand and stretching out her arms she herded us together, almost pushing us along the street, chattering all the time, her husband following, sentry-like. "You must be tired, have you travelled far and all alone? Did you come by coach? Not on foot, I hope. Have you eaten? We must find some supper for you, will cold cuts suffice? We had a good piece of mutton earlier - there is plenty in the pantry - is there not plenty left over, husband?" I heard a single sound from behind. "And will it not be nice to have two such young ladies as our guests? Our house is just along here, be careful it is becoming quite dark now, there is a step, oh yes, and another." The door opened and in a moment we were inside and it clicked shut behind us.

"Here, please allow me to help you with your cloaks," the man said.

"Why, what red hair you have, my dear," the woman said as Gwen's hair fell free. "Now, do sit by the fire, there is such a chill in the air this evening."

The candles lit a goodly room and Gwen and I were pleased to be ushered into the two stout chairs set either side of the fire. "I shall ask Dora to light a fire in your chamber," the woman said and followed her husband out into the hall. Gwen and I exchanged a glance, almost a shrug - here we were, too weary to question the offered bed for the night.

"Our father has sent for us to join him in London," I explained to Mistress Porter the next morning.

"Then you will need to get the coach from the High Street tomorrow, it leaves at seven of the clock."

"Oh!"

"But it is no problem, you must stay here and rest today so you are prepared for the remainder of your journey. My husband is gone to Chatham on urgent business but I shall stay with you – the town is still awash with sailors, so it would be better if we all spend the day quietly at home."

Gwen spoke before I had my thoughts in order. "You are very kind, mistress."

"It is our pleasure to have you here. When you are ready why not take a stroll in the garden, it is a pleasant enough morning." Our plump hostess slid out of the room.

"Another day passing," I whispered to Gwen as we sat at the table, finishing our meal with bread and butter.

"But we are safe here," Gwen said, "out of the way." The image of Skinner trotting along the towpath towards Maidstone flashed into my mind. Before I could reply Mistress Porter came back into the room, smiling, she was always smiling.

"We shall get our cloaks and wander outside as you suggest," I said.

"They are so generous to strangers," Gwen commented as we climbed the stairs. Her words added to the unease I had felt since we had met the couple: an unexpected civility from persons of rank towards strangers, it reminded me of nothing less than Sir Neville's early attentions: future betrayal hidden behind present kindness. My breath caught in my throat.

"Are you unwell?" Gwen asked, seeing me sway on the stair.

"I think not." I put my finger to my lips and hurried on. "Where was it? Where was it?" I cried when we were once more in our room.

"What?"

"The window, the window with the scratch on it." Gwen regarded me in bewilderment. "Did you not notice it yesterday? It caught the candle light."

"What did, what are you talking about?"

"I *must* find it." I went over to our window, my eyes racing over the surface of each pointed pane held in place by its metal framework.

"Tell me what it is?" Gwen implored me.

"I saw it last night, a scratch on the window glass."

"But why is it so important?"

"Because it reminded me, reminded me of something I had seen before. Look, just look, will you?"

Gwen gave a sigh of resignation and stepped out on to the landing. "Do you mean this?" she asked a moment later.

I ran to join her. "Yes," I replied slowly. My hand traced the marks, the letters J and L intertwined and encircled with ivy leaves. How could I have been so foolish a second time, I asked myself. I pushed Gwen back into our room. "We have to go," I said.

"What? Why?"

"We have to go now, no time to talk, we are in danger here."

Gwen queried me no further but began gathering our few belongings into our bags. "We must hide them beneath our cloaks as best we can," I said. "We should seem to be merely doing as she suggested, taking the air in the garden, we must not allow her to be alerted to our going."

We moved as smoothly as we could out into the garden with our bags clamped to our bodies beneath our cloaks.

"Morning, miss." Our attention was drawn to a young man scratching at the earth with a rake.

"Good morning," I replied, my voice catching in my throat. I tried to remain calm but the boy must have seen my eyes searching through the trees, seeking our escape.

"If you are wishing to visit the town you'll need to go out the front way, miss," the lad said, "the back gate's locked for some reason."

"Thank you," I said, "but it is no matter, we wish to see the garden."

"There's a bench by the pond," he called after us. Were we being watched from indoors? I could not resist glancing back at the house and there, above the door from which we had just stepped, carved so deeply that lit by the morning sun they seemed to stand proud of their surroundings, were the initials NL with ivy leaves. I allowed a gasp to escape my lips, causing Gwen to follow my gaze. We had both seen the same sign at Wilderness Hall. There was no doubt now, this must be one of Sir Neville's many properties.

"It's a walled garden," I cried, "we're trapped."

"Keep going," Gwen said. We walked on slowly taking a feigned interest in the clusters of primroses dotted about beneath the budding apple trees until we found the bench, hidden by a thorny rose bush and sank down on to it.

"What now?" I asked, more of myself than Gwen.

"Wait." Gwen stood. "When I say 'ready' make for that strange tree, see, the one with the huge flat leaves, right at the back of the garden." She stood on tiptoe so she could watch the garden boy. "Quick, he's gone to the back of the wood pile." Our footsteps grated in the gravel, surely loud enough for the whole house to hear. As we reached the tree Gwen dropped her bag, hitched up her skirts and stepped up onto the lowest of the thick, scaly branches. "Fig tree," she said as she pulled herself up, "there was one at the Hall." I marvelled at her agility; her limbs worked in easy union and instantly she was above me and within arms' length of the wall. "Bags," she hissed.

I held up the bags for her and she dropped them over the wall. "But," I began. But I could not do as she had done.

"Quick!" Gwen reached down a hand. I took it and clambered on to the lower branch.

"No, I can't."

"There!" Gwen commanded, pointing to the branch I must reach for next. The moment I let go of her hand she dropped out of sight behind the wall. I felt I had been torn in two as she disappeared, the wound of my missing son opening up within me. "Gwen!" I cried, and pushed and pulled and scrambled and with the bough creaking beneath me I reached the top and fell behind the wall. I repressed the cry that would otherwise have risen from my lips.

"Come on," Gwen urged me, pulling me to my feet. Pains came at me from all directions, but none of them sharp enough to prevent me from following Gwen along the alleyway to the lane beyond.

Chapter 28

"How did you know this was Sir Neville's house?" Gwen asked me in a whisper as we emerged on to a back street of the town.

"The scratch on the window - I remembered it - from Wilderness Hall, I'd seen it there. It was…" I hesitated, it was difficult to utter the name. "Jacob, it was his initials, JL, Jacob Lattimer. Jacob has stayed here. It was no accident we ran into the Porters in the town - Skinner must have told them and they were looking for us."

"You think Skinner's been here?" Gwen's voice betrayed her fear.

"We only just missed him, he was on the road to Maidstone, I saw him from the boat." We were walking quickly between elegant houses. Had Skinner visited any of them? Did Sir Neville have other friends in the city? Were there other eyes searching the streets for us?

"You saw him!" Gwen stopped, her eyes blazing anger.

"Yes."

"And you didn't tell me."

"You were asleep."

"But later."

"I didn't want to…" I broke off, knowing how feeble my words would sound, "to worry you."

Gwen's eyes flashed accusingly. "Is there anything else? Anything else you have decided not to trust me with?" Words could not come, they died on my lips. She held my gaze for a long time, the silence between us louder than thunder, then walked on without a word. My guilt made the point of her accusation all the more sore. She had never accused me of endangering her when I asked her to bring my baby to me; she had never accused me of separating her from her family when we were taken to the farm, or of standing by when she was whipped - but she accused me of not trusting her, of not believing in her strength. She stomped on as tears fell from her eyes.

Shame flooded through me washing away every other emotion. Lies had fallen from my lips time and again, to wagon drivers and coachmen, to friendly farmers and kindly fellow travellers, even to Margaret and Matthew with that first lie about my name. But those lies, all of them, had been for survival. Nothing shamed me more than my lack of trust in a friend who was the most trustworthy person ever to take breath; the person to whom I owed my very existence. Without her where would I be? Skinner's slave on the farm? Dead?

"Forgive me." They were the only words in my head, the only words I could speak. "Forgive me."

She was silent. We hurried on, moving as quickly as we could without drawing attention to ourselves, passing between the cathedral, its towers reaching skywards, and the castle, standing firmly upon the earth. "There is no alternative, we have to cross the bridge," I said. Gwen nodded her acknowledgement but said nothing. If we had been missed at the house they would rush to the bridge - our route to London. The castle stood on its hill, keeping its watch over the city and the river, and over us - was it on our side or with Skinner? I tapped Gwen on the shoulder.

"What?"

"We must separate - they are expecting the two of us to be together. There, go with them, I'll come behind." I pointed towards a group of children crossing behind a tall woman dressed in black. Gwen's glance was as sharp as a scythe. I stood back and watched as she went, walking away from me and that feeling of loss, of being cored like an apple, overwhelmed me again. Was I losing her? I could only blame myself. Pain caused by one's own mistake is always the hardest to bear. I watched as Gwen's diminutive figure added itself to the line of children. I could see from the inclination of her head she had engaged one of the children in conversation and smiled to myself, knowing how, even in her anger, she was thinking her way through. I hesitated; I must take the bridge myself - beyond it did not lay safety but upon it lay the greatest danger, it was the pinch point and I could feel it cutting close.

Coaches, wagons, animals and pedestrians vied for space across the bridge, held close by its tall iron railings, its feet cutting the river into narrow channels, the boats carefully manoeuvring through beneath the arches. I dived into the melee waiting, waiting for a hand to grab at me, to pull me back into my nightmare. My heart was pounding in my chest; my fingers reached out but there was no Gwen to calm my nerves. I took my place on the moving carpet making its way across. The stone of the bridge gave way to wood, then back to stone and I was over; the carts rattled on and the pedestrians spread out. My eyes searched and rested on a stationary figure. Gwen was waiting for me. "Do you?" I asked.

"What?"

"Forgive me?"

She could not say the word but nodded. I knew it was a forgiveness of the head but not the heart. I had finally pushed her too far: she would suffer any hurt for me, but not hurt *from* me.

From the fisherman's cottages close to the river and the fine church, almost a rival for the cathedral, the road rose steadily and we continued in silence. It was a steep chalk escarpment and we were soon weary but dared not slow our pace. The road was straight - it was our obvious route and all the more vulnerable for that. We took a lesser road off to the right and attached ourselves to the back of a group of travellers then walked beside coaches and carts, taking any action to lose ourselves in the flow of travellers from the city.

"We must get off the road," I said. "They'll guess we are here, on this road."

"Right, where do you say we should go then?" Gwen's voice was full of bitter anger.

"Let's just get off the road."

"Into the field?"

"Yes, into the field, behind the hedge, out of sight."

Gwen stomped off and I followed her. We stood and looked at one another like soldiers regarding each other from enemy camps.

"I'm not a child," Gwen said at last.

"I know."

"Trust me then."

"I will, I do."

"But you didn't! I could have killed that man at the inn."

"You didn't."

"But I could have - yet there you are deciding what you think I can bear and what I cannot - what information to trust me with."

"My name is Ruth," I said.

"What?"

"My name is Ruth."

"I don't understand."

"Hope was my sister, she was killed in the raid at our farm. I stole her name when I found I was pregnant. Hope was married to Henry Ashton, not me. I was a maid. Sir Neville was correct - my son is his grandson - though I would give half my life to make it not so." Gwen stood back as if seeing me for the first time. "You are the only person alive to know that. You can see how I have lied and lied - even to dear Margaret. I have lied to cover the shame of my child; it is not his fault, what that villain did to me, yet he would have borne the mark all his life - but I cannot lie to you any longer. I trust you with everything." My voice broke. "Do not think badly of me." I waited. I dared not reach out to her but need not have feared, for her arms were about me as the sobs choked me and my body rocked as I released the dam of deceit that had built up within me.

I sensed a shadow fall over the land as clouds built barricades across the sky. My tears had ceased, but I found I could not open my eyes - if there was a world beyond my reach I did not wish to see it. Finally, we stood in silence.

"I do," Gwen said.

"What?"

"Forgive you. There was never anything to forgive - I was feeling tired and..."

"Do not explain, I was at fault, not you."

"Should I still call you by that name, should I still call you Hope?"

"Such I must remain for the world, I do not think I would answer to Ruth now. I left her in the ruins of our farmhouse - I fear she is lost."

"Come then, Hope, we must be on our way."

We walked on, quiet, but in harmony, a feeling I had quite forgotten but it was there in my past, with my sisters, with Hope and Jessie, when we were tired at the end of a day, when all the energy, all the teasing, all the quarrels had faded, and we would sit together. Sometimes Jessie would lie across our laps and we would plait her hair. Such was the feeling that embraced me now as we continued along the hedge leaving a trail of footprints in the soft earth.

"My mother's sister had an infant by the squire when she was but a child herself," Gwen said as the sunlight threaded its way through the clouds. "My mother said I had always to remember the burden was my aunt's but the shame was the squire's."

Chapter 29

"Here!" Gwen darted through a rough gap in the hedge.

"Wait!" But she was gone. I followed her through the sharp-fingered opening on to the road. A heavy open wagon filled with passengers pulled by two great horses was drawing close. "But," I began.

But Gwen was stumbling, falling. A cry of fear broke from my lips; the driver yelled and pulled hard at the reins; Gwen was prostrate on the ground, her cloak spread out about her. I ran towards her, waiting for the crack of bone as she was hit but the heavy black hooves fell still beside her. I dropped to my knees as the driver jumped down.

"Is she?"

"What is this?" a strong voice demanded as a black-garbed priest climbed down from the cart.

"'Twas not my fault." The driver's voice shook at the sight of the limp body. "She fainted, right in front of me. It's a miracle she wasn't killed."

"The driver did well to stop the horses," I said, shocked at how small and fragile Gwen seemed, lying there, beside the strong, obedient animals.

The priest seemed satisfied. "We must put her in the wagon." The driver gathered her in his arms and lifted her gently. The passengers who had been peering forward to see what had happened moved round to allow space for Gwen to be laid on the bales of hay making up the seating.

"Come, my dear," a gentle voice invited me to join them.

I climbed aboard and knelt beside Gwen, running my hand over her pale brow. She sighed and her eyelids fluttered open.

"What happened?" she asked in a shaky voice.

"Be still. You fainted, I think you must have knocked your head and…" My words ceased as my thoughts caught up with the situation. "And these kind people stopped."

"How is your companion? Is she hurt?" enquired the priest.

Gwen moved a little on her straw bed. "I believe there is no harm done," I replied. "We should trouble you no further." I saw a frown momentarily cross Gwen's brow.

The priest stood beside us, stroking his grey moustache. "Where are you bound, may I ask?"

I took a moment, the shock of the preceding few minutes still racing in my veins. I had to remind myself of our story. "We are on our way to London; our aunt is ill and father says it is an urgent matter."

"It must be so, for you to travel so far unaccompanied. But then," he seemed satisfied by my response and the happy outcome of the accident, "the more the merrier. Do we not all agree?" he added, addressing the passengers. There was a rumble of assent as he took his place beside the driver and the horses began to pull away from their unexpected stop.

"Pass the flagon, Jake." The priest reached a hand out to one of the three men seated behind him and was presented with the jar from which he took a good gulp.

"What plans do you have?" the priest asked me, wiping his mouth with the back of his hand. "As for ourselves, we are on our way to Gravesend and from there we take the Long Ferry to Southwark."

"You have had a fright, my dears," said the woman seated beside me. "Is your sister injured?"

"I think not." Gwen opened her eyes, held her head and attempted to sit up. "Don't you want to lie down a little longer?" I asked her.

"The jogging of the wagon…" I could see the same sickness that overtook her on the water possessed her as she lay there.

Gwen sat up, giving herself a little shake. "What happened?" she asked. "Did I faint or trip on the road?"

"Only you can answer that," I replied, my suspicions showing in my voice.

Gwen closed her eyes and I closed mine also. Two of the women kept up a steady chatter as a song came from the front of the wagon, all the men joining in, but I could hear little of it: the haunting image of Skinner on horseback had been replaced in my mind by the sight of the horses running towards Gwen's inert body on the road. I recoiled at the thought of it. This near catastrophe, together with the anger and antagonisms of the day, the seemingly never-ending chase in which we were the prey, Sir Neville reaching out for us in the person of Skinner and his web of connections, whirled within my brain. I could not accept the danger Gwen had put herself in yet again. I reached out and touched her hand and her fingers curled round my own. Perhaps we should not try to reach London but change direction, go elsewhere, any town or village where Sir Neville or Skinner would not seek us. Perhaps then I would lead Gwen into no more danger – I could give up my quest for my son - Sir Neville doubtless cared for him in his own way and would ensure he was well looked after. What could I give my child other than myself –

would he think it sufficient when old enough to measure such things. Perhaps it was Gwen I should save, remove from harm.

"We shall be arriving in Gravesend very shortly," the priest shouted over his shoulder.

"Gravesend," Gwen echoed, "doesn't sound very cheerful."

"The long ferry will take us right to London Bridge," one of the men explained.

Right to London Bridge, this very day! My thoughts of giving up my son, my surrender to the forces of Sir Neville, evaporated with the thought of our journey's end.

"Long Ferry?" queried Gwen.

"To London - long ferry," the man replied, "over the river to Tilbury - short ferry." He picked up his bottle again.

The wagon rolled downhill, the bustle guiding us towards the river and the busy port. Carters, carriers and porters vied for access to the quayside and other travellers stepped out of the surrounding inns glancing about, checking the sky, feeling the breeze for their forthcoming voyage. A line of boats swayed against the pier, crewmen in knitted caps and canvas jerkins busily stowing cargo, boxes and bottles at the rear.

"How could you do that?" I asked of Gwen as the two of us stood alone on the dock wall staring out at the grey sky alive with screeching gulls.

"What?"

"Lay down in the road to stop the wagon: you could have been killed." I was still shaken, angry.

"I tripped."

"You could have been killed!"

"But it worked." Now Gwen could no longer hold on to her pretence of innocence, she smiled. "We were in a hurry."

"You know I couldn't face all this alone, don't you?" I protested. "Without you…"

"But you are not without me," Gwen said.

"Never again," I insisted. "Promise."

"All right, never again," Gwen conceded. "And no more boats," she added. "This must be the last."

"It will be. London's the end of our journeying - for good or ill."

As we waited we were joined by the priest. "Did you know my own small church, St Mary Colechurch, was where the venerable Thomas a Becket was baptised?" he asked with not a little pride. I shook my head. "Ah, it is not as well-known as it should be," he continued. "You must come and see it while you are in London, it's just off Cheapside, but I should warn you - walk too quickly and you will pass it, it is so *very* small."

An hour later I showed our tickets as Gwen and I, holding our bags tightly, stepped carefully on to the shaky gangplank and were helped into the boat by one of the sailors. The vessel was crowded with twenty or more travellers but other than the shouts of the sailors the voices were low and I could but believe that like myself they were listening to the slap of the waves against the wall and wondering how we would fare on this crowded, heaving river. We all sat close upon one another to gain what benefit we could from the canvas tilt that gave us some protection from the spray. The boat was moving against the jetty, the swell constantly raising our small craft and then allowing it to drop with a hearty splash.

Cries broke into the quiet conversations and activity increased. A sailor loosened the rope from the capstan on the quayside and the four rowers pulled hard on their oars, the sail was unfurled and under the guidance of the steersman the boat began to move out into the broad river. Gwen flashed me a weak smile and I smiled in reply to think our days of journeying would be soon over. With a gentle rocking movement we moved away from the wooden houses, quays, slipways, wharves and activity of Gravesend. The river was as busy as any highway I had ever seen. Large seagoing vessels with huge white sails, like so many sheets hanging on a line, hogged the mid-stream, while the smaller boats such as ours kept closer to the shore. We had waited for the tide and now it was carrying us towards London.

For a long time the straining rowers and full-bellied sail moved us between quiet flat shores, a marshland inhabited by the seabirds I could see resting on the waves made by the many passing craft. Occasionally they flapped into the air, circling until they saw some prey onto which they could dive beneath the water's surface. The river did not run in a simple straight line, at moments we could see nothing but land ahead, then it would twist and a new vista of the river would appear. After one such change of direction a town appeared on the shore beside us, but we sailed past its busy quays and not long after another town came into sight where we could see the skeleton of a ship. Now the river was narrowing and the towns came more quickly, suddenly the shore as busy as an ants' nest.

"Is this London?" Gwen asked.

"Why no," Father Joseph replied with a smile, "this is Woolwich. Next, you'll see Greenwich, then the naval yards at Deptford. Do not worry, you will recognise London when you see it, it cannot be missed."

The river beside us became a dull grey and was seemingly used as a rubbish dump judging by the detritus floating on its surface. A formidable castle built strong and square came into view, the outer walls sitting tight by the water. "It's the Tower," the priest explained, turning in his seat to speak to us. "If you have sharp eyes you may make out traitor's gate." Gwen and I peered to our right trying to make out the dreaded place but a small craft with a brown sail overtook us ruining our view to our disappointment. "Oh!" A cry escaped me as I turned my gaze forward again to see a great wall soaring above us, crowded with four and six storey houses.

"London Bridge," said the priest. "Did I not say you could not miss it?"

We pulled up on the shore a little before the bridge for which I was glad as I could see the strong currents pulling as the water flowed through its many arches. The rowers splashed ashore to secure the boat. Father Joseph told us he must hurry and wished all Godspeed as he clambered over the side and marched away, his cloak flying about him.

We held our breath as we beheld the bridge and the houses that must surely topple into the river if there was so much as a sudden breath of air. What place of wonders was this?

London at last.

Chapter 30

"Oy! Outta the way." I felt the tug on my skirt as a precariously loaded cart brushed past along the quayside. I spun round to view the whirl of activity surrounding us. No busy market or spring fair had prepared me for the London waterside: the embarking and disembarking ferry passengers stepping carefully ashore watching their belongings; the porters, hauliers, carters and wagon drivers vying for trade; the flash of the silk or velvet clothing of the well-to-do, bright against the well-worn woollens and linens of the working people; the rowing boats jostling at the river's edge; the many wherry-men reaching out their hands for the next paying customer to be ferried across the river. "Watch it, miss," came another voice. I was too slow for this place; its heart was beating fast and I guessed I would have to match its rhythm if I wished to prosper here.

I grabbed Gwen's hand so we wouldn't be separated in the crush and wished our erstwhile companions Godspeed as they headed towards the bridge. We began to wander along the embankment; we were quiet as we walked, the ever-changing scene before us taking all our energy to absorb.

"Over there." The cheerful Blue Anchor Inn sign hung outside a large weatherboard building; entering its dim interior seemed like stepping out of a rushing river.

"Good day, young ladies," a voice boomed at us out of the darkness.

I beheld a woman as tall and square as any I had ever seen, her face deeply pock-marked. "We require a room," I said, finding my voice, "possibly for a week."

"Then you are welcome," came the reply just as the door behind us opened again. Before I could answer I saw the woman's eyes dart over my head. "Out!" she yelled, "I've told you before!" The door crashed shut. The woman returned her gaze to us with a smile. "One room, then?" she continued. I nodded. "This way - I'll give you a quiet room, I can see you are not Londoners and the causeway can be noisy - the Hope Theatre is close by." She grabbed a bunch of keys with a powerful hand and led us outside and upstairs to a long wooden balcony running the whole length of the building above a gravelled courtyard. We entered the fourth room and a smile found its way on to my face; this small chamber with its bed, wash-stand and fireplace felt like a safe haven.

"There you are, my little chickens. Just remember, behave yourselves and you'll have no cross words with Jenny Grey." We murmured our agreement only for her to add, "But if you put a foot wrong!" We did not wish to learn what would happen in that circumstance. "Windows to be kept closed at all times, no use to be made of the back staircase at the far end of the balcony unless the place is on fire." Now we were suitably impressed her voice softened. "Watch yourselves, you are in London, and there's many a malign face hiding behind a silken mask. Any problems - let me know, I run a respectable house here." We did not doubt it and paid for two days in advance to prove our good intentions.

There was a little daylight still available and having laid out our few items of clothing we donned our cloaks and headed outside with a feeling of slight trepidation and much excitement. We walked along the river path planning what we would say if we were challenged as to our purpose in the city.

"Tickets, tickets! Best show in the city," a rough voice yelled. We paused, just a hesitation in our steps, but enough to draw the attention of a red-faced, unkempt man. "Come on, wenches, buy your tickets for the bear baiting." I shook my head as we backed away.

"What's it like? A bear, I mean," whispered Gwen.

"A sort of big animal," I began but broke off as the crowd parted and voices lowered and we heard the clanking of chains against the ground. A bear with a muzzle shuffled towards us, as tall as the men surrounding it, its shaggy coat of brown fur dull and matted, long chains attached to each of its limbs trailing on the cobble stones. "Look at the sores on its wrists and ankles," I cried; the bare red skin attested to its pain as it was forced towards a narrow alley named Bear Gardens, four men prodding it on its way with the metal points of their batons. We heard its shrieks of anguish as it tried to swipe at its tormentors with its large clawed paws but failed to reach them and each protest against the cruelty led only to the batons striking again.

"Come, Gwen, I can't listen to any more of the poor creature's agony." We stepped away only to face half a dozen vicious dogs hardly restrained by the two men hanging on to their leads.

"Never mind him," said the man, "he will best the biggest of dogs, rarely does the bear lose the fight."

"So what happens to the dogs?" Gwen queried, but the men laughed at her question. Seeing the snarling animals with their spikey collars, saliva dripping from their yellow teeth, it was difficult to feel sympathy for them, though it seemed they were doomed to be victims too.

Our view of the city as a place of marvels had darkened a little, but immediately we were caught up in a more cheerful crowd gathering nearby. There were brightly-dressed clowns juggling wooden batons and men on stilts striding through the assembly waving fiery brands, which, to our amazement they thrust into their mouths. Would they not die upon the instant? I wondered, but no, the flaming stick re-appeared and was triumphantly waved to the applause of all. Acrobats threw themselves into the air, twirling over, but still somehow landing upon their feet with a smile and a flourish.

"Watch where you're going," cried an elderly lady about to climb into her coach as Gwen stepped backwards on to her foot.

"So sorry," said an embarrassed Gwen as she stared at the woman's tall powdered grey wig, an imitation bird sticking out of it as if about to topple to the ground. The man accompanying her, not to be outshone, wore a wig of cascading curls topped by a hat bearing a foot-long feather.

"Country bumpkins," cried the woman scowling at us both. "Out of the way, child, we are going to the theatre."

We moved on, our gaze caught across the river by the tall wooden houses, all higgledy piggledy, a crush of shapes and sizes, leaning towards each other like gossiping women. Above it stood the tower of St Paul's cathedral with its ragged top, badly in need of repair. We had never seen such a concentration of fine buildings, a scramble of gold domes, turrets, weather-cocks and coloured windows glinting in the last of the evening sun. When we lowered our eyes the view was not so refined: the tide had receded from the bankside exposing rubbish deposited in heaps upon the foreshore and boats lying at awkward angles stuck in the mud. Those small ferry boats still afloat were forced to unload their passengers onto wooden boxes and mats in the hope they could make it to the shore without ruining their shoes.

The light was fading as we made our way back to the inn, grateful to have an evening without fear - but for how long were we safe?

"Do these people never sleep?" I murmured as midnight came and went and I turned over in bed for the tenth time as the laughter and cries and yells drifted up from the street.

"And she said this was a quiet room," Gwen groaned, pulling the blanket over her head.

I was longing to see London Bridge for myself and with money in our pockets we were impatient to get going but first we needed to think of our mission. After breakfast, I asked Mrs Grey where we might find the Inns of Court.

"I'm sure their inns aren't as comfortable as this one, we shall not be leaving," Gwen put in, not wishing to annoy our landlady.

Mistress Grey let out a bellow of laughter. "Oh, my dears, my dears," she cried, "that's the best one I've heard in a twelvemonth." Gwen stood back, disconcerted, and lowered her eyes.

"We have to find an ecclesiastical lawyer," I began, but my voice failed me.

"I'm sorry, take no notice of me." Jenny Grey wiped a tear from her eye. "Now tell me."

"We have to find this lawyer," I began again, telling the tale Gwen and I had agreed upon. "A certain John Nichols, to seek his advice concerning our uncle's ill-begot marriage - a delicate matter. Our uncle is crippled and is following us to London but at a slow pace so we volunteered to go on ahead and seek out the lawyer and make arrangements for his visit as time is of the essence and we were warned the law can move extremely slow."

"I see. All the *Inns*," she stressed the word and was barely able to restrain another laugh, "of Court are off Fleet Street, over the river." I started to utter my thanks, but she immediately interrupted me. "Hold on, you don't intend going dressed as you are, do you? That will never do."

"I have a slightly better dress - black velvet."

"Let me see it, go put it on."

Jenny Grey clucked her tongue when she saw me coming down the stairs and shook her head. "An old-fashioned gown, I have to say, not good enough to get you beyond any lawyer's clerk. They will assume you are a time-waster. You'll need something better." She fingered the fabric of my gown and must have seen the expression of concern on my face. "Don't worry, it doesn't have to be brand new. There are several shops up on the bridge selling good quality second-hand clothes." She pulled at the neck of my now-discredited dress. "Something a little more daring will help you charm your way in."

"Really?" I sighed.

"You should be able to sell this dress, it's good velvet. In fact, wait until you have told me what the shop offers, I might be able to get you a better price for it from the undertakers, they often rent out clothes to the bereaved." She regarded us as the naïve young women we were. "Going to law is an expensive business, surely your uncle knows that." She resumed her seat behind the desk. "Your sister could pretend to be your maid, that'll give you more status and her dress doesn't need to be anywhere near so grand."

I heard a sound from behind me, Gwen's disappointed "Oh."

Gwen and I made our way towards London Bridge, past the busy wharves and chandlers' stores, the chop-houses and the tiny ramshackle shops selling everyday essentials. We queued impatiently on the slope leading up to the bridge to enter through the gatehouse. There was much pushing as the road on the bridge was scarcely more than the width of a country lane. Wagons, handcarts, coaches, horses and pedestrians all had to negotiate their passage through. Now I could believe Jenny Grey when she said it could take an hour to make one's way across. Below us in the first arch of the bridge there was the great wheel of a water mill and granary; the scent of baking bread drove us into the baker's shop above and we bought ourselves pasties to eat later.

"Have you ever seen…" I began but Gwen was not beside me. There was a moment of panic before I saw her at the edge of the road bent over the figure of a young lad, a slender boy with fair hair, his outstretched hand holding a begging bowl. His face was clean but his clothes were pitiful and dirty and a threadbare blanket covered his legs which appeared to be set at an awkward angle. The short branch of a tree, fashioned to make a crutch, lay beside him.

"You gave him your food," I said when she came back to me.

"I know too well how it feels to be hungry, his hand was hardly strong enough to hold his begging bowl. Anyway, it wasn't so generous," she added with a cheeky smile, "I know you'll give me half of yours."

We laughed and walked on in the torrent of people. How long before Skinner came searching for us in London? Surely we could manage to lose ourselves; this was a city of some three hundred thousand people, or so the priest had said.

"What a fine place this is to get lost," I murmured.

"But I think if we go along the river we'll be all able find our way…"

"No, Gwen, to lose ourselves. Who would notice us in all this chaos?"

"Make way, there." A loud shout made us step back quickly as we came near to being knocked over by a sedan chair. The carriers elbowed their way through the crowds heedless of those in front of them on the heavily shaded streets. We pushed our way along past the shops, selling everything you could want from vegetables, meat, fish, coal, candles, to clothes and furs. It was with some relief we reached a widening of the road where the houses stopped leaving a gap before the north gatehouse; it was where a fire had taken place back in the 1630s we heard someone say. We could still make out the charred boards and railings. We stood eating our pasty and viewed the city for a while before carefully traversing the road and retracing our steps a little until the shrill blast of a horn made us hold our cloaks tightly in fear of having them torn from us as a coach rushed past with a roar, sending a spray of dust and debris against our feet. Stepping back, we saw we were leaning tightly against the door of a dress shop bearing the grand name of 'Madam Blanche' and went inside.

"Oh, Gwen!" I exclaimed as we moved between the lines of gowns, almost as grand as the one Sir Neville had provided for me to parade in before his friends. "Who would sell such garments if they were lucky enough to own them?"

"How little you know," a voice replied from behind a gown of cream silk being held to a voluptuous body. "Many a wealthy lady can afford to wear an item just once or twice." A pert, pretty face beneath a torrent of black hair smiled at us and we found ourselves smiling back. She tapped her nose. "They trade them in for pin money unbeknown to their husbands." She stepped out of the shadows and I heard a quick intake of breath from Gwen as we saw her bodice was cut so low it barely balanced over her breasts - I thought she must be afraid to lean forward. She caught my expression. "I know," she said softly, "but 'tis the fashion, and one must be fashionable."

Not that fashionable, I thought.

"No, do not try that one," she added as she saw me pick up a blue gown, "it doesn't go with your complexion, trust me. Try the dark red one over there and for you," she moved towards Gwen, "you with your luscious hair," she reached up and ran her finger along a lock of Gwen's hair, "there's a green taffeta at the back." So saying she disappeared into the next room.

"Why Gwen, you are no child now," I cried a few minutes later as she stood before me her pale skin and radiant hair glowing in contrast to the dark forest green of her dress.

"And you are dressed as a lady should be," Gwen replied with a smile.

Her words tore at my heart; I did not wish to think of myself as Lady Lattimer. All this, all this running, hiding, seeking, it was all for my son. I swallowed hard. "I think we will do very well," I said. "Good enough for any lawyer."

We paid a deposit and agreed to call back later in the day when Gwen's gown had been shortened a little. "I suppose we can sell them back to the shop later," I said, "if we want to."

At the door, we ran into the young woman we had spoken to earlier. "We took your advice," I said.

"Advice you're handing out now, is it, Hannah?" The shop owner glanced across at her.

"Indeed, it is," Hannah called back, "and you have sold two dresses because of it." Stepping out into the street she asked, "Have you been to Fleur's? She sells the most beautiful chemises and nightgowns at reasonable prices, and make-up, too, and young ladies, you have no make-up, and that will never do. I'm going there next, why not come along with me, it's not far – just at the north end of the bridge."

In truth, we were in need of such underclothes, ours were little more than well-darned rags, and caught up in the delight of buying new apparel we cheerfully followed Hannah to the next shop where she seemed equally well-known.

"You have the advantage of me," Hannah said, "you know my name but I do not know yours."

"This is my sister Gwen and my name is Hope." In alarm, I realised I had given our real names - London had made me feel safe.

"And why are you in London, may I ask?"

I was dismayed to think everyone we spoke to could recognise us as strangers. My thoughts must have been plain upon my face, for she added, "You have the breath of the country about you and a soft burr in your voices."

I stuck to the story of our uncle but heard myself being evasive when asked when he would arrive.

"If you are going to be in London for some time you should find somewhere cheaper to stay than an inn. Come to think of it, you may be in luck, I believe my neighbour has a room to rent. It is a good place - for young ladies only. I think it will suit you. I shall check and leave word for you at Madam Blanche's."

"What is it?" I asked Gwen some time later. We had spent a pleasant few hours admiring the amazing variety of goods in the shops. I had noticed her peer over her shoulder for the third time as we started our return journey to Madam Blanche's. I could see the unease on her face.

"I don't know - I think someone is following us."

The lightness of the day disappeared. "Who? Where?"

"I'm not sure, maybe I'm imagining it."

"Skinner?" My voice cracked as I said his name.

"No, a boy, I think."

"Then we must talk to him, find out who sent him."

"Skinner or Sir Neville, what does it matter?"

"At least we'll know." I tried to sound calm though my heart was thumping in my chest. "Gwen, wait in the shadow of the shop doorway while I walk on, see what happens."

Gwen was no quiet observer when we were under threat. As the boy passed her she pounced and grabbed hold of him. I heard him let out a cry as I hurried to her aid. "You cunning, deceitful, little boy, pretending to be lame."

"No Mistress, that's not true."

"But I saw you begging."

"No mistress, not I." he pleaded.

Gwen shook him, "Are you are telling me my eyes have deceived me, you little cheat? I gave you my pasty!"

"Mistress please, I'm Jack, you have seen my brother, Walter."

"A likely story," I said.

"Right," said Gwen, "we are going that way now and you are coming with us." Keeping a firm grip on his arm we made our way back towards the south gatehouse.

"Well, where is he?" Gwen began as we approached the building, but as she spoke the flow of people eased a little and we saw the boy lying as he had been earlier, beneath the window of the bakery. "Twins!" Gwen seemed annoyed at being proved wrong. "So why were you following us? Hoping to steal from us?"

Jack hung his head, "No mistress, no. Please don't be so angry. I have my brother to take care of, he can't walk since being hit by a coach." He went to his brother's side and stroked his head.

Walter regarded us nervously. "A man asked me to keep watch for you."

So Skinner was here, dear God. I felt sick. My voice shook as I spoke. "What makes you think we are the girls you are looking for?"

"He told me what you looked like and he gave me this." He held a strip of material from Gwen's skirt, blue with a black line in the weave. "He said it was given to him by a friend of yours called Margaret to help him find you both and he needs to talk to you."

Who could this man be, this man who had persuaded Margaret to aid him, this man who 'wanted to talk to us'?

"You have been kind to me, I wouldn't do anything to hurt you." Walter was close to tears. "The man seemed nice, we thought he meant you no harm." The pale, ragged boys waited for some punishment to befall them; I could not stand the beseeching expression in their eyes. I took two pennies from my pocket and handed them to Jack whose fingers quickly encased them.

"When I got back to Walter mid-morning he said you had already passed this way so I went in search of you. I thought I could find out where you were staying and let the man know."

"What's he like, this man?"

"A tall man, a gentleman, no doubting that, with blue eyes and light brown hair."

Not Skinner, thank God, but the man we had left unconscious in our room in Maidstone? Surely, he was no friend of ours.

Jack leant forward. "I know where to find him," he said.

Chapter 31

"I don't like it." Gwen's expression was troubled as we hurried along, trying to keep up with Jack as he pushed through the afternoon crowds. She grabbed hold of my arm and pulled me to a halt. "What if this is some trick of Skinner's?"

"I think Jack is telling the truth." As I spoke I indicated for Jack to wait for us.

"I don't doubt Jack."

"We have to take the chance of help," I replied, trying to dispel my own fears.

"Hope, it could be a trap." Gwen let go of my arm, despairing of me listening to the truth in her words. "Remember, maybe by now Sir Neville knows - that man, that man from the Maidstone inn, he could be a gentleman - and a friend of Jacob's."

No other words could have brought me more suddenly to a stop. Gwen was right, but we needed help, and if help was on offer we could not afford to spurn it.

"But," I reasoned, "he is waiting for us in a public place, he can hardly steal us away from there. But…" but, of course, I must protect Gwen though without her knowledge. "To be certain, will you stand guard outside, just in case of trouble? I will feel safe then and I'll send Jack for you when I am convinced the man means us no harm. Will you do that for me?"

Gwen nodded. "It's a risk."

"It's a risk we have to take, since leaving the farm we have taken so many, and so far..."

"So far," Gwen repeated.

We walked on till Jack stopped outside a large white-painted building resembling something of a mixture of shop and inn. Gwen slipped into a shaded gap between two houses on the opposite side of the road from where she could keep watch on the door of the coffee house. I noted the expression of concern on her face and I knew it was reflected in my heart – but we both had to hold our nerve and trust, trust in the boy standing beside me, and the man within.

Jack opened the door for me. The room beyond was large, noisy, smoke-filled and with the heavy aroma of coffee; I knew the scent from my time at Wilderness Hall but had never tasted it. It took a moment for Jack to scan the room and find the person he sought.

"There!" Jack pointed to a corner table with but a single occupant, his head facing away from me. As we drew closer I thought there was a familiarity to the figure.

A moment of quiet fell upon the room; I saw Jack and I were objects of interest in this mostly male space. It seemed the man heard the silence too and turned towards us. The movement seemed to take an age, my toes clenched as I prepared to run. The movement complete all my fears dissipated. It was the face I had seen in Kingsdown and again at Wilderness Hall - a fine, open face, one I knew upon the instant could not dissemble. He stood as he saw us and smiled.

My moment of pleasure melted away from me: this was the man I had believed I would never see again - I had taken the name of my sister and in so doing I had claimed kinship of a sort with him.

"I had not thought to meet my brother's wife in such circumstances, I am your servant."

"Sir Edward." My voice had almost deserted me in my moment of doubt.

"Pray, be seated." Sir Edward indicated one of the leather-backed chairs scattered about the place. His attention moved away allowing me a moment to collect my thoughts. "Well done, Jack, you richly deserve your reward." Sir Edward opened a large purse and extracted a sovereign. Jack's mouth fell open at the glint of gold. "There, that is for your good work in bringing my sister to me this day, and this..." he found a matching coin, "is for your brother."

"Please sir," Jack's voice wavered as he spoke, "have you nothing smaller? I fear trying to change such a large coin some might think it was stolen, how else would the likes of me get such a thing?"

"Of course, forgive me for not being more considerate, let me give you some crowns instead." Pausing in handing over the coins Sir Edward asked, "And where is Gwen?"

"Oh Lord! Jack please go and get her," I said, coming to my senses a little, "tell her all is well and bring her in."

"Oh, no!" Gwen stopped short when she saw Sir Edward.

"What is it?" I asked.

"Is he...?"

"I believe we met in Maidstone," Sir Edward said.

"That was you?" I could see embarrassment overtake my friend. "I'm so sorry, we believed..."

"I am a friend," Sir Edward declared, "though I believe I was taken for a foe."

"Are you... quite well?" Gwen asked in a whisper.

Sir Edward threw back his head and laughed. "Quite well, thank you, though I do not believe such was your intention." Gwen's face glowed pink. "An honest mistake, young Gwen, and in defence of your friend." He stood and bowed to her, only adding to her discomfort. "Please come and sit, I gather my family has much to thank you for."

"Your family?" Gwen said, glancing in my direction.

I gulped at the air trying to calm myself. "This is Sir Edward, my late husband's brother by marriage," I explained, wondering whether I should wish I had not told Gwen of my true identity - having done so I had implicated her in my deception.

"A brother both in name and affection, if not in blood," Sir Edward added.

Sir Edward raised a finger and a waiter ran over and took an order of hot chocolate for Gwen and myself.

I fought to arrange my thoughts. "I believe you have been to see my friend Margaret," I said.

"Yes, it was her idea to give me the piece of material to help me track you down. And it worked - here you are."

"So..." So, I had to put my story into words yet again - my story, Hope's story, entwined and interwoven as they were, but Sir Edward could read my thoughts it seemed, for he interrupted me.

"I have heard of the terrible occurrence at your farm in West Penton, your..." he hesitated before the words, "your marriage, your cruel treatment at the hands of Sir Neville, and of your son, my nephew." I could see determination cross Sir

Edward's face. "This is a family matter and I am here to help and to protect you while you seek your annulment."

"I cannot presume upon your kindness," I said. "You owe me nothing – we have never met until this moment."

"I trust I would assist any woman in your position," Sir Edward said, "and you are of my brother's family."

Even as I tried to resist the lure of allowing myself to depend upon Sir Edward I felt the muscles in my back and shoulders release a little as the burden I had been carrying for so long was lifted from me. Sir Edward, I thought, would find no load too heavy to bear; he was a soldier - he had a soldier's valour.

"I see I have upset you," Sir Edward said.

"No, no, please do not think that. I am grateful for any help you can give us."

"I went to West Penton not merely to seek out a brother after a long absence but to ask him why he had not replied to my letters, the letters I had sent him months before," Sir Edward broke off, "telling Henry his father had died."

"I am sorry to hear it."

"I could not believe Henry was so angry with his father he would refuse to reply to such a letter."

"Indeed, he would not." I recalled Henry's unhappiness at his father's refusal to meet Hope, or even to discuss the matter of marriage with him. I remembered his anger, his defiance, his "Let him disown me, I shall make my own way. I would rather be a happy farmer than a miserable slave to my father's every wish," but I knew one hesitant step by his father in his direction would have been answered by Henry running to his father's side: there had been anger between them, not hatred. "He had hoped for a reconciliation," I said.

"Squire Ashton felt the same before he died. He forgave Henry for marrying without his consent. He had been angered and sought to punish Henry but he thought to see him again, to bring him home, with you at his side, of course. He did not know his time had run its course and he had left it too late."

"Too late, indeed. You must forgive me, I was unwell for a long time, and in my distress, did not wish to send word to Squire Ashton. I especially did not want him to learn of my condition or think I wanted anything from him, knowing how misjudged he considered our marriage." I found I was speaking as Hope now, as my sister would have spoken had she been in my place instead of the other way around. We were working people, we did not expect to be plucked to safety, away from any disaster that overtook us.

We sat in silence awhile, our thoughts too loud in our ears for the conversation to continue. "Ashton died some seven months ago," Sir Edward began, speaking quietly so it seemed it was just him and I in this large room. "I had wished to take the sad news to Henry myself - but a commission from the king, one that was oft-extended, kept me far away until finally I knew I must delay no longer. I wrote to Henry at Hamblemere Farm but by then Oliver Whitby had been installed there; he could not read the letter, but gave it to Sir Neville."

A gasp escaped me. "Sir Neville knew!"

"He knew all right, even before the letter, and it was I who told him. I came across him on my travels and we spent an evening together, I spoke to him out of respect and friendship for his older son, Robert, a brother soldier. I told him then of the death of Ashton and he withheld that information from you." A deep line creased Sir Edward's brow and there was anger in his eyes. "He knew that as Henry's widow you were not without support in this harsh world. He is the vilest of men and will get his comeuppance, believe me." Edward grabbed my hand. "Dear girl, if you will permit, I shall help you obtain the annulment of your marriage and the return of your son."

The sudden smile that lit his face made me feel all this was possible, not only possible but within reach.

Chapter 32

As we emerged from the coffee house I stepped into a ray of sunlight piercing between the chimneystack of one house and the gable roof of another; it lit my face so fiercely I was forced to close my eyes for a moment against its glare. I exhaled, then breathed deeply of the horse-manure, river-mud, rotting-vegetable, human-sweat filled air, and it was sweet to me. When I opened my eyes Gwen's excited face was before me, the wisps of hair escaping from her hood a glowing halo.

"We'll be all right."

"Yes."

We had informed Sir Edward we were staying at the Blue Anchor and he said he would meet us there upon the morrow. When we collected our dresses there was a note awaiting us from Hannah, giving the address of her friend's property and confirming there was a room available.

Childlike we swung the ribbon-handled parcels containing our dresses to and fro as we walked back to the inn but I found my pleasure could not be as unalloyed as Gwen's - all my dealings with Sir Edward must perforce be coloured by my deceit.

I put out my hand to open the door beneath the Blue Anchor sign, but stopped, my hand stilled as I heard a horse whinny. The sunny day disappeared and we were back, in flimsy dresses, rags tied about our feet, in the snow on the farm, standing beside Cassie's stable. I crept forward and poked my head around the corner of the building. Gwen made to follow me but I put out my hand to bar her way.

"What's the matter?"

"Quiet!" I hissed, "Cassie's in the courtyard." I took a step forward and gazed up at the window of our room; a figure passed by on the inside; it stopped and stood to angle something towards the light. The lanky black hair fell back revealing the face I knew too well - Skinner.

We moved out of sight under the balcony and stealthily made our way to the other end of the inn. Fear flooded through us as if it was our natural state - whispering and tiptoeing, hearts pounding, sweat breaking out on our brows, ready to run for our lives. We mounted a few steps of the back stairs and waited until we heard the door of our room open and close, followed by heavy footsteps making for the stairs at the other end. As soon as we heard him start down the steps we scurried forward, silent, close to the wall, like mice. We both let out a long breath as we heard the clatter of Cassie's hoofs as Skinner rode away.

"How did he find us?" That was the question racing through our brains, Gwen the first to put it into words.

"An inn beside the river near London Bridge - we felt too safe, we were stupid."

"He might be back, we have to go, don't we? We can't wait for Sir Edward." Gwen gathered our things together as she spoke. "Oh no, we don't know where Sir Edward is staying, we didn't ask."

"Just hurry," I said sharply, trying to hide my own despair at such a foolish error. "What was Skinner doing so long in our room? What was it he was looking at?" A moment earlier, when I had thrown a shawl into my bag I had seen my document pouch safely inside where I had left it but now I burrowed down to bring it to the surface. It was too light in my hand and fell open – empty, the letters from Margaret and the Reverend Wilkins, the letters to put forward my case for annulment, all gone.

I had no time for the tears threatening my eyes, I blinked them away: I needed anger, not self-pity. We must get away. I found the piece of paper the shopkeeper had handed me lying on the bed where I had dropped it in my haste. "We have to go to the place Hannah has found for us," I said. "Wherever it is." On the stairs once more, I tore off the blank bottom half of Hannah's note to write a line for Edward explaining we were going to stay at a friend's house, giving the address. At the door I handed the note to the porter, explaining as I gave him a shilling he should hand it to Sir Edward when he called upon us in the morning. He would receive another shilling from him for keeping the note safe. He must tell the mistress we had gone. Nervously we headed off towards the bridge.

We queued impatiently on the slope leading to the gatehouse, constantly checking about us, recalling, as we inched forward, what Jenny Grey had told us with great pleasure - it once displayed the heads of traitors on spikes.

The bridge was nearly as busy at night as it was during the day. We struggled through the throng with our bags and parcels in the evening gloom. The houses on either side leaned in over the roadway, blocking out the sky and now in my despair, felt menacing. If it had not been for the candles and lanterns in the shops it would have been impossible to see our way. Gone now was my earlier admiration when I had marvelled at how each floor hung over the lower one by a couple of feet as the buildings rose above us five floors and more. I pondered if the bridge had been wider how many more storeys there could have been before it all came tumbling down like the tower of Babel.

The address on the piece of paper was The Cygnets, Swann Lane. We knew it was in the city but on nearing the north end of the bridge in the gathering darkness we still had no idea where to go. Not wishing to speak to any stranger in the street or waste the precious minutes holding us ahead of Skinner, we hurried back as far as Madam Blanche's and entered seeking the owner.

"Well, that was quick - I would have bet against it, but what do I know?" the woman at the desk said, though I knew not what she meant. "Swann Lane be five minutes from the bridge. Take a sedan chair, it'll save you getting lost in the dark - and you'll be able to afford it."

There was a clutter of chairs waiting by the north entrance of the bridge. I took a deep breath, stood as tall and calmly as I could, and gave the address. A smile passed between the men and I guessed we were about to be charged excessively for our journey but it was a matter beyond my concern at that moment.

"It's like a privy with cushions," Gwen commented as she stepped inside.

It was a strange and not particularly comfortable ride but I was thankful for the anonymity it gave us. When the jogging and footsteps ceased and the chair came to rest on the ground once more I emerged before a pair of smart three storey Elizabethan houses with the sign of an arching young swan before it, properties with front gardens and room for coaches. Paid, the men and chairs disappeared into the night.

"They've taken our money and left us at the wrong place," Gwen complained. "This can't be Swann Lane."

"But it is," I replied, pointing out the street sign.

"Well, does this seem a cheap lodging place to you?"

"Let's wait and see, anywhere out of the way will be good with Skinner on our trail." As we made our way up to the door of the house it opened unexpectedly and two laughing young women emerged, their silk gowns of grey and dark blue reflecting the evening colours. We stood aside for them to pass, shimmering apparitions glowing in the dancing light from the torches flaring either side of the door. We turned back and found the bright eyes of a plump maid staring in our direction. "May I help you?"

I stepped forward. "We were... recommended... by Hannah." I realised as I spoke I did not know her last name. "We have come about the room."

I saw the girl's face clear. "Miss Hope and Miss Gwen? We were expecting you tomorrow."

"I'm sorry."

"It is no matter, do come in." The blazing fire in the large hall was a welcoming sight; we stood beside it for a moment, rubbing our chilled hands. "Miss Hannah has arranged rooms on the first floor for you. I will tell Miss Georgia you are here. Please be seated while I fetch her."

"Upstairs? Surely not," I began, knowing there was nothing but a basement room we could afford in such a house but the young woman had walked away.

"Hannah has deceived us," Gwen muttered, "how can this be cheaper than the Blue Anchor?"

"Not that we can go back there," I put in as a door to our left opened and a lady with black ringlets framing her face came towards us, smiling, her hair impressively dressed with cream feathers matching her satin dress. The maid followed her and waited patiently.

"I'm Miss Georgia, I am pleased to meet you both. You have arrived at a busy time, so let me show you the rooms. And allow me to arrange for some mulled wine, the evening has become so cold. Marie, fetch some wine and bring it upstairs."

We followed Georgia as she glided up the steps. She opened a tall dark door. "Miss Hope," she said, then opening the opposite door, "Miss Gwen."

"Two rooms?"

"Of course."

I followed Gwen as she took tentative steps into the room. "I've never had a room to myself," she whispered, "and a room like this?" The room was almost as fine as mine had been at Wilderness Hall with a large bed and a huge wardrobe in which our few belongings could easily be lost. "Let's see your room."

We passed a full-length looking glass on the landing, a luxury I had never seen before. We stood in front of it and laughed at our reflections: was that us? - thin, a little dishevelled after our journey, our cloaks engulfing us, holding our bags and leaning towards each other as if afraid to be parted.

"You can have my room if yours isn't as nice," Gwen said.

"Oh, Gwen!" I hugged her closely and we followed Marie as she carried a jug of wine and a plate of biscuits into an identical chamber.

"It's so lovely!" Gwen sat on the bed sweeping her hand across the quilt, revelling in its softness.

"They will do then," Georgia smiled as Marie left the room.

"Oh yes," I replied frowning. "But how much?"

"How much?"

Georgia's laughter rang out but she checked herself. "Talk to Hannah later," she said. "Well now, why not unpack, the evening is still young and a party is about to begin next door, you must come. I will ask Marie to come upstairs in a few minutes to help you dress. Hannah said you both bought the most becoming gowns so will not feel out of place."

"But…"

"No buts. Hannah would not forgive me if I did not bring you along to meet the other ladies who live here. It will be fun." She smiled. "There will be some important people here this evening, possibly a few lawyers. A chance for you to meet them, Hannah said you were seeking legal advice. Oh, and there will be food served later if you are hungry."

She hurried out of the door leaving us regarding each other in amazement.

"Do you think they have got us mixed up with two other girls?" Gwen asked, kicking off her shoes.

"Called Gwen and Hope? I don't understand but at least we should be safe here."

Nervousness and fatigue had made us both thirsty and I poured two glasses of wine.

"Perhaps Hannah thought we were well off having bought the gowns and other bits and pieces. Anyway, we have the money from the box sewn into our garments so we can afford a few nights."

"To Sir Edward," Gwen said, and I smiled - if we had Skinner on our trail, we had Sir Edward on our side.

We had eaten nothing since the pasty on London Bridge so quickly devoured the biscuits and more wine as we smoothed out our skirts on the bed. We washed before putting on our new chemises. The sensuous feel surprised me as my first silk undergarment moved over my body.

"Makeup! Makeup!" Gwen chanted, diving into her bag. "We should put on some makeup."

"I don't know how."

"Can't be so difficult," Gwen decided, pouring another glass of wine, "not if you can milk a cow."

"And we can milk a cow." We picked up the pots Hannah had insisted we buy the previous day, trying to recall what was supposed to go where. "Too much rouge, Gwen," I laughed.

"Me?" Gwen almost shouted, "See yourself!" She gave me the hand glass and I saw a pantomime clown staring back at me. We laughed and glanced at each other and ourselves again until tears started to roll down our faces causing our makeup to run in stripes, only to heighten our laughter further.

"Mon Dieu!" cried Marie as she entered the room and we collapsed on the bed giggling. "Too much wine. Go wash your faces. The wine has made you so flushed you won't need rouge on your cheeks, just a little on your lips and between your breasts." We were puzzled. "You both have much to learn, the colour will make them appear deeper than they are, trust me, so much more alluring."

We caught each other's eye and burst out laughing again. "Alluring?" cried Gwen.

"Well, we must feed you up first, you are too thin at the moment, but with a little help…" She cupped her hands and made a lifting movement. Once our make-up was washed off

Marie set about showing us how it should be applied lightly; she brushed our hair and curled it with fierce tongs; our hands, an apparent disgrace, were covered with lotions, and rose water was dabbed at our throats. We slipped into our beautiful full skirts and tightly-laced bodices, before placing silk pumps upon our feet. Marie walked us back to the full-length mirror; we seemed hardly to be related to the two girls we had seen earlier - here stood two elegant young women, so changed on the outside I could but wonder how they could be the same within.

"Now, away with you both, go next door and enjoy the party, shoo, shoo," and she ushered us to the door. "Go - enjoy yourselves."

We quickly descended the stairs and out into the cold air, hurrying next door, where the gates were open wide and flaming touches flared this way and that in the wind. We could hear music and laughter as we approached. Several coaches lined the roadway outside. As the door opened a sedan chair could be seen coming down the lane.

"What now?" Gwen asked.

Chapter 33

"I don't know." Gwen stopped at the door; the room ahead was brightly lit, filled with the sound of swirling silk gowns, female laughter and strong male voices.

"It will be all right," I whispered, entranced.

"Of course it will!" Hannah slipped between us and wafted us forward. This was the room of my dreams - the room conjured in my imagination from my mother's stories of being a maid in the squire's house. Once she had accompanied the family to some great manor and her description of the ball had haunted my imagination for a long time. That evening she had been unable to do more than peep through the door, but I was within, I was one of the lovely ladies dressed in silk, waving like so many daffodils floating in the passing breeze of a gentleman's attention. Crystal candleholders trembled with light, crimson curtains were gathered thickly beside wide windows, notes from a harpsichord flitted in the air and bright flowers flowed from vases all about the room. Every glance showed me something beautiful. This was what had been missing from Wilderness Hall I thought, remembering how solidly masculine the house had been; rich but heavy, weighed down by its wealth.

"You both look wonderful." Hannah appraised us each in turn. "As I am sure you know." I saw Gwen's concerned eyes alight upon the bold black spot placed a little to the left of Hannah's mouth moving with her words and smiles. Her dress was cut away to a level that was surely beyond fashion. "Here, take these." Hannah handed us each a glass of wine from a tray on a side table and I watched as Gwen swallowed hers in one gulp. We were steered across the floor towards an antechamber where a side of beef sat between baked fish, their iridescent scales glowing like our silk gowns. "Come meet the others. Sarah," she called softly and a young woman with bright blue eyes and curling pale hair came over to us.

"Miss Hannah?"

"This is Gwen and Hope, new to London, you must make them feel at home."

Hannah moved away, taking some gentleman's arm, switching on a beguiling smile.

"Is this your first?" Sarah asked, her voice soft and girlish.

"First?"

"Place."

I nodded though I did not comprehend the question.

"They treat you well here - as long as you obey the rules, of course."

"What rules?" Gwen broke in, her words a little slurred. "We haven't heard of any rules."

"Tomorrow," Sarah said.

"We just wanted a place to stay," Gwen continued.

"Ah, yes." It seemed Sarah was recalling some past event. "There is nowhere better than Miss Georgina's and Miss Hannah's, not really." She gave a sad smile. "Do you want something to eat?"

We were hungry and the food was sumptuous, though some we hardly recognised as food at all, so decorated was it. We each took a plate and were served a slice of beef.

"What's in the back room?" I asked seeing a young man being ushered in, the door quickly closing behind him.

"Oh, things like gambling," Sarah replied, "but you have to be invited."

"Is it a regular thing then, if they keep a room just for that?"

Sarah seemed discomforted by the question. "Yes, but you need not worry, there is never any trouble, Hannah and Georgina are very careful about their guests."

I heard a muffled sound beside me, a choking, gasping noise. "Gwen!"

"Quickly, this way." I took Gwen's arm and followed Sarah through doors and passages, leaving the splendid rooms behind us, descending into a dim kitchen with a flagstone floor. "Here."

A bucket was placed before Gwen and as her hands flew away from her mouth a spout of yellow liquid shot forth. "Sorry," she mumbled as she was sick again.

Sarah grabbed a rag and wiped Gwen's face, its rosy complexion replaced with a deathly pallor. "It's probably the wine - if she is not used to it."

"She isn't, I don't suppose she has ever had more than a glass at some celebration at Wilder…" I began but knew I had drunk a similar amount and must take care to mind my words.

"Sit down, sit down here," Sarah said, leading Gwen to an old wooden chair. "I must go back, I will be missed; you should come with me."

"No, I can't leave Gwen."

"Yes, go," Gwen said, "I'm feeling better now. I just need a minute."

Sarah took my hand. "Come now."

I was pulled away. "If you are sure," I called to Gwen. "I'll be back in a few minutes."

I focused my mind on the route to the hall so I wouldn't get lost on my way back to the kitchen, wondering why Sarah was so pressing about our return. We had but stepped into the room when a gentleman, well-dressed and portly, came towards us and I saw his plump fingers slide over the pink satin of Sarah's dress and around her waist. She smiled.

"I hear you are new to this establishment, fresh from the country," a voice addressed me. Before me stood a tall bewigged gentleman. His hand reached out to me.

"Excuse me, just a moment," I said, my voice a hoarse whisper. I manoeuvred between the pretty women and the wealthy men and ran towards the kitchen and Gwen.

Gwen was still seated on the kitchen chair, pale, and by the light of the one candle on the table, I could make out the course of tears on her face.

"Are you ill?" I cried.

Gwen shook her head wearily. "It's Hannah and Georgina. I heard them, outside in the passageway. I heard them talking about us."

"About us?"

"Georgina said she had three bids for me and two for you, the best price was offered for me if she could confirm I was... a virgin."

"What?"

"'A good night's work,' Hannah said." Gwen lifted her distorted face to mine. "She said she was sure we would join her girls when we realised we would be better off with her than working the streets ourselves."

"Working the streets!"

Gwen wiped her face with her arm and coughed. "She said she never believed our yarn of being in London to see a

279

lawyer; she told Georgina she had seen us in the coffee house with a fine gentleman. She said you ingratiated yourself so quickly you were obviously well used to the business."

"How dare she?" Anger coursed through my body, my hand went to my so-carefully arranged hair and pulled out the flower placed by my ear; I dropped it on the floor and stamped on it. We had been evilly deceived by Hannah but I knew my foolishness was equally to blame. I eased Gwen to her feet and supported her with my arm. "We must get to our rooms."

The laughter and music coming from the salon sounded ugly to me now but at least it covered our footsteps as we hurried out of the kitchen and through the alleyway between the two houses.

Marie opened the front door when I knocked. "Mon Dieu," she cried when she saw Gwen, obviously her reaction to any unexpected event; she tutted as she helped me take her up the stairs. I helped Gwen out of her gown and into her everyday dress and did the same myself. We lay on the bed waiting till there was a hint of light in the sky. I packed the rest of our belongings and gazed about the room one last time wishing things had been different but I knew now what I should have understood before: this comfort came at a price, one we would not pay. We left the house without a sound, leaving a crown to cover our board - I could not bear to be indebted to such a place.

The chill of the night air awakened us like a cold bath. In our old clothes and cloaks we were able to pass unnoticed by the coachmen and sedan chair carriers. We did not pause until we had left Swann Lane a dozen turns behind us.

"We must keep out of the way for now," I said, "till we are able to mingle among the early risers on the street." We found a corner between two grimy walls and stood silently together. Gwen held her head and closed her eyes. I had been intoxicated too, and not merely by the wine - I was more foolish and more venal than I had ever thought. A pretty dress, an elegant house, had turned my head: my mother would have been ashamed of my foolishness. And I had led Gwen into danger once again – not the ugly danger of Skinner but a seductive danger hiding behind the silken mask Jenny Grey had warned of.

We wandered along the riverside not sure where to go.

"Oh lord," I cried, suddenly horrified, "what will Sir Edward think when he receives our note, I have given him Hannah's address – and he will find a whorehouse."

Gwen reacted as if she had been slapped in the face. "And he will find us gone and have no idea where we are."

Tiredness overwhelmed me, my legs buckled and I slumped down on to a low wall. Gwen sat down next to me. We were alone and chilled and lost. But if I had learned one thing from my experiences it was self-pity was a crippling emotion. I banged my fists against the crown of my head to wake myself up. "We will have to get a message to him somehow," I said, "perhaps via Jack, though we dare not cross the bridge ourselves, not with Skinner after us." I tried to think, though the wine was still clogging my mind, like sand in a cog; at last a decisive thought got through. "First, we have to find ourselves a room and quickly, then if we can get a message to Jack he can tell Sir Edward where to find us."

"Do you think the priest on the ferry would know somewhere?"

"Father Joseph? Gwen, you're right. What was the name of his church - St Mary's something?"

"St Mary Colechurch, but do you think he would help?"

"We won't know unless we try."

The church was close to the corner of Old Jewry and Cheapside. It was an odd building balanced on a mound with steps leading up to the entrance. We made our way to the top and found the old priest had just finished an early service. "Well, bless me," he chuckled, "I know I invited you to come and see the chapel but I never expected to see you this early in the day. Is everything all right with your aunt?"

"Aunt?" I had almost forgotten the story we had told. "It's not that. We need your help to find somewhere safe to stay. Can you help us?" I was unable to stop the desperation in my voice. "We can't go to an inn. Please, Father Joseph, we need a place, just a single room, we can pay." I ceased speaking not knowing how much more I should say, but the words "We are in danger," escaped me.

"Good Lord, of course I will help. Just let me think. Yes," his face lit up, "at the back of the church there are some alms houses," he pointed over his shoulder, "just a few alleys away. Potter, that's her name, our good mother Potter - her son has just gone on his first voyage and she could do with a few extra pennies. Yes, I am sure it will suit - *she* will be happy," he smiled, his impish, gleeful smile, "and *you* will be happy, now let's get some breakfast. Come to the vicarage. I will see you are safe, never fear. But first, allow me to show you the small chapel where Thomas a Becket was baptised."

I could not refrain from smiling to myself at the almost childlike joy of Father Joseph as he led us forward into the smallest of the church's three chapels. "Here," he said, "baptised in this very font, I am sure there is no doubt of it, is it not beautiful?" Gwen and I stood for a moment and made murmurings of appreciation before he led us to his home.

The breakfast was good enough though I could barely eat it, so tense was I at the prospect of telling my story yet again; it seemed like some ancient legend growing more distant with each repetition. Once the housekeeper had left the room I told the good father of my marriage and the loss of my son and all that had befallen us since.

"I can see you are in sore need, my children, though I hope you know annulments and divorces are rarer than hen's teeth." He heard my sharp intake of breath. "The level of deceit will stand in your favour," he reassured me, "I will do all I can to help."

"And we need to get word to Sir Edward, he will know what we should do now the documents have been stolen."

"I take it you cannot venture far yourselves but never fear I shall be going over to the bridge tomorrow as we have a church there, St. Magnus Martyr, and I can take a message for you to young Jack, let's pray he is still in contact with Sir Edward."

We pulled up our hoods and shielded our faces as we followed Father Joseph out into the noisy, crowded streets once more. The mound upon which the church stood was pierced with shops and a lively tavern. "A very convenient arrangement," he chuckled, "its cellar is part of the crypt. This is one church that will never run short of communion wine if you take my meaning." With relief we followed as he guided us along two very narrow alleys, neither of which was wide enough to take a coach, stopping outside a tiny terraced cottage in sweetly-named Angel Row.

Though surprised at having unexpected guests, mother Potter, a tiny but vigorous woman of later years, welcomed us, saying she would be glad of the company and for a few pence a day she would provide our meals as well as a bed.

We followed her up the narrow steps to the room on the left. "You have this room – the bed is larger - and I shall have my dear Will's room." We regarded the bed with its pot beneath, the rough walls, the homemade chair, the basin and its accompanying pitcher containing water for a morning wash. "A home," I muttered, "a real home. Thank you, mother Potter."

There was more than a day to wait until Father Joseph would go to try to find Jack; calm, domestic days such as Gwen and I had never before passed together. We sat in the tiny parlour in the cottage in Angel Row happily mending ancient linen - darning a hole here, sewing a hem there, pausing to reflect on the treasure that was peace.

Chapter 34

"I've found them!"

It was evening, the last rays of sunlight retreating across the floor, and the contentment of the day had been replaced by tension as Gwen and I had waited for news. We had both been holding a slice of bread smothered with honey when the door burst open.

Father Joseph had not waited to knock or be ushered in; he shot through the door and with a step was halfway across the room, removing his hat as he did so. Mother Potter came in to see the cause of the commotion but upon seeing her visitor tactfully retired.

"I've found them," he repeated.

"So the boys were there - at the baker's?"

"Yes, well no, not exactly. I got there as early as I could following the evening service and they were nowhere to be seen but I asked the chestnut seller - wonderful chestnuts - I bought some but gave them to the boys - and he pointed down the alleyway - so tight it was I could feel the walls brush my shoulders - and there they were, huddled together, said they could feel the warmth of the oven through the wall."

"And?"

"And I told them who I was - they know me of course but it was dark - and that I was there on your behalf." Father Joseph fell onto a chair wiping sweat from his brow. "Oh, forgive me, I have been hurrying. The boys have seen Sir Edward - he went to them, indeed, saying he had been

285

searching for you as you had departed the Blue Anchor and left no word for him."

"But there was a note."

"He did not receive it. No matter, Jack will find Sir Edward tomorrow and ask him to come to St Mary's at ten of the morning and tell him to make sure he is not followed on his way."

"Tomorrow," I murmured.

"It may not be tomorrow," Father Joseph corrected me. "I said I would be there every day at ten."

But tomorrow it was. As the morning hours slipped past I found myself becoming more excited, more anxious. Gwen seemed content, there with her sewing, but my needle failed to obey me and I pricked my finger more than once. At last there was a fierce knocking at the door answered by mother Potter.

"Father Joseph has sent me," I heard the voice declare, its tone both familiar and urgent.

I dropped my work and stepped forward as good mother Potter waved him inside before she took herself out into the street, closing the door behind her.

"There you are, I thought I had lost you."

Sir Edward's words echoed my thoughts exactly.

Gwen stood beside me and we both curtsied. I did not know whether I should wait for Sir Edward to ask us to be seated, or if, as his host I should speak first.

He sensed my confusion. "We should waste no time on ceremony," he said, "please tell me, are you both well?"

"We are." For a moment the reply seemed to be an end unto itself, to settle everything.

"You saw Father Joseph, Sir Edward?" Gwen questioned into the silence.

"Indeed, I did. He was most careful; after giving me directions he kept watch from the church to ensure Skinner was not on my tail. When I reached the corner he signalled he had seen nothing untoward. He is concerned for you."

"He has been very kind."

"He told me Skinner appeared at the Blue Anchor, that you were lucky to escape and you left a letter for me. I asked if there was a message of the landlady, as formidable a woman as I have ever had the acquaintance of," Gwen gave a sudden laugh, "but she said no, I asked the porter also but nothing was forthcoming."

"Then the porter was false to us, I paid him a shilling to give you a note saying where we had gone." I wondered how much more I should say but Gwen broke in.

"Perhaps we should thank the porter," she said, "seeing what happened."

I saw the question in Sir Edward's eyes and resolved not to flinch. "We, Gwen and I, had been given an address where we might stay but found it was a house of ill repute," I hurried the words, "and we left immediately we understood the nature of the place, with no harm done."

Sir Edward burst forth a cheerful roar of laughter. "'With no harm done', what adventures you two are having."

"It did not seem so amusing at the time," I commented.

"I shall never walk down Swann Lane again as long as I live." The pain of what might have been was still strong in Gwen's heart.

"Ah, Swann Lane - it has a certain reputation. Now explain to me more of what the good father said, about losing your documents."

"Skinner took them - the letter from Margaret, the document from the Reverend Wilkins at the Archbishop's Palace in Maidstone, everything I needed, everything that might help explain…"

"The porter," said Sir Edward, "must have been the one who gave Skinner the key to your room, no wonder your message went astray. All is not lost. Those documents are essential to your cause, it means I must return to West Penton and to Maidstone to obtain fresh copies for you. It is a pity, it will take me away."

"For how long?" I asked, my voice wavering; London seemed a safer place knowing he was in it.

"Just a few days. And, oh Lord, I have arranged for a meeting for you with the lawyer for tomorrow at noon. I found John Nichols' office at the Inner Temple and spoke to him. He is prepared to take a deposition from you both and have it scribed ready for your signatures and he wanted to study the papers we no longer have."

"We could still go to the meeting," I suggested.

"Alone?"

"Perhaps Father Joseph could arrange sedan chairs for us. Skinner may well believe we have left London as without the documents we would have little chance of proceeding."

"If he has the note from the Blue Anchor inn he will be looking for us at Swann Lane," Gwen observed.

"The sooner I leave the sooner I shall come back to you," Sir Edward said, bending to kiss my hand. "Miss Gwen." He bowed to her as he took his leave. "When I return, I shall go to Father Joseph in case you have moved on. I shall not lose you again."

The following morning Gwen and I prepared with care, putting on our new dresses, the dresses that had so nearly brought us to disaster; I must become as close to being Lady Lattimer as fancy clothes could take me. Gwen brushed and arranged my hair as fashionably as she was able and tucked her own hair beneath a cap and wore a shawl and apron to give her more the appearance of my maid. We took the ordered sedan chairs from the church to The Strand and the Inns of Court. Carried in my curtained chamber I shuddered to think of all that hung on this forthcoming meeting. "Rarer than hen's teeth," Father Joseph had said speaking of an annulment. Surely no-one could believe mine had been a true marriage, I had never been a wife, merely a chattel, a vessel; but for many, too many, that was exactly what marriage meant. Mine was but an extreme case.

The lawyer's office reminded me of the one at Maidstone; lawyers it seemed existed amid piles of papers, books, and scrolls, but the man in its midst was very different - a man of thirty or so with bushy eyebrows, dressed in dove-grey robes and a powdered wig.

"Lady Lattimer," he said, "or would you prefer me to call you Mistress Ashton?" I knew he had been well briefed by Sir Edward so I might feel more comfortable.

I took the proffered seat, Gwen taking a seat at the back of the room as arranged, though I sorely wanted her by my side. A scribe sat, black-robed, a little to one side at a small table, his head lowered as if trying to be as inconspicuous as possible.

"Will Sir Edward be joining us?" the lawyer asked.

"Sir Edward has urgent business to attend to and shall be away for a few days." My voice shook a little. I took a deep breath to steady myself. "He suggested we should start the preliminary work and he will accompany…" I found I wanted to say *us*, "accompany *me* here for my next visit and provide the documents he told you of."

I had thought the lawyer had a harsh air but now, now that he regarded me from beneath those eyebrows I found bright, inquisitive brown eyes and felt a little less afraid, but what he asked of me made me shiver. "In that case we may as well start with the details of the raid, your wedding and the journey to Wilderness Hall."

I tried to detach myself from the voice telling the story of my rape and Sir Neville's courtship, the wedding and its non-consummation and my separation from my child. Gwen stood to give her statement of events. I was grateful Sir Edward was not present, I did not believe I could have spoken of such intimate matters if he had been in the room. I felt humiliated; I kept my eyes low - like the scribe, I was trying to disappear.

Tired and drained as I was I preferred to walk a little in the fresh air before seeking a chair to take us on our journey back - perhaps the smart breeze could blow away the foul flavour the words had left in my mouth.

"That was terrible," I said.

"It's over," Gwen replied gently.

"I wish that were the case, I fear it is only the beginning."

I was lost in thought and almost walked into a man who had stopped to pick something from the ground. At the same time I was aware of an "Oh," from Gwen behind me and with a push at my waist I felt myself shoved into an alley. Suffocating darkness descended as a sack was thrust over my head; I almost choked on dust and the smell of rotting cabbages as my feet were lifted off the ground. From the cry behind me I knew they had Gwen too. I kicked out but missed my aim. Strong arms held me in an iron grip as I was carried along the alley. I opened my mouth to yell but the sackcloth filled it. I heard the heavy clink of chains and horses moving in their harness.

"Quickly!" a voice commanded.

Skinner!

"Get them in the wagon."

So, he had us after all.

Chapter 35

I continued to kick out at the man holding me so tightly but despair filled me, draining me of energy, of hope. I managed a cry, more of pain than for help, and was struck across the face, the gritty sack biting into my skin. I was lifted, thrown, crashing against the floor of some sort of wagon as it lurched forward, my breath being forced out of my lungs. Gwen landed beside me, almost atop me, a gasp of shock uniting us, our cries muffled. I was pushed over and heard the rattle of chains as my arms were pulled forward so iron shackles could be fastened around my wrists. My legs were tied together a little above the ankles with sharp rope to stop me lashing out.

He had us in his power once more. The days and nights of moving, hiding, believing we might have fortune on our side with the warning signs and sightings that had allowed us to evade him, had come to nought; now he held us fast, at his mercy, though of that I knew he had none.

As the wagon moved off I manoeuvred myself on to my side. I could hear Gwen kicking against the cart as best she could to draw attention to our plight.

"Thought you had got the better of me, eh?" jeered Skinner, "with a false trail leading to that whore house? I had only to keep watch at the lawyer's office," he laughed, "a few coins to the lawyer's clerk was all it needed to find out when you would be there."

Of course, he had the letter addressed to the lawyer - I had not thought how he could make such use of the information.

I found my breath, my strength. "Murderer!" I yelled.

"Murderer?" I heard a voice echo with alarm.

"Shut up if you want to be paid," Skinner hissed back.

"Murderer," I repeated. "Help! Help!" I knew our stifled cries were lost in the sounds of the city; words were weak weapons but all we had. "Murderer!"

"On!" Skinner urged as the wagon slowed and I heard the crack of a whip and the horses pushed forward. They were brought to a shuddering stop a moment later as a clear cry bellowed forth.

"Stop in the name of the king."

I shook with relief within my chains. "We're saved," I whispered to Gwen. The wagon rocked and I knew the men beside us had jumped off, no doubt hoping to disappear into the crowd before they could be apprehended.

"Let them go, we've got the ringleader," a strong voice commanded. "You, you there, why are these women hooded and chained like criminals?"

Relief allowed me to breathe more easily beneath my sack. I opened my mouth to thank whoever had come to our rescue but Skinner spoke first.

"It's all right, sergeant, I have papers."

"Murder, murder!" Gwen cried beside me.

"He's stealing them away, sir." It was Jack's young sweet voice.

A snort of contempt came from Skinner. "Stealing them away, eh? 'Tis the other way about, I'm taking them back. Collecting two runaways and returning them to the farm where they belong."

"No, no sir," I yelled, moving round as best I could, hoping I was facing the officer. "The boy is right."

Skinner brazenly held his ground. I heard the soft hiss of paper being unrolled. "Thieves, as I said, here's the reward poster."

"Let me see," the voice commanded.

"Lies," I protested.

"Silence!" the voice insisted.

I held my breath.

"It's all in order." The voice dismissed Skinner. "You can be on your way."

"No, no!" Tears fell down my face and the sack was being drawn into my mouth as I gasped for air, choking me further.

Jack's voice, light and childish, called out. "It's not so, sir, he is abducting Lady Lattimer and her maid. Sir Edward told me to watch out for them both while he's away."

"You again," yelled Skinner. "It's all nonsense. I caught this boy picking my pocket earlier and this is how he repays me for letting him go with just a cuff to the head." I heard the crack of the whip as Skinner stirred the horses into movement.

"No. Don't believe him," Jack shouted again as the wagon began to move. "He's a lying villain. Sir Edward will explain all."

"Halt!"

"What now?" Skinner hissed in anger.

"That is no way to address an officer of His Majesty's army."

Skinner mumbled something that could have been an apology.

"Boy," the officer said, "Lady this, Sir that, if you are lying it will be a bad day for you."

"I'm not, sir, I'm not lying."

"Corporal, take the reins. Men - fall in around the wagon, they can come with us to Newgate. I am going to make it my work to find the liar here."

The wagon shook as men climbed aboard and to my relief the sacks were loosened and pulled up over our heads. Light dazzled my eyes as I took in deep draughts of fresh air. At last I could see the man who could be our salvation: he was tall, his scarlet uniform and the glinting steel of his sword and those of his men bright, contrasting with the clothes of the group of passers-by who had assembled to watch the proceedings; for them nothing but a distracting few minutes in a humdrum day. Rough hands untied our legs and sat us down but the chains about our wrists remained in place. Gwen and I were grateful at least to be able to see what was happening but were not reassured to see the soldiers were also guarding a group of prisoners, now lined up behind the wagon. Skinner sat upfront still, his demeanour seeming to show a confidence I found troubling.

One of the men lifted Jack into the wagon beside us. "You're coming with us, lad, till this matter is settled."

"But," Jack began, dismay written over his face.

I wanted to reach out and hold his hand but my shackles held me fast. "Bless you, Jack, for saving us."

"Are we saved?" Gwen asked.

"Of course, of course we are. Sir Edward..." But Sir Edward was away, he would be away for days yet, until he was here in person he was but a name, an empty word we could only endeavour to use as a shield.

The wagon and its trail of prisoners continued its course through the city streets with its military escort. "How did you find us?" Gwen asked of Jack and I was pleased to have the distraction from my thoughts.

"Sir Edward asked me to keep an eye on you while he was away," Jack whispered, his eyes darting from the officer to the prisoners and to Gwen and myself, as he tried to comprehend all that was happening to him. "He told me you had an appointment and where it was. I saw you go in to the lawyer's office and waited." His face crumpled with pain and concern. "I must get back to Walter."

"You will, I promise." I regretted the words as soon as I had spoken them; I was in no position to promise anything.

The wagon stopped, caught up in the confusion caused by a cart with a broken wheel in one of the narrow streets. A voice close at hand broke through the general hubbub. "Well, bless my soul if it isn't one of the Courtney girls from Kingsdown, what have you been up to, girl?" My breath caught in my throat to hear my family name. "Never thought to see you in chains. Your father's an honest wheelwright and would be heartbroken to see you like this."

The thought of my father seeing me thus in chains, being pulled through the streets of London, instantly brought tears to my eyes.

The sergeant had heard the words and accosted the man. "You say you know this woman, you are coming with us, we will need your statement."

"Here, here who are you pulling about? I have no time for this," cried the man.

"Unless you want me to arrest you, you had best come quietly."

The man was familiar to me, though I could not recall his name. I found my voice. "Sir, that was before I married and my family moved to West Penton."

"See, the boy is a liar," Skinner jumped in, taking advantage of the man's words. "Lady something or other, my eye. The kid's in their pay, pimping for them and a thief to boot."

"It's not true, don't believe a word he says," I shouted, gesticulating towards Skinner. "He's a liar and a murderer. He killed my family."

"Enough, I will hear no more till later."

My eyes were closed by tears but I felt Gwen's fingers lightly descend over my own. My defiance had melted with the words of the man who knew me from Kingsdown; he did not know my story but told me how we, Gwen and I, seemed to the world: prisoners being dragged to their just punishment. I hung my head in shame.

As we approached the sombre walls of the prison the gates opened and we passed within. The line of prisoners was led away. The sergeant dismounted, entered the guardhouse and called for Skinner to be taken in. We remained in the wagon, united in silence.

A few minutes later we were helped down and led into a bare, echoing room with benches and a desk behind which sat the sergeant.

"Fine dresses - are they stolen, too?" he observed as we stood before him.

"We bought them at Madam Blanche's on the bridge - ask her," I replied, pleased to be so sure of my ground.

"Money from theft or whoring?" Skinner interrupted.

"No, my own money."

"And where did that come from?"

How I could say it was dug up from beneath an ancient tree? "An inheritance."

"You, boy," the sergeant addressed Jack who instantly stood to attention, "I see you have new shoes. Where did you get them?"

Jack looked down at his shoes and then at the sergeant, a puzzled expression on his face. "The market, sir."

"Come forward to the desk and empty your pockets, come on, be quick about it." A startled Jack did as he was ordered and placed three crowns, a shilling, and a few pence on the table. "Where did you get the money?"

"From Sir Edward, for finding Mistress Hope and Gwen for him." His face betrayed his alarm.

"Looking for whores, was he?" Skinner interjected.

"No, sir, nothing like that."

"Sit down over there, lad, no, leave the money," the sergeant commanded. I heard a whimper from Jack as he retracted his hand and walked away, his shoulders slumped.

"Did I not tell you he was a thief? How else would he have so much money on him?" Skinner called from the side of the room.

"Quiet!" The sergeant set his eyes on me. "You, whatever your name is, come forward."

I raised my eyes and stood up tall. "I am Mistress Ashton, I was widowed last year when my husband and family were murdered by Skinner and the men with him. I married Sir Neville Lattimer at Christmas but prefer to be known by the name of Ashton."

"Madam, the only thing I know for certain is you once lived at Kingsdown and your father, Master Courtney, was a humble wheelwright and blacksmith. This," he said waving the paper, "is from the carter we met earlier. It is his completed witness statement to that effect. As we use him for deliveries for the barracks and the quartermaster has known him some years I trust his word."

"My father's name was Courtney and he was a wheelwright, I have never claimed otherwise. But, sir, since that man saw me last much has happened to my family. I married Henry Ashton and my family moved to West Penton. We had not been there long when the farm was raided by renegade soldiers and only I, only I," I repeated as my voice broke, "escaped with my life."

"Courtney, Ashton, Lattimer, I am not interested in who you claim to be, just take that piece of paper and copy it out in your own hand." I copied the note and handed it back to him. He picked up another sheet of paper and compared the two documents. "Enough of your fantasies, woman. I have a note here addressed to a man called Edward, no doubt a follower of yours, a note in your own hand saying you were going to The Cygnets in Swann Lane - a well-known whorehouse. And I believe this lad," the officer's bright eyes caught Jack who winced as if from a blow, "has been pimping for you. I have no doubt you have corrupted this young girl too." His hand waved towards Gwen.

"Don't call me corrupted," Gwen intervened.

"I'll call you whatever the evidence says I may, now be quiet." The officer turned to Skinner. "I have read the documents you gave me signed by these *females,*" he said the word as if it were an accusation in itself, "saying they agreed to work without pay on your farm rather than face justice in court for theft. Take these two runaways back to wherever it is they belong."

Gwen grabbed my hand. "Please Sir, those papers were never signed by us," I implored. "See, those marks, they are not ours, we can write, why would we make a mark?"

Skinner let fly a harsh cackle. "I warned you she was a good liar and so cunning, signing the paper with a mark, pretending to be unable to write her name, that's a good one." He lowered his voice, as if speaking confidentially to the sergeant. "Their families were glad to be rid of them, said they were out of control, unwilling to work." Skinner leant towards the sergeant. "They feared for their morals." He moved away, then added, "This document is witnessed by Sir Neville Lattimer, would you doubt his word?" The officer's attention was all on Skinner now. "They drugged me, nigh on killed me to make their escape, stealing what they could. Hope Courtney is a dangerous woman." Skinner was beginning to strut about the room as his confidence grew. "Sir Neville could have them hung for theft but he is a forgiving man. I have a more secure farm in mind for them now. It is laughable to say that farm girl, fancily dressed though she may be, could be Sir Neville's wife; she, poor demented woman, has been locked up in an asylum and he left with no mother for his young son."

"So that is why she thought she could get away with using the name." The sergeant seemed to believe he had solved the case.

"Father Joseph!" Gwen cried, "Father Joseph of St Mary Colechurch and the lawyer we visited today they know our story, they will speak for us."

I nodded vigorously.

"But what can either tell me other than what you have told him?"

"Please sir, when Sir Edward gets here he will explain all," Gwen tried again. "And he will bring proof from a lawyer that Hope is suing for an annulment of her marriage to Sir Neville and for the return of her son." I understood as she spoke there was little point in involving lawyer Nichols as all he knew was hearsay, we had not been able to provide him with any proof.

"I see no need to wait for this Sir Edward if indeed he exists, and if he does he no doubt has been duped by your lies, you have nothing whatsoever to back up these astonishing falsehoods. I know Sir Neville Lattimer is here in London for the celebrations, he can confirm the truth of these papers." He gave us a sharp look as he heard the gasp from Gwen and myself, and seemed to take it as an admission of guilt rather than a cry of despair. "Enough time has been wasted. Lock the women and the boy in the holding cell." Jack instantly began to weep, while disbelief brought a cry of "No!" from Gwen and myself.

"Silence now or a whipping will be in order." I lowered my head in submission. "You'll be locked up for the night." He regarded Skinner whose saturnine features had opened up into an alarming smile. "Providing Sir Neville backs up your word I will give you two guards to help to take these miscreants some of the way back to your farm as a favour to him. No doubt you will have your own idea of a fitting punishment for these women's actions."

301

We had thought of the farm as a prison but it was luxury compared to the real thing. Drunken yelling, cries of anguish, simple weeping, filled the stinking air. We were held in a separate small cell away from those housing convicted felons, the only light coming from a window high up, the shadow of the bars slowly fading against the opposite door as evening fell. We were silent; there could be no comfort in words. We had come so far and all for nothing. My heart ached as I thought of my son; I would never see him again. Would Sir Edward try to find us - how would he know where to look?

It was a long time before I closed my eyes only to be plagued by fears of life on his farm and whether Skinner would carry out his promise to take Gwen by force if she failed to marry him - as his wife she could not give evidence against him. I held my hand tightly over my mouth to stem a sob, unable to sleep, waiting for the dawn and the fate it would bring. Jack's head rested on Gwen's shoulder and at last she closed her eyes. Sir Edward would not be back in time and would not know where Skinner had taken us.

God help us, I prayed.

.

Chapter 36

As the dawn light crept through our little window I watched as the bare walls of our prison cell slowly became visible. The night had been long, interrupted with the cries and moans of other women's pain. I envied Gwen and Jack the embrace of sleep as they lay huddled together in a corner but found that comfort unavailable to me.

As Jack stirred he mumbled Walter's name and I thought of that poor child, bewildered by his brother's absence. I was sure Father Joseph would go to him seeking information about our disappearance; yes, he would take care of Walter. As I sat on the floor, the silk dress in which I had taken such pleasure now battered and filthy, I could feel the ripples of disaster that flowed from me, capturing so many other people in its wake.

A shout and banging against the bars of our cage brought me back to the present. "Breakfast. Here," an old woman, hands blackened, held portions of bread and cheese but as I reached out, she grabbed them back. "If you can pay," she cried in a cracked voice. "Otherwise…" She held up a stale crust, the mould already taking possession of its edge. "There's small beer - if you can pay." She watched with greedy interest as I took out a few of the pennies hidden in my underskirt. I took the stale bread as well for with the crust torn off it could be softened in the beer. Gwen and I each gave Jack a little of our share saying we were not hungry. Though our stomachs cried out for food it was the least of our concerns; as soon as confirmation of Skinner's lies arrived from Sir

Neville as they surely would, we would be on our way to some new hell. My mind churned over the facts and the likely repercussions: the evidence against us from the sergeant's point of view appeared overwhelming. What would happen to Jack? Would he be charged?

If only Sir Edward were here.

Mid-morning, we were let out for a while to take exercise in a grey courtyard; I took deep breaths, the stale air less putrid than that in our cells. We walked in circles beneath a square of sky bright in the morning light. I put out my hand to rest on Jack's shoulder, noticing he kept his eyes on the ground - he seemed lost in thought unable to take any respite from his burden of cares.

"Why just shoes?" I asked, to distract him a little.

"What, mistress?"

"Why did you just buy shoes when Sir Edward gave you money enough to buy new clothes?"

His face lit up. "Would be bad for business," he replied, amazed at my ignorance. "Walter and I rely on people's pity and generosity, we may never see the like of such money again. But the shoes, the shoes help me run errands." I smiled to think of the shrewd mind behind the child's face. "We'll get something warm for winter we can wear under our old clothes and when the snow comes we'll be able to afford a few nights in a hostelry."

"You've got it all planned," Gwen smiled but her words were interrupted by the call for us to go back to our cells. "Not back inside already," she complained.

An officer overheard her words. "You'd better get used to it, Sir Neville is currently away I hear."

He seemed to take pleasure in imparting bad news but it gave us a glimmer of hope Sir Edward might complete his mission in time to save us.

Though the hours dragged dreadfully we feared their coming to an end - we would be moving from one form of captivity to another, but one without the possibility of salvation. Poor Jack fretted about Walter. I tried to console him but Gwen was far better at the task than I, thinking of little games for him to play, even holding two beetles in her hand for a moment while Jack had to guess which would climb the wall faster - she must have played such games with her brothers and sisters, I thought.

"Out!" The guard stood beyond the bars, a massive key in his hand. The single harsh word broke me from my reverie. Too soon! It was too soon! "Come along you three, the sergeant wants to see you."

"What is it?" Jack asked, immediately catching on to our despair.

I took his hand. "It will be all right," I said, though my voice shook and I knew he could see through my lie. We were to be Skinner and Sir Neville's chattels, to do with as they pleased.

I found my legs could barely support me, the weariness of all that had befallen me, of all the days and all the miles, overwhelmed me, and it was only Gwen, taking my trembling hand in her own trembling hand, that allowed me to move forward.

We were led into a large room, full of stifling silence except for the shuffling of our own feet. We were brought before a long table behind which sat three men, one of whom I recognised as the sergeant who had arrested us. I felt Gwen flinch as we entered the room aware Skinner was sitting smirking in the corner.

"The document provided by Squire Skinner has been authenticated by Sir Neville," the sergeant began briskly. "There is no need for further delay." Gwen's grasp of my hand tightened so I felt she could break my fingers. I fought to bring my eyes from the floor to the sergeant, though it took the last of my strength to do so. One of the other men seated at the table addressed Skinner. "We have not yet received the major's authority for the guard to escort you the first ten miles from the city. It should arrive shortly, then you can be on your way." I heard Skinner rise to his feet and come forward.

"There is one other matter," the man continued, "the boy Jack, do you wish to bring charges against him, Squire Skinner? If so, you will have to wait here until the case is heard, it will take a few days. What do you say?"

I felt Skinner's approach with every nerve in my body but he stayed a little back so I could not see him.

"I need to get going, but the boy has to be punished." I caught my breath and heard a sob escape from Jack. "May I suggest you keep him here a few days more for disturbing the peace, fine him and take his ill-gotten gains before letting him go? That way he won't be able to follow us and cause further trouble."

From Skinner this could be said to be mercy but we knew it was merely expedience. The sergeant thought for a moment. "It seems a reasonable request. I will give it consideration." Poor Jack began to weep. "You should count yourself very lucky my lad if my superior agrees to this suggestion - the courts could have sentenced you to transportation."

Jack was about to protest his innocence once more when I shook my head. "Thank you, sir," he whispered.

"Take them back," the sergeant commanded over our bowed heads. I could feel the smile on Skinner's face.

I knew I must do whatever I could for Jack as he would be alone here once we were taken. I offered him what money I had left which was little enough, the remainder still being sewn into our old clothes but he refused it with a grin. "We still have the other sovereign," he whispered, "Walter has it safe." I approached an older woman, a wreck of a human with sparse grey hair hanging limply over her face, her bones visible through her taunt skin, but I had heard her express a kind word on behalf of another as the woman had been led away.

"Not yours, then," she said in a voice that seemed to be scraping over stones.

"Oh, no!" The thought of leaving my own son in such a place tore me and left me ashamed. "Will you keep an eye on him when we are gone."

"If he'll behave himself."

"He will." I tried to explain. "He's only here because…"

She held up a feeble hand. "We are all one in here, awaiting our punishment. Tell him to come to me - just a few days, you say, I should have that long."

I thanked her, not daring to ask the obvious question.

It was becoming evening and it seemed we would not be leaving until the morrow, not that a few hours would make any difference to our fate. As I stepped out from the privy I saw a soldier peering into the cell where Gwen sat with Jack. He opened the door. "I am the major of the guard organising the escort for your journey, are you the woman calling herself Mistress Ashton?" Gwen shook her head.

I gave a little cry. "Major Lawson?"

The man turned and I saw the pain in his eyes. "Hope, is that you?"

I wanted to run, to take his hand to ensure he was not a ghost created by my desperate mind.

Chapter 37

"Major Lawson!"

"Hope, don't tell me you did away with your child," he whispered, his face anxious.

His words stopped me where I stood. Gwen regarded me in puzzlement. I felt reprimanded for an old sin. I held myself still against the current of the words circulating about me. "Never, never!" I said, gathering myself against such a thought, such a deed. "I, we," I indicated Gwen, "are here because I am fighting for my child. To have him returned to me by my husband."

Relief flooded Major Lawson's face. "A husband. Then I shall do everything in my power to help you. Come, let us find a quiet corner of the yard where we may speak, you must have much to tell me."

I allowed myself to be led away by him, outside into the cold air of the courtyard where there was a bench in a quiet corner. "Your words have stirred such memories," I confessed, still feeling their blow. "I did not know what I was doing - that day by the river - it was never my child I wanted to destroy but myself, and all that had happened to me."

"Shh, no explanations are needed as I told you then. What of your child?"

"My son, my husband has him in his care and has cast me aside, imprisoning me on a pig farm from where I escaped."

"And what is this about Lady Lattimer? Is that you?"

"Sadly, it is."

"I was asked to provide the guard detailed to accompany you out of the city. Dangerous criminals, that's how you and your companion were described but all I see is two underfed young women. When I heard the name Hope Ashton I knew I had to see for myself though I could not imagine it could be you. How did all this happen? And your son - what is he called?"

"Ja… Jacob." That hated name - it hurt my mouth to say it. Then the story came spilling out of me, the words rushing towards the kindly major in such a torrent I was surprised he was able to follow them.

"So, the girl with you is Gwen, the one with the red hair?"

"Yes, my Gwen."

"I feel my own part in your troubles keenly, to think I trusted Sir Neville's word concerning Oliver Whitby."

"But you have only ever been kindness itself to me."

"But if I had checked elsewhere things would have been very different, your son would have inherited the farm and you could have been living there. You may yet do so, Whitby will be given his marching orders, I will see to that."

"No, no more disturbances, Whitby was deceived by Sir Neville, his lies embraced so many people. No, if I can but be free. In truth, there is one thing only I desire at the moment - freedom. Without it, there is nothing. Freedom for myself and Gwen and little Jack. Freedom to be with my son and walk away from Sir Neville."

"But you are his wife."

"I did not know what chains I was putting on with my wedding ring."

The night was cold, eager drops of rain were beginning to splash the barren earth around our feet. "We must go in,"

Major Lawson said, guiding me towards the forbidding walls of our prison.

"Sir Edward?" he asked as we moved from one kind of darkness into another. "You say you are awaiting this gentleman's return."

"He is my late husband's brother by marriage. We can but wait and pray he will be here tomorrow."

"I think I can do better than that," Major Lawson said, his face brightening.

"How?"

"There are documents - from my time in West Penton. I must go, I have a busy night ahead of me." As we reached the door of our cell he lent forward and kissed my brow before depositing me back to Gwen's side. "I will see you are well fed this night even if at present I can do little else. Justice must be done. Have faith."

Just as it seemed life on the farm with Skinner had been better than our present incarceration we guessed even this place of despair and anguish would be preferable to what awaited us. Sleep came as no respite to me but as fragments of chaos - of bleak landscapes, sudden violence, and Skinner's face, always that face, drawing ever closer.

As the morning light arrived movement resumed in our prison. I knew we had but minutes before we were taken off. Major Lawson said he had documents - would they be sufficient to save us? Did he have them to hand? Could he defeat Sir Neville's plans? We were silent, trying to stretch the minutes we had left, imagining Sir Edward galloping ever closer with the documents from the lawyer and from Margaret that would prove what I had said - or was he breakfasting at an inn still twenty miles hence? Unaware, all unaware?

"'Tis time," the keeper called. Gwen and I kissed Jack goodbye and he moved across to the old woman who held a thin arm out towards him.

"Tell Father Joseph we thank him, won't you? And Sir Edward..." I could say no more.

"Bring the boy!"

"What?"

"Bring the boy."

I held out my hand towards Jack, was he to be charged after all? I believed I caught a flash of disappointment on the old woman's face as we walked away.

We went one last time along the stinking hallway to the daylight beyond. We did not enter the courtyard but were led to the left and into the chamber where we had been questioned before. A whisper of hope took hold of me and I could see from Gwen's face she was unsure whether she should allow herself a smile.

Four soldiers fell in behind us so any improvement of our spirits immediately evaporated. The double doors opened as we approached, the soldiers following us in, the doors closed and the soldiers spread themselves across the way. Had they been convinced we were desperate criminals after all? But there was Major Lawson, he saw my eyes upon him and turned his head, guiding my gaze - to Sir Edward. Gwen instantly touched my arm, her face one joyous smile as she saw both Sir Edward and Father Joseph sitting tight against the wall, and between them, the tiny pale figure of Walter.

Despite the certainty we were saved I had only to hear the name 'Squire Skinner' called and hear his footsteps as he approached the table to feel the old dread take hold of my heart. Then I saw the same expression I could feel on my face written on that of Skinner. The sergeant, with whom he had got on so well, who had believed every one of his lies, had been replaced by an older man of higher rank judging by the decoration on his uniform.

"I bring this meeting to order," the officer proclaimed. "I am Deputy Governor Smithson and I am taking charge of this hearing." He took in the room with his bright beady eyes. "Jack Barnes, please rise." Jack got shakily to his feet, reaching out to Gwen for re-assurance. "You, young man, have been called a thief by…" he glanced down at the paper before him, "by Squire Skinner and had sixteen shillings and four pence on your person when you were apprehended. What have you to say for yourself?"

"Please, sir, the money was not stolen, it was mine, given me by Sir Edward."

"A large sum for a gift."

"I earned it, sir," Jack protested.

"Squire Skinner, please come forward. The statement you made three days ago says you caught Jack Barnes trying to steal from you and you let him go with just a clip on the ear."

"Yes, sir, that's correct."

"No, it isn't, he made it up," shouted Jack, "because I brought the guard to stop him stealing the two ladies away."

"Quiet!"

"But he just wants to make me look bad." Jack could not control his indignation.

"Rubbish," Skinner yelled back. "Of course he is a thief, how else would the likes of him have that sort of money if not by thieving? It stands to reason he stole it."

"His word against yours."

"The word of a beggar, the word of a street urchin."

"No, sir." The voice rang out clear and bold. "You have my word too. I gave the money to the boy."

"You are?"

"Sir Edward Ashton-Somerville."

"Are you prepared to swear to your statement?"

"I am."

"I told you I never stole it," Jack crowed, jabbing his finger towards Skinner.

"Silence!"

Jack's jubilation could not be stemmed by a simple word. "There, we got him, Walter." He bounced in his new shoes until Gwen held a restraining hand on his shoulder and whispered in his ear.

Skinner set his jaw in stubborn resistance but his eyes darted about as if seeking an escape.

The gavel slammed down on the desk. "Sit down, boy. I may have to dismiss this charge but one more word from you and I will find another with which to lock you up."

The clerk on the governor's left handed him another set of papers. "Now," he said, "this brings us to the case brought by Squire Skinner against the two women before me, Hope Courtney also calling herself Mistress Hope Ashton even Lady Lattimer, and the maid Gwen Dixon. The reward poster I have here," he waved the dreaded poster in his hand as if thereby spreading its contents, "who had it printed?"

"I did," said Skinner.

"So, we only have your word it is true." He shuffled the papers again.

"Sir Neville Lattimer has confirmed the matter."

"What had Sir Neville to do with the case?"

"Both women worked for Sir Neville and they colluded to steal from him." Skinner glanced about him, perhaps wondering how well his story would be accepted. "It was his kindness that stopped them being transported - or hung."

"It's nonsense, sir," Gwen cried, getting to her feet.

"Silence."

Gwen sat down heavily, resentfully, but the fear that should have taken possession of us on hearing Skinner's words was dissipated by the knowledge that Sir Edward was there, seated against the side wall. My eyes sought his face for reassurance.

Smithson gazed sharply at Major Lawson. "You have a statement I gather."

"New charges, Sir. I bring murder charges against Squire Skinner as he likes to call himself." Major Lawson approached the desk with a sheaf of papers. "I lay before you the witness statements I gathered at West Penton last year and my report of the investigation into the raid on Hamblemere Farm. It was where I first met the widow Hope Ashton following her harrowing ordeal."

I wanted to close my ears to the story, my story, being spread out with all its fire and blood and pain before this assembly. I fought to keep my head from sinking low as Major Lawson spoke of the statement given by the boy. The boy who had saved me, the boy my mind had been unable to remember until it was too late, the boy who had put a name to one of the murderers - the one who had escaped justice in West Penton – *Skinner*. The boy was saving me again, though I had not reciprocated in kind. I had my guilt, too.

My own statement was read, describing the scar on Skinner's face, made all those months ago when once more my voice and memory had come back to me. It was enough for Governor Smithson to dismiss the charges against us for it was obvious Skinner had good cause to imprison us to save his own neck and nothing he said could be believed.

When next I was aware of what was happening about me Skinner was shouting, "Lies, all lies, Sir Neville will vouch for me," as manacles were placed around his wrists. As he was led away to a prison cell to await trial Gwen and I were being told we were free to go and Jack that all charges against him were dropped. Jack dashed across the room to fling himself at his brother; Gwen and I embraced, tears flowing, shaken to know we were free at last, as if, in all our chasing we had never believed such a thing was truly possible. Major Lawson's face was lit by the greatest of smiles, and there, in the background, stood Sir Edward, with an expression I found hard to read.

It was only at that moment that I realised I was not free at all - I was still married to Sir Neville.

Chapter 38

The heavy gates closed with a shudder. We stood in the blustery wind stunned into silence as our victory sank in. Sir Edward held Walter in his arms, the child's head resting against his shoulder, Jack stood next to him, their happiness at being reunited evident in every expression and gesture. We hardly knew what to do, Gwen and I, but stood waiting and watching the populace going about their business as if today were some ordinary, commonplace day.

Major Lawson, though, could not hide his elation, coming up to us, embracing us, kissing us on both cheeks, Gwen's face becoming almost as red as her hair. "Well done."

"But it is you who have done well," I murmured, with tears born of mixed emotions filling my eyes. "It was your evidence that carried us out of there."

"But it was your courage that brought you to the city to start with. We must celebrate, come to dinner this evening at my house, it's just off Cheapside. In fact, the top floor is currently unoccupied, stay with me, yes, of course, that is what you should do." His enthusiasm seemed too much for him to contain, he waved his arms expansively in a most unlikely manner for a soldier in uniform.

"You are too kind."

"No, it will be a treat for me - some young blood in the house - Mistress Turner, my housekeeper - will be so pleased, she always says how dull the house is since my daughter married."

"Then we accept with gratitude."

"Settled then." Major Lawson clapped his hands in pleasure.

"There are a few things we must do first."

"Of course, I shall not hold you up, come when you are ready, oh, and you must bring the boys." Major Lawson strode off calling for a messenger while our little party stood for a moment not knowing which way to go. There was no need for haste, the chase was over; strangely, the sense of relief was overwhelmed by the feeling of being at a loss for what we should do next.

Sir Edward broke the silence. "I have arranged for a coach," he said, "it will be waiting on the corner. I propose we go to collect your things from Angel Row after taking Father Joseph to his church."

We started to make our way following Sir Edward who still carried Walter as if he were but an infant.

"What did he mean - we could go too?" Jack asked.

"That you should come with us," I replied. "Major Lawson wants you to stay tonight."

Jack's face showed a series of emotions. I compared his reaction to this news to that when he could so quickly sum up a difficult situation - kindness, it seemed, caused him to flounder in disbelief. Gwen took his hand. "Race you to the coach," she said, spying it a little way ahead. She picked up her skirts and ran and Jack chased after her.

Sir Edward moved to my side and we walked on in silence. "I have the letters from the Reverend Wilkins in Maidstone, and from Margaret, and the family bible, too. But Major Lawson had the satisfaction of saving you, so you did not need me at all."

"Please do not say that." The words were out of my mouth before the thought had entered my head. A little flustered I continued. "I... I mean Gwen and I, we are so thankful for your assistance - it gave us hope."

"And it has brought Hope back to me."

I could feel my cheeks become as rosy as Gwen's. "You are playing with my name, Sir Edward."

Walter began to rally and stretch out his thin arms; he smiled to find himself carried so easily.

"Come on, my lad, I think we should chase after your brother, and *hope* that Mistress Hope can keep up with us."

Walter's giggles echoed along the road behind him and I did my best to run but found I was laughing too much.

Jack begged to be allowed to sit up top and Sir Edward volunteered to sit beside him in case excitement got the better of him. Father Joseph, Walter, Gwen and I nestled within. The horses pulled away and we could hear a whoop of delight from Jack. Gwen smiled at me, the tightness that had claimed her face in recent months gone at last. "We're free."

Our arms slipped around each other. I could not say the obvious, the question still nagging at me, would I ever have the freedom to be with my son?

Mother Potter opened her alms-house door with a cry of "Oh, my ducks, there you are! Whatever happened to you? You left here as great ladies and return as scarecrows." There were much hurried explanations and handsome recompense for the loss of her paying guests with coins to the surprise of all but myself, Gwen cut from the hem of her old dress. Within minutes, with kisses and hugs and good wishes and waved handkerchiefs we set off for Cheapside.

Major Lawson's house on the main thoroughfare was a large black and white Tudor building. As we entered the hall the aroma of roasting meats coming from the kitchen made my mouth water. I had forgotten how hungry I was.

"My housekeeper has laid out a few sweetmeats for you," Major Lawson said, "but has told me to remind you dinner will be ready at four of the clock and I should add that upsetting Mistress Turner is not good for the next day's dinner. Now, help yourselves." Jack immediately grabbed at the mince pies, taking one in either hand; knowing how hungry he must be I could not blame him but reprimanded myself when I saw him carry one to Walter who was propped in a corner chair.

"These are wonderful," Gwen mumbled, her mouth full. "We used to have them at Wilderness Hall, at least - we ate the left overs, all that meat and fruit, too good to miss."

"Come now, lads," Sir Edward said, as the boys started on their third pies, "you won't be able to eat your dinner."

"I could eat a horse," Jack replied.

"Then its fortunate that is exactly what is in those pies," Major Lawson teased.

The boys seemed aghast for a moment, then, "Wouldn't be the first time," Jack shot back.

Major Lawson spoke briefly to Sir Edward and indicated for Gwen and me to join them. "You should all rest awhile before dinner and later we will work out our next plan of action," he said. "We may have Skinner where he belongs but Sir Neville will not be so easy to deal with."

I was so tired I fell asleep in the chair after dinner and Gwen and I climbed to our upper chamber only minutes after

Sir Edward and Major Lawson had carried the boys to bed. I was asleep immediately but woke before dawn. I could not trust this freedom I had; it was but a temporary state, a few hours of respite before some new incarceration at the hands of Sir Neville. He retained his power over me - he was my husband. My son was his property, as was I.

I did not stir from my haven until I became aware of the sounds coming from below and knew the house was waking and the business of the day beginning.

Gathering a blanket around my shoulders I ran downstairs and found Mistress Turner in the scullery, our gowns hanging from hooks in the ceiling.

"They're not perfect," she warned me as she stirred the coals of the fire, "but they're clean."

"But I could have washed them myself."

"Major Lawson said you would need them today, I just hope they will be ready in time."

"Today?"

Going upstairs I found Sir Edward and the Major ensconced once more in the study but my lonely wanderings soon came to an end as the men emerged and Gwen and the lads joined us for a breakfast of eggs and meats, warm bread and golden butter.

Gwen and I were instructed to spend the morning in preparation for an afternoon visit. We bathed, and dressed each other's hair, luxuriating in hot water and time.

After a light dinner we put on our freshly laundered gowns as instructed, wondering what was the necessity of dressing so elaborately.

"I thought this dress was the loveliest thing I had ever seen," Gwen said as I laced her into her bodice. "Now I hate it, it just reminds me of the prison." She sat down heavily. "All those others, those other prisoners, they aren't out, are they? At least if they are - they are moving on to something even worse."

It was thus, feeling rather sombre despite our new comfort, that we descended the stairs to see Sir Edward waiting for us with two large fans surprisingly held in his hand.

"Here, you'll need these," he said.

"Why?" We immediately found opening the fans with any degree of grace more difficult than it appeared.

"We are going to confront Sir Neville at his home at Chelsea. The coach will be here shortly."

"What? No, I can't," I cried, dropping the fan to the floor.

Sir Edward stooped to pick it up and return it to me, encasing my hand in his as he did so. "You are not alone in this battle now." He moved away then came back to my side. "But then you never were, were you? You had Gwen."

No amount of reassurance could make me feel at ease as we approached the large house in Chelsea surrounded by its precisely hedged garden.

"You will give me a few minutes, Lawson?"

"As we arranged," the major replied.

"Is not Major Lawson coming with us?" I asked.

"Sir Neville is aware Major Lawson knows your identity, I want to catch him out in his lies first."

Sir Edward took my hand to help me from the coach. "Nothing bad will happen I assure you, on the contrary, this day is important because it will mark the beginning of your freedom." Gwen was half-way out of the coach before Sir Edward remembered to go to her assistance. "Now take care to make good use of those fans to hide your faces as we enter," he said as he mounted the three steps to the great door and knocked loudly.

"It's George from Wilderness Hall," Gwen whispered under her breath. We both raised our fans to an unnatural height so we could barely see where we were going.

Sir Edward introduced himself and waited in the hall to be announced, asking George to show Gwen and myself into the garden as we wished to take the air. Gwen stood close behind me as George knew her well but he led us forward with a bow, paying us no attention. With relief we descended the steps into the gently sloping rear garden where two men in jerkins and thick leggings were busy hoeing a bed of foxgloves. They glanced up as we approached but soon went back to their labours. We moved slowly, both impatient and wary, the skirts of our dresses swaying in the breeze.

"Sir Edward, this is an unexpected pleasure." The voice was that of Sir Neville - it chilled my heart.

"There!" Gwen whispered from behind her fan, indicating a casement window a little above our heads standing slightly ajar. We sauntered towards it, feigning interest in a piece of topiary in the shape of a bird.

"There is no pleasure in this visit." Sir Edward's voice was hard, determined.

"Then tell me what matter has brought you to my door."

"I have heard rumours of two girls claiming to be your wife and her maid."

"I have heard such also." The words left Sir Neville's mouth like a yawn of boredom.

"You will understand my concern, your wife being the widow of my late brother."

"Indeed. Pure fabrication of course."

Gwen tugged at my elbow. "Have you seen the apple tree?" she asked in a false voice I hardly recognised. She indicated with a flash of her eyes the gardeners were coming towards us. We walked on until we could hear their footsteps fade, then hurried back to our spot beneath the window.

"You claim the girls were previously in your service and are guilty of theft."

"Attempted theft – of the Lattimer jewels, no less." I could hear Sir Neville's tone had changed, he sounded more defensive, at bay against the chasing hounds.

"But you know well they are no such thing."

We heard Sir Neville get to his feet, riled, his voice moving about the room. "My wife has been locked up as a lunatic and I care not to be reminded of such a distressing matter."

"That is untrue," Sir Edward shouted in reply.

There was a pause, a silence in which Gwen and I exchanged glances. What excuse would he give now?

"Believe me, you have been misled, my friend." Sir Neville's voice was calm again, his tone friendly. "Liars always have a plausible story to tell, they are good at spinning yarns, otherwise they would not last long at their chosen occupation. I repeat, with sadness, that my wife, my dear wife, has lost her mind and had to be removed to a place of rest for the safety of herself and others, and most especially the safety of her child. Who could say..."

Hearing that voice, the gentle tones with which he had once wooed me, brought forward a tide of anger. I was not afraid of this man, I was filled with contempt for him, contempt and loathing. I did not think - I acted. I tossed the fan into the bushes and marched up the steps and inside, Gwen hurrying behind me as I pushed open the door.

"Am I not your wife, Sir Neville?"

Chapter 39

"Hope!" My name escaped Sir Neville's pale lips before he could prevent it.

"I have Skinner in custody." Major Lawson had entered the room behind me.

"You have ganged up on me, this is preposterous - out! Out with you all, I will not have you in my house. George!" Sir Neville picked up the bell beside his chair and rang it as well he could with a shaking hand.

"Your wife is to start proceedings for an annulment of your marriage." Sir Edward stood over his foe and I could see the soldier within him. "The court will surely be full to the brim to hear of your lies, your deceit, and the vile deeds of your son…"

The door opened. "Sir?" George stopped. "Gwen! We were told you were unable to leave the mistress's bedside," he glanced in my direction, "but you are here, my lady." He looked to his master for an explanation.

Sir Neville got to his feet, waving his hand towards George. "Go! Go! You are dismissed; leave this house, leave it now." His voice rose with each word then broke as he fell back into his chair, his left arm crossing his body.

"Get the physician," Sir Edward commanded George who was standing confused in the centre of the room, disbelieving the scene before him.

"Go!" Gwen said and he did as he was bid.

"Quickly!" Major Lawson and Sir Edward rushed to Sir Neville's side, loosening his neckerchief. There was a commotion outside as George called for assistance and servants came running, and there, in the cacophony, was the sweet sound of a baby crying.

"My son." I flew from the room, following the sound, Gwen at my heels. I ran up the stairs, opening door after door until I saw a cradle in a dim room, a nursemaid seated beside it making gentle cooing sounds.

He was in my arms before I knew what I was doing. He was in my arms. In my arms. I held him close while Gwen calmed the nurse. I did not see where she went; did not hear the exclamations or the explanations. He was in my arms. He was warm, moist, his movements sudden and strong. He pulled his head away from my chest and saw his mother's face properly for the first time, and it was smiling. His bright inquisitive eyes sought mine. Time could stop now, I thought.

"Hope." Sir Edward's voice broke my long reverie.

"Sir Edward?"

"He wants to see you."

"Who?"

"Sir Neville."

"Tell him to go to hell." I was amazed at the ferocity of my anger; it had not been assuaged by the happiness I felt in holding my son, instead my senses were lit by all I had missed.

"He could be on his way there, the doctor fears for his life."

So what care I? was my thought. I had no desire to see his face again.

"Hope," Sir Edward repeated, "surely you have much to ask him, to tell him before he goes to meet his Maker." And there was Gwen beside me, holding out her arms to accept my infant.

"Indeed there is," I replied, following Sir Edward from the room.

Sir Neville's chamber was almost dark, the curtains drawn against the bright afternoon sun. Two candles had been lit. There seemed to be half a dozen men around the bed but Sir Neville dismissed them all with a wave of the hand as I approached. The door closed behind them and all I could hear was his laboured breathing. I hung back having no intention of being within his reach but when he spoke it was in a whisper so I was forced to draw close to the side of the bed.

"You want to see me?" My voice was hard.

"I do. I think you believe I used you badly."

"Believe! You lied to me. You deceived me into marriage. You had me drugged after the birth of my son and you took him from me and locked me away to become Skinner's slave. And you punished Gwen for merely being my friend. You cannot refute any of that."

"I did what I must."

"Must. Why?" I wanted to know, needed to know. I leaned close, seeing the weariness in his eyes.

"My wife died in childbirth," he began slowly, "my third son, he would have been my third son if he had lived - but they died together. But I had two sons, I was content. My first born, Robert, was the apple of my eye - so clever, loving, the opposite of Jacob - Jacob missed his mother and was jealous of his brother." I listened, compelled by the effort it took Sir Neville to speak. "When the war came, Robert was determined to fight for his king, I was loath to let him go but knew I must. I kitted him out with the best of everything and prayed for his safe return. Every day I watched for a messenger, for any word of how he fared. Several missives arrived in the early months - one said he had been injured but was on the mend. I wanted to go to him but it was not possible. Then Jacob said he was off to be a soldier. I forbade him to go, he was still so young, but he sneaked off one night when I was away, Skinner and one or two of my men going with him. He emptied the strong-box before he left." Sir Neville shook his head and I thought I could detect the beginnings of a tear in his eye. "But I would happily have spent more on him, so did not begrudge him the money if it kept him safe. It was only later I heard he had joined Cromwell's Army. I dreaded the thought of my sons going into battle against each other. With one in either camp, I fastidiously kept myself neutral, I did not wish to take sides between them." He paused. "I did everything I could to be fair." His voice wavered. "Robert died in battle, it broke my heart." The tears began to form and run slowly down his face; he did nothing to stop them. "I wrote to Jacob, asking him to come home, telling him he was the heir to my estate, hoping when the war was over… but he preferred the soldier's life. I saw him rarely and then a year ago he sent Skinner to say he was on his way home."

Sir Neville began to cough. I looked about me and found a water jug and glass on the table. I knew he would not be able to hold it steady enough to drink, so put it to his lips, suspecting it was less through kindness than the desire to hear more.

"Thank you," he whispered as he gathered himself and for a moment I saw the man I had first known at West Penton; the gracious man with a gentle air. "I had everything prepared for his homecoming, killed the fatted calf - had the fire lit in his room..." The memory brought the hint of a smile to his face. It was gone in an instant. "When he did not appear I sent Skinner to find him and you know what he reported back to me." His eyes cut into me. "That Jacob had died at your hands."

I stepped back from the bed. I no longer wanted to hear what he had to say.

"When I heard you were expecting a child I had to ensure it became my heir, the last Lattimer, no matter what the cost. Do you think it was easy for me to sit beside you in idle conversation when I knew what you had done?"

"What *I* had done?" I cried, no longer able to restrain myself.

"No matter. The child is mine, and so he will remain, there will be no annulment or divorce, I shall not survive the night." There was a hint of triumph on his face.

"What do you expect of me?" I asked. "Do you want me to feel sorry for you – to forgive you? I cannot. It is too much. You took my son from me - you knew what it was to lose a child..."

"You could have other children but this was my last chance to keep the Lattimer name alive."

"Other children?"

"After a few years, when I was dead and little Jacob had inherited - Skinner had instructions to let you go."

"So you think that exonerates you?" I was bursting with anger. "Imprisoned by Skinner, you gave him the power to do as he pleased with us. You should see the scars on poor Gwen's back, see what price she has paid for your evil plans."

"I did not tell Skinner to treat you so badly, war has changed him and the suffering of others has come to mean nothing to him."

"But you allowed him to put up a reward for our return dead or alive when we escaped from the farm."

Sir Neville winced. "I could have no stories circulating about little Jacob's conception, surely you must see that - for his sake."

"Do not put all this on me!" I walked away from the bed and circled the room. "I was but an innocent girl when your son destroyed my family, all of them killed, as I would have been had I been in the house, instead I was violated and would have been killed too, had I not defended myself. If that pitchfork had not been to hand I do not doubt I would have died in the barn. I did what I had to survive."

"As did I," Sir Neville whispered, "for the survival of my family."

The candles flickered, a bird sang outside the window, a lonely song. I took a step away from the bed in order to gather myself and when I turned back towards Sir Neville he was holding a pistol in his hand.

"Swear!" he said, using all his remaining strength to hold the gun steady.

"What is this?"

"What you just said, 'innocent girl.'"

"I meant nothing by it."

"Swear then, swear before God that Jacob is not my grandson."

I was silent.

The pistol fell from his hand. "Your silence is sufficient," were the last words he uttered. His head dropped back on to the pillow and I ran outside to summon help.

Chapter 40

I knew not what happened in the following days. A fever took me, a cold sweat held possession of my body as on those winter days on the pig farm, lost in the mist and mud, working the fields in the bitter wind. I thought Gwen was beside me, soothing my brow, or was she brushing my hair in Wilderness Hall? Or was it at home? Or was it Hope? Was I not Hope? Who was Ruth, where was she? I sought her through our journeys: the long ferry to London, the castle in Rochester, Father Joseph's church - was she there? At Swann Lane where Hannah and her girls laughed as they rustled to and fro in their silk gowns? or at Wilderness Hall, or Hamblemere Farm? No, it was in that bedroom in the vicarage in West Penton, that was where she sat, abandoned.

My eyes fluttered open at odd hours of day or night. There was Gwen, her face all concern; a man I did not know pronouncing only time would tell; Sir Edward, his eyes on me, so that I took his face into my dreams and was reassured. Finally, I slept.

Sunlight moved across my eyes and I heard Gwen say, "Close the curtains just a little, the sun is on her face."

"Gwen?" My voice was nothing but a rasping whisper coming from my parched mouth but my dear friend reacted as if she had heard a nightingale sing.

"Hope, Hope! You are back with us." She brought a glass of water to my lips and raised my head from the pillow.

I was exhausted with the effort of speaking that one word but smiled to find myself at peace.

"Quick, tell Sir Edward," Gwen called over her shoulder and a figure hurried away.

"My son, is he safe?"

Gwen bent close to me. "He is. He is downstairs with his nurse, she takes good care of him."

This sipping of water, this flickering of eyes, reminded me of Sir Neville; then I had been the watcher - and so angry; then I had been in a different world to the one I now inhabited.

I felt a draught as the bedroom door flew open. "The maid said..." Sir Edward began, then our eyes met and he rushed to the bedside, taking hold of my hand. "Thank God you are safe, my dear girl, my dear, dear girl."

A little later Gwen fed me some broth and I felt strong enough to hold my sleeping son awhile.

I drifted in and out of sleep for another day.

When I awoke it was dawn, a sliver of rosy sky visible between the curtains. Gwen was asleep, curled up on the leather armchair that had been placed beside the bed. I slid from under the covers to walk barefoot to the window. My legs shook but I had no fear of falling. I rested my elbows on the windowsill, my head in my cupped hands. A new day was coming. The garden beneath my gaze was bright with flowers and long shadows lay dark across the gravel paths. Today I would bathe and dress, today I would go downstairs, today I would hold my son, today I would try to thank Gwen for everything she had done for me; today I would be with Sir Edward again.

"Much has happened since you became ill," Sir Edward explained a few hours later as we sat in the garden. "Skinner's trial has taken place, it was a brief affair, Gwen gave evidence."

"What happened, his sentence?"

"Penal servitude in the West Indies."

"So, he will be the servant now."

The sound of horses' hooves and the clatter of a coach broke into the quiet afternoon. "Are you expecting a visitor, Sir Edward?"

"Yes, I am, excuse me. Do not move."

"I have no intention of doing so." I was content where I was but also gathering strength to make a confession.

"Hope, Hope, look who's here." Gwen was running across the garden, her arms waving. I followed her gaze to the small woman standing at the top of the steps leading from the house into the garden. She was dressed in black with the most brilliant red hair. "My mother, it's my mother." She flew up the steps and into her mother's arms. Sir Edward approached round the side of the house.

"You brought her here," I said.

"It was the least I could do; Gwen must have her joy too."

His hand was on the side of my chair; before I knew it, I had lifted it from its perch and kissed it. "Thank you," I said and found I had not blushed, or experienced any embarrassment, as I surely should. Sir Edward echoed my gesture with his own, kissing my hand with the softest of touches.

"I shall take Robert now," I called across to the nurse who lifted my son from his blanket and brought him to me, placing him on my lap.

"Robert?"

"Sir Neville wished him to be called after his son, but I think I have the choice of which son. You told me once Robert was a good man."

"And such he was."

"Then perhaps we can both be satisfied, both Sir Neville and I."

Robert reached up to grab at my hair, holding it between his fingers, fascinated.

"There is something I must say," I began, "something I had not faced until… until the other day, when we met." Instantly Sir Edward's fingers were upon my lips. "Shh. Do not speak. I sat by your bed when you were ill, heard your sorry words as your mind wandered through your past." He allowed the import of what he had said to settle in my mind. "When the war was ended," he continued, "I told every person on my estate the past must be put away, whether they were on this side or that, what each did for good or ill must be forgotten and forgiven, for we must come together, start again, be united, if we were to move into the future."

"But…"

"Do you wish to hear my confession, too? It will take some time, the war left none of us as innocents."

My heart raced. "But you should not call me Hope…"

"Regardless of your past, be it as Hope or be it as Ruth you will always be Hope to me, you are the personification of hope, of hope against all the odds, against every tribulation. You are *my* Hope if you will allow. Will you?" I smiled as he lent towards me, his face just inches from mine. "You cannot wish me to be… *Hopeless*." He kissed my hand again. "Have I the hope of love? The love of Hope?"

"I fear you are playing with my name again."